No, Don't Ever Stop

OTHER TITLES BY MARNI MANN

The Billionaires of Boston

A Million Times, Yes
No, Don't Ever Stop

The Weston Group Series—Erotic Romance

The Arrogant One
The Wildest One
The Mysterious One
The Irresistible One
The Forbidden One

The Spade Hotel Series—Erotic Romance

The Playboy
The Rebel
The Sinner
The Heartbreaker
The One

Praise for Marni Mann

"Sucked in completely and jealous of such a clever story! You won't put this one down. Marni will have readers desperate for every soul-gripping page . . ."

—Rachel Van Dyken, #1 *New York Times* bestselling author

"If you're reading a book by Marni Mann, I'm warning you now: Grab a glass of cold water because her spicy stories are going to set you on fire!"

—Monica Murphy, *New York Times* bestselling author

"Marni Mann is my spice queen! She delivers every single time. With smoldering chemistry and impeccable writing, her books are utterly addicting."

—Devney Perry, *Wall Street Journal* bestselling author

"This book is perfection, and that's not even a good enough word! Chef's kisses!"

—Natasha Madison, *USA Today* bestselling author

"If you're looking for your next wickedly hot read, look no further. Marni Mann will have you fanning yourself all the way through."

—Laurelin Paige, *New York Times* bestselling author

"Sierra-approved sexiness on every page."

—Sierra Simone, *USA Today* bestselling author

The Dalton Family Series—Erotic Romance

The Lawyer
The Billionaire
The Single Dad
The Intern
The Bachelor

The Hooked Series—Contemporary/Erotic Romance

Mr. Hook-up
Mr. Wicked

The Agency Series (Stand-Alone Novels)—Erotic Romance

Signed
Endorsed
Contracted
Negotiated
Dominated

Stand-Alone Novels

Before You (Contemporary Romance)
Even If It Hurts (Contemporary Romance)
The Better Version of Me (Psychological Thriller)
Lover (Erotic Romance)

The Bearded Savages Series—Erotic Romance

The Unblocked Collection
Wild Aces

The Moments in Boston Series—Contemporary Romance

When Ashes Fall
When We Met
When Darkness Ends

The Prisoned Series—Dark Erotic Thriller

Prisoned
Animal
Monster

The Shadows Series—Erotica

Seductive Shadows
Seductive Secrecy

The Bar Harbor Series—New Adult

Pulled Beneath
Pulled Within

The Memoir Series—Dark Mainstream Fiction

Memoirs Aren't Fairytales
Scars from a Memoir

No, Don't Even Stop

MARNI MANN

This is a work of fiction. Names, characters, organizations, places, events, and incidents are either products of the author's imagination or are used fictitiously. Otherwise, any resemblance to actual persons, living or dead, is purely coincidental.

Published by Montlake, Seattle

www.apub.com

EU product safety contact:
Amazon Media EU S. à r.l.
38, avenue John F. Kennedy, L-1855 Luxembourg
amazonpublishing-gpsr@amazon.com

ISBN-13: 9781662529498 (paperback)
ISBN-13: 9781662529481 (digital)

Cover design by Letitia Hasser
Cover image: © Michelle Lancaster PTY LTD

Printed in the United States of America

What do you do when you find a man who's the right mix of alphahole, arrogance, and assuredness?
You make him realize he can't live without you.
And you make it his life's mission to make you his.
Because you're sassy like that.

PLAYLIST

"Touch Me Like A Gangster"—Jessie Murph

"God & Guns N' Roses"—Tyler Braden

"What I Want"—Morgan Wallen, Tate McRae

"I Don't Wanna Know"—Chase Matthew

"Last One to Know"—Gavin Adcock

"I Like How I Look"—Jessie Murph

"The Way I Wanna"—Max McNown

"Back in the Saddle"—Luke Combs

"Think I'm in Love with You"—Chris Stapleton

"Oil Money"—Graham Barham

"Might Be Dangerous"—Tyler Braden, Kaitlin Butts

Get the playlist at: https://marnismann.com/books/no-dont-ever-stop

PROLOGUE

Emily

I'm the kind of girl who takes one for the team. Only my best friend's team, that is, since tonight was supposed to be girls' night. But instead of grabbing drinks at a bar, breaking down my nonexistent sex life for Maya, and gossiping about everyone we worked with, I was at the Boston Bears arena, on a double date with her and Jordan, her soon-to-be boyfriend, and his seven-year-old nephew, Ben.

The plan for this evening had been simple: leave work, go to our favorite cheap pub, and have way too many cocktails.

A plan that had completely derailed the moment Jordan showed up to the rehab center where Maya and I work as RNs. Maya's ovaries had exploded when she caught sight of Jordan, his hand clasped with Ben's. While she was mentally picking out the names of their future children, Jordan suggested that Maya and I should come skating with him and Ben. That was all it took and, boom, we were here.

Now, clutching Ben's small, semi-sticky fingers, I wobbled toward the ice rink with the thought *Please don't bust your ass* repeating in my head.

I couldn't even remember the last time I'd skated.

And although Ben was the most adorable kid on the planet and I enjoyed every second of watching him inhale the private dinner his uncle had arranged for us in the owner's suite and the cupcake he had for dessert, this girl needed a drink.

Preferably a cabernet sauvignon that was extra jammy, in a wide, breathable glass, with a second round already ordered.

I squeezed Ben's hand, mine on the verge of sweaty. "Come on, kid. Show me what you've got, and do not let me fall," I begged as the tip of my skate hit the ice.

Ben gave me a red-rimmed smile, the rawness around his top lip from the milkshake mustache he'd worn throughout dinner.

Jordan, now retired, was in the NHL and had taught Ben how to skate. I had full faith that this tiny human could guide me around the rink and make sure I left in one piece.

That didn't mean I wasn't obsessing over the possibility that I could face-plant at any second and Maya would have to unbreak—or re-break—my nose.

It seemed that whenever we were at this arena, something dramatic happened. Like last time, when Maya and I came to watch a Boston Bears game. Of course, that was before Maya knew Jordan was the owner of the hockey team and he, along with Gavin, Ben's dad, walked onto the ice to give a $1.5 million check to a nonprofit organization. My best friend hadn't realized that Jordan, the dude she'd been running with every morning—even banging under a bridge—wasn't just a normal nine-to-fiver. He was the owner of the seats we'd been sitting in, along with half of Boston, with a net worth of over a billion. As someone who wasn't a fan of the rich, Maya lost her shit over the news.

I did, too, but for an entirely different reason.

As I stared through the glass that surrounded the ice, I found myself speechless—something that never happened—my eyes bugging out of my head, my hands rubbing the thighs of my jeans to release the tingles that were building.

All because I couldn't stop gawking at the man standing next to Jordan.

Gavin Worthington.

There wasn't anyone in this world more yum than him.

He was around six feet, four inches tall, with broad shoulders, like he still played in the NFL although he was retired, muscular legs that his pants hugged, and an ass that looked rock hard. Besides a body that could rival any non-retired athlete, it was his face that surprised me the most. His serious expression was all steam—hard edges and sharp lines with a well-trimmed beard, a blend that made my heart pound. The cherry on the Gavin sundae was his smile. One full of cuteness, like I'd found his vulnerability and I was tickling that spot relentlessly.

A combination I still found myself thinking about, especially as I gazed at his son.

"Faster, Emily! Faster!" Ben shouted as he skated backward, guiding me toward the first turn.

My knees were locked, my shoulders almost as high as my ears. Even my lips were straining as I squeezed them together, trying to breathe through my worry.

"We're gonna get past this corner and then we're gonna fly!"

The only flying I wanted to be doing was in a plane.

"Be careful with me, Ben. Don't forget, I'm a beginner."

There was a piece of vanilla icing stuck to his dark-brown locks that I hadn't noticed while I was washing his face after dinner, and he had the most beautiful blue eyes, which lit up even brighter as he giggled. "I didn't forget."

Jordan and Gavin's grandmother, Bettie, was one of our patients at the rehab center, a fun, mind-blowing twist that neither Maya nor I had been expecting. But ever since I'd found out they were related, I secretly hoped Gavin would pop in to visit her during one of my shifts.

Because he hadn't, I still wondered if he was as handsome close up as he had been that night I saw him on the ice.

And as I looked at Ben, who shared the same smile as Gavin, I wondered if his gorgeous blue eyes had also been inherited from his father.

CHAPTER ONE

Emily

"Make it stop," I groaned as my phone rang, my toes hovering over the lip of the bathtub, seconds from dunking in. The water inside was full of sparkly bubbles from the bath bomb, taunting me with its peach scent and promise of relaxation. I took my phone off the counter, and a quick glance at the screen showed me I had no choice but to answer. "Hey, it's Emily."

"I'm sure I'm the last person you want to hear from right now."

I laughed at my coworker, a triage nurse for Dr. Kaplan, a concierge doctor I worked for a few times a week, tonight being one of them, so I could actually pay all my bills and save a little each month. "If I wasn't about to soak in a much-needed bathtub, I'd probably be a lot happier to hear from you." I checked the time on my phone. I had an hour until my on-call shift technically ended. "Whatcha got for me?"

"I'm going to text you an address. The patient's file will be in the system, should you need to access it. The visit shouldn't take you too long. Heck, you might even get back before your bathwater gets cold."

I snorted.

When it came to anything medical, at this hour of the night, nothing ever moved quickly.

"I'll leave in two minutes," I told her.

"If you need me, you know how to find me."

"Sure do."

I lifted my towel off the closed toilet seat and wrapped it around me before loosening the plug in the tub, mentally waving at the peach-bombed water now going down the drain. I sighed as I left the bathroom and went into my room to throw on a fresh pair of scrubs. Once I was dressed, I tied my long blond curls into a high ponytail and grabbed my nursing bag. After entering the address into my Maps app, noting the distance was a bit too far to walk, I ordered an Uber, the car arriving by the time I got outside my apartment building.

Nestled into the back seat, I pulled up the last text I'd gotten from my best friend and shot her a message.

Me: I'm fully aware that you could be having sex right now (and if you are, a part of me hates you, LOL) and you might not see this until tomorrow morning before your run. I just need to tell you, I miss you. I miss you not being home. I miss not talking to you every second of the day.

Me: And I miss you not being in the bedroom next to mine so I can pop in and bitch about being called in to work an hour before my shift ends, like I was tonight. Currently in the back of an Uber on my way to see a patient. FML.

Maya: I'm getting ready for bed. Don't worry, sex already happened on the kitchen counter while we were making dinner. Ha!

Me: I really do hate you.

Maya: You LOVE me.

Maya: I'm sorry you're off to see a patient. I bet the only thing you want to do is take a bath and go to bed.

Me: In ways only you understand.

Maya: Will it be a hard case?

Me: Don't know. Haven't even looked. I just want it to be over with so I can get home and go to bed.

Maya: Text me when you get back, I don't care what time it is. And see you tomorrow at work.

Me: XOXO

The car came to a stop in front of a large, fancy high-rise, and I held my bag against my side as I got out of the back seat and headed to the entrance. The door to the lobby opened when I was only halfway up the sidewalk, the doorman saying, "Nurse Emily Wren," while he stared at me.

The scrubs gave away my occupation, and the badge across my breast—if he could even see it from there—showed my name, but it was still a little jarring to be addressed before I even got to the door.

"Yes," I replied. "I'm Emily."

Dressed in an all-black suit and tie, he was the size of a linebacker, with a gaze as intense as a hockey goalie. I imagined not even an ant could get past someone with his stature and build.

"We've been waiting for you. Would you mind showing me some identification before I escort you to the elevator?"

As soon as I reached him, I pulled out my ID and handed it over.

He studied the photo and returned it. "Follow me, please."

Since my territory was within the city, I was used to the protocol of high-rise buildings, providing identification and sometimes filling out paperwork—a much different process from the nurses who worked in the suburbs and just had to ring someone's doorbell.

I assumed he was going to lead me to the bank of elevators to the left, but we walked right by them and down a short hallway, a single elevator sitting at the end.

He hit the button next to it, and as the door slid open, he moved to the side to let me in. "I'll see you when you come down, Ms. Wren."

I nodded. "Thank you."

The door closed, and I pulled out my phone to check the patient's file, something I still hadn't done. But as the elevator climbed, my service got worse—a common theme in elevators in this city. Since the app wouldn't open, I returned my phone to the pocket of my scrubs and focused on the monitor, the digital screen showing each floor that I passed. There were only two buttons on the control panel: "L" and "PH." So I had no idea what floor the penthouse was on, but I figured I had to be getting close.

I was right. Within a few seconds, the door slid open.

But I didn't step out.

Because a man was standing only inches away on the opposite side, a distance that caught me off guard, his stare moving right through me, especially as I took in his face.

His handsomeness.

Features that were shockingly familiar.

"Ms. Wren, I'm glad you're here." His tone was a little frantic. "Follow me—"

"Gavin?"

He was mid-turn and halted at the sound of his name. "Yes." His eyes narrowed, closing in around the deepest blue irises. Eyes just as stunning as his son's, proving Gavin's smile wasn't the only thing Ben had inherited. "Do I know you?"

I could tell he was raking through his memory, trying to answer that question on his own.

"No. I know you. Well, I don't really *know* you, know you. But I know you through Maya, your brother's girlfriend. It's . . . oh God, a long story."

What the hell am I saying?

Do I sound like some NFL groupie who thinks I know him because I follow him online?

That worry quickly faded as the realization of why I was here hit me hard. Dr. Kaplan was a pediatrician. If I had been called to Gavin's house, that meant . . .

"What's wrong with Ben? Is he okay?"

He pointed over his shoulder. "He's in the living room. Come with me."

Once I stepped out and saw that I was in Gavin's foyer, the location of the elevator at the end of the private hallway suddenly made sense. I followed behind him as he led me deeper into the condo, doing everything I could to keep my eyes on his back.

But I was failing.

Miserably.

My stare focused on one thing and one thing only.

His ass in those gray sweatpants.

Holy mother, it was perfection.

"I'm not sure how much Dr. Kaplan told you," Gavin said, my gaze rising as he peered at me over his shoulder, "but I tried taking Ben to the ER, and he wouldn't have it. I tried to get it out, and he wouldn't let me touch it. Tonight has been fucking hell."

Get it out?

Now I wished I'd prepped myself and dug into Ben's file in the Uber.

"Forgive me, but I didn't peek at Ben's chart before I came over. What exactly will I be getting out?"

Due to Gavin's height and my position behind him, he'd mostly been blocking Ben. But as he moved around the oversize ottoman and took a seat beside his son on the sectional, I saw there was something definitely wrong.

Ben's hands were covering his face, his eyes red and watery.

"There's something lodged up his nose," Gavin informed me.

My last client visit had been running a rehydration IV for a six-year-old with a severe case of the stomach flu. I had a feeling this wasn't going to be nearly as messy.

"Well, let's get this thing out." I drenched my hands in antibacterial gel and slipped on a pair of gloves before I knelt on the floor in front of Ben. "Do you remember me?" I smiled. "I'm Maya's best friend. You taught me how to ice-skate."

"Emily!" His hands stayed in place, his voice muffled as it came through his fingers. "The lady that loves strawberry cupcakes like I love vanilla ones!"

Not quite, but I wasn't going to correct him. So I laughed and said, "Can I take a look at your nose?"

Slowly, he unmasked his face. The width of whatever was up his nose was widening his nostril as far as it would go.

Oh, Ben, what did you do?

I was sure Gavin's big, beautiful living room had more lights than my entire apartment, but there were only a few lamps on, the soft glow not bright enough to show what was up his nose.

I found a flashlight in my bag and held it in front of Ben, making sure he was comfortable with each step I took. "I'm going to shine this up there"—I pointed at his nose—"and see what we're dealing with."

"No!" He re-covered his face. "It's gonna hurt!"

"This is what happened when I tried to get it out earlier." Gavin kissed the top of Ben's head, and I completely melted, turning straight into the heart-eyed emoji. "Which then led to a total breakdown."

I nodded. "I won't hurt you, Ben."

"Daddy said that and it hurted." He glared at his dad.

"I'll make a deal with you." I held his knees. "If I hurt you, I'll send you an entire box of vanilla cupcakes." I paused. "How does that sound?"

Ben's bright-blue eyes widened. "With extra icing? That's swirled like an ice cream cone? Just like the ones we had at the arena that Uncle J got us?"

I squeezed his knees, knowing I'd won. "No, they'll be even better than those because they'll have triple the frosting."

"Triple?"

"Yep." I smiled. "I promise."

"Deal." His hands dropped.

My heart pounded as soon as I connected eyes with Gavin. "I'll explain why I know vanilla is his favorite once I get whatever this is out of his nose."

I tilted Ben's head back and aimed the flashlight. Whatever was in there was about halfway up, wedged in horizontally, and whitish in color. It didn't seem to have any edges, telling me it was probably round.

I dug through my bag until I found a pair of tweezers, and I showed them to Ben. "I'm going to need you to hold super still, okay?"

"Emily, that's gonna hurt!"

"It's not, you have to trust me."

When he didn't interject, I inserted the metal, and once I surrounded the object, I could tell it was plastic and there was absolutely no wiggle room. Ben, I assumed, had been playing around, and as he'd tried to pick it out, he actually jammed it higher. Whatever this thing was, it wasn't moving.

"Any idea what it might be?" Gavin inquired.

"Not a clue."

"Do you think you can remove it?"

Gavin knew nothing about me aside from my name and occupation. Therefore, he had no idea that I wasn't someone who gave up. That when it came to all things medical, my nine years of experience served me well. "Oh, I'm going to get it out." I rummaged through my bag until I found the lubricant and squirted the clear gel onto a Q-tip, showing it to Ben. "This is going to be cold, and it might tickle a little. Just try to stay as still as you can."

Gavin wrapped his arm around Ben's shoulders. "Hang tight, buddy. You've got this."

An idea came to me, and I went into my bag again and handed Ben the small stuffed dog I kept inside. I normally didn't bring out my furry friend unless I had to give a patient a shot, but this situation seemed as relevant.

"Can you do me a favor, Ben? Can you hold my dog for me?"

"Why do you have a doggy in your bag?" He took the stuffed animal and moved it close to his chest.

"I love dogs. They're my favorite animal. And this one was given to me by a very special patient who's about your age. I don't like to leave the dog alone, so I always bring him with me."

"It's so soft."

While he rubbed its ears, I dabbed the Q-tip around the inside of Ben's nose, trying to get it as slick as possible, leaving globs of the gel around the plastic. The only way this was going to work was if I came at it from both sides, so it was double the force.

I pulled the Q-tip out and said, "Do you want to guess what his name is?"

"Mmm." He stared at the dog. "Golden?"

"Such a good guess given that he's a golden retriever, but no. I named him Fenway."

"I love Fenway!"

"Then how about you hold Fenway until I leave? Take care of him for me, okay?"

"Okay." He petted the top of the dog's head.

I got a little more comfortable on my knees, moving my bag behind me, so I was in the best position possible to do this. "Here's what I'm going to do. With this hand"—I waved my free hand in the air—"I'm going to push on your nose to hopefully pop out the plastic. And with this hand"—I lifted the one holding the tweezers—"I'm going to try to pull on it. Does that sound okay?"

"Please don't let it hurt."

A simple sentence that had my chest aching. "I'm going to do everything in my power to make sure I don't."

I tapped on the outside of Ben's nostril and felt the plastic. If I drove down too hard, I was afraid I'd really cause him pain, and that would result in a trip to the ER since I had a feeling Ben, at that point, wouldn't let me do any more. Somehow, I had to find a balance and hope that the lube would do its job.

I gently massaged the outside of his nostril, taking my time while I attempted to slip the tweezers around the plastic. Fortunately, the pressure from my finger got the plastic to move the tiniest amount and that was all it took. The plastic then shot right out.

"You've got to be kidding me." Gavin picked up the culprit, which had landed on Ben's lap. "A button?" His voice was getting louder with each word. "You put a button up your nose?" He waved it in front of Ben's face.

"Looks like it could have come from right here." I pointed to the missing button at the top of Ben's dinosaur-themed nightshirt.

"I was just playing with it, Dad . . . and it got up there." As Ben hugged the dog, I could tell he was trying not to laugh, where his father didn't think any of this was funny.

"Why in the hell would you play with it up your nose?" Gavin shook his head. "You know what, we'll talk about this later. Upstairs. Now."

I got up from the floor so Ben could stand.

"See ya, Emily," he pouted, handing me Fenway before he ran for the stairs.

Gavin's hands were in his ink-colored hair, pulling at the longer strands that were gelled and styled in a sexy-mess kind of way. "I can't fucking believe that kid."

I put the tweezers and lube back in my bag. "If it makes you feel any better, this is super common. It's not the first thing I've picked out of a kid's nose, and it certainly won't be the last."

He looked at me through his long, dark lashes. "But a button?"

I laughed. "At least it's not a LEGO."

"You've fished out a LEGO? How did that even fit up there?"

I smiled. "Don't ask."

"Jesus," he groaned.

I hung my bag over my shoulder and took off my gloves.

"I'll take those." He held out his hand.

As I set the latex in his palm, our fingers grazed, and something instantly happened. It was a burst, swirling inside my stomach, lifting to my chest.

It came on hard.

Fast.

And it didn't stop with one wave—the longer we touched, my fingertips frozen against his palm, his gaze intensifying by the second, the more ripples blasted through me.

I couldn't move.

All I could do was part my lips and take a deep breath.

When his hand pulled back, clutching my gloves, he asked, "How do you know Ben?"

Had he felt that?

Was his body on fire like mine?

Who is this man, and how did he have the power to make me feel that?

"And his love for vanilla cupcakes?"

Answer, Emily.

Speak.

My hand dropped to my side, my tongue dry and heavy like lead in my mouth. "I'm best friends with Maya. We're roommates and coworkers. Your grandma is actually one of our patients."

"No way. That's fucking wild."

"One evening, not too long ago, Jordan was looking after Ben, and the four of us had a little date at your arena. Your son basically taught me how to skate." I shifted my weight, my body suddenly fidgety. "He's really fabulous, Gavin."

He stood from the couch, towering over me, the movement sending me a strong breeze of his scent. An equal mix of ginger and cinnamon, creating a spicy and mysterious aroma.

"He is."

I ran my tongue over each lip, trying to wet them. "I won't tell you what that kid inhaled for dinner, but it became pretty obvious how much he loves vanilla cupcakes."

He chuckled. "My brother gives my son anything he wants." He gripped the back of his neck. "It's too much."

"It's only out of love."

"I know."

The room turned silent, and I took that as my cue to leave. "I'll let Dr. Kaplan know there's no need for a follow-up. If Ben has any pain later tonight or in the morning, you may want to bring him into the office tomorrow. If not, I think he'll be fine." I nodded toward the direction of the elevator. "I'll let myself out."

As I was about to take a step, he beat me to it and walked over to the wet bar on the far side of the living room. "I don't know about you, Emily, but I could really use a drink." He lifted a bottle off one of the shelves and poured the liquor into a short tumbler. "Would you like to join me?"

I let out a long, semi-moaning exhale. "I'm on the clock. I have to stay liquor-free in case I get called to another emergency button situation." I offered him a smile. My head tilted as the regret of my on-call status dug deeper into my chest. "Another time?"

"Sure."

It felt weird to push the topic any further. Besides, I had a feeling our paths would eventually cross, considering how connected we were.

I moved in the opposite direction of where he stood, and when I got to the corner that separated the living room from the foyer, which would block us from seeing each other, I turned toward him.

He was still looking at me, something that shocked the hell out of me. But his expression was unreadable, and his eyes seemed almost haunted.

"Don't be surprised if Jordan brings Ben a box of vanilla cupcakes with extra frosting."

He dragged his teeth over his thick bottom lip, a gesture that screamed of hotness. "From you?"

"He was an amazing patient."

"But he lost the bet—you didn't hurt him."

"To be honest, I have a feeling I did. I think he was just being tough." I smiled and rounded the corner, pressing the button for the elevator. It was already here, the door opening, and I stepped inside, resting against the back wall after I hit the "L" button.

Just as the door was closing, my phone beeped from my scrubs pocket, and I pulled it out, reading the text on the screen.

Dr. Kaplan's Office: Your shift is over. As soon as you're done with your patient, let me know and I'll clock you out. Thanks, Emily.

CHAPTER TWO

Gavin

There was only one thing to do when the most gorgeous woman I'd ever seen in my life turned down my offer and walked out of my condo. That was to pour myself a scotch and immediately bring it to my lips, staring at the last spot where I'd seen her, swallowing until the glass was empty.

Emily, I don't know who the hell you are aside from the woman who just rescued my son . . . but damn, girl, you're fucking beautiful.

The entire time she was helping Ben, I couldn't take my eyes off her. The gentleness she used with him, the patience. The stuffed dog that was aimed to distract him. How she showed him everything she was going to do before she did it so she wouldn't scare him off.

And that smile, shit. I couldn't get enough.

I glanced away from the wall that she'd disappeared behind and looked at the ceiling, knowing I needed to get my ass upstairs and deal with Ben, addressing the drama he'd stirred up tonight. That boy had scared me half to death when he came down from his room, screaming and panicked that he couldn't get that goddamn thing out of his nose. And when I'd tried to remove it, more shouting erupted.

If Dr. Kaplan hadn't sent Emily over, we would have been at the ER for probably most of the night. But even though it had only taken a phone call and Ben's issue was solved, that wouldn't always be the case, and Ben needed to understand that. He needed to know that just because I had every resource at my fingertips didn't mean there weren't consequences.

That was the talk I was about to have with him as I stepped away from my wet bar to head upstairs. I didn't make it more than a few paces before I heard the elevator, the low-pitched ding that went off when it arrived, the sweeping of the door as it opened.

I halted by the edge of the couch, listening to the sound of rubber soles move across my wooden floors, and when they silenced, Emily was peeking around the wall that divided the living room and foyer. "I hope it's okay that I came back?"

"Did you forget something?"

She leaned her shoulder against the edge. "No. I got a text from Dr. Kaplan's office that I'm no longer on duty." Her smile was soft yet charming as hell. "I thought I'd take you up on that drink." She paused. "As long as you still want one."

Having a drink with her was all I wanted.

Fuck, that wasn't true.

But a drink was a solid place to start.

"Make yourself comfortable. I'm going to go check on Ben. I'll be right back."

"Hold on." Even though she was looking at me, I got the feeling she was taking in the entire space around me. "Ben's mom or someone who isn't Ben's mom isn't going to be upset that I'm joining you for a drink . . . are they?"

A fair question.

And a question I'd never been asked by any other woman.

"You have nothing to worry about, Emily."

She nodded. "Okay."

While she made her way to the couch, I went to the stairs, taking them two at a time until I reached the top. Ben's room was the second door in the hallway. Although his light was on, he was in bed, tucked under the covers, sound asleep, cuddling his stuffed hockey stick that Uncle J had gotten him a few years ago. Something he not only slept with every night, but it traveled with us too.

I pulled the blanket up to his neck and kissed his forehead, keeping my lips there for a few extra seconds to breathe him in.

I knew this wouldn't be the last time he would scare me half to death. My son was an athlete. He had hundreds of games ahead of him. Situations where he could break all his bones. But tonight could have been avoided, and in the morning, I'd make that clear.

"Good night, my boy," I whispered before turning off his light and returning to the staircase, the angle in which it was built giving me a direct view of Emily.

Fuck me, she was perfect.

Dressed in light-pink nursing scrubs, the top tucked in so the material hugged her tits and waist, jetting out toward her hips and rounded to her ass—curves that were exceptional.

That were just right.

That were everything I craved.

Her eyes were a piercing blue, and she had a cute splatter of freckles under her eyes and across her nose, pouty lips, with long blond hair she wore high on her head.

The total package—one hell of a face with a body that fucking rocked.

A body I wouldn't mind devouring.

"Is he okay?"

She caught me staring as I reached the bottom step, and I headed for the bar. "He's sleeping."

She looked at her watch. "It's late. Besides, tonight was probably a bit traumatic for him."

"Tonight is going to be the main topic of conversation when I talk to him in the morning."

She smiled knowingly. "I don't doubt that."

I stilled at the bar, my hand on the bottle I'd been drinking from earlier. "What can I get you to drink?"

"Anything. I'm really not fussy."

I held the bottle in the air. "Scotch?"

"Sounds delicious."

I refilled my glass and poured one for her and brought it to the couch, handing it to her before I took a seat one cushion away.

She held the rim to her mouth. "This isn't how I expected tonight to end."

"This isn't the end, Emily." I reached across the space between us and clinked my glass to hers. "This is only the beginning."

Her cheeks flushed as she took a sip.

"Question." I had to force myself to focus only on her face because everything below her chin was just as fucking enticing as everything above it. "How did you know it was me? You called me by name when the elevator opened. We've never met . . ."

"I saw you at the arena at a Boston Bears game. Your grandmother actually gave Maya and me the tickets to go. You and Jordan walked onto the ice and handed over a check to a charity." She ran her palm over the top of her forehead. "An evening I'll never forget for several reasons."

"I believe I know the one you're talking about. That was the game when Maya realized who Jordan was, am I right?"

Her hand left, and her brows lifted. "Jordan told you the whole story?"

"Oh yes." I chuckled. "Bettie too."

She smiled, and it was better than art. Hell, it was better than a fucking touchdown.

"You have the best grandmother, by the way." She tucked her legs underneath her and positioned herself to face me more. "I'm dying for her to get out of rehab so Maya and I can take her out."

"You're going to . . . take her out?"

"Are you kidding, she's going to be a blast."

She was good with kids, and she liked hanging out with an older generation.

Emily was getting more interesting by the second.

"Let me get this straight. You work at the rehab center, I'm assuming during the day. And you work for Dr. Kaplan at night?"

"Just a couple nights a week, but yes."

I took a drink. "Two jobs. That's tough."

"For the most part, it's easy. The nights, anyway. I'm on call for about four to five hours. I don't always end up visiting the patient. Sometimes I can speak to the patient's parents and get things worked out over the phone." She smiled even larger. "But sometimes, like tonight, it's unavoidable, and I end up at their home."

And I wasn't mad about it.

When it came to what Ben did—yes. But having her here—no.

"Still, that's a lot of hours each week."

"Unfortunately, it's necessary. This city is completely outrageous. The amount of money I pay in rent, and still have three roommates and we all have to share a bathroom—it should be illegal." She glanced around the living room like she was in awe. "You know, problems that fit into the normal-people category."

"As opposed to?"

"Your category."

"Which is?"

"Not even close to normal." Her hand went out. "What I mean is, you're a retired NFL player and an executive at Worthington Enterprises. I can't imagine your pay stub has the same amount of numbers as mine. Or your bank account." She bit her lip as her gaze returned to me. "Maya filled me in on what you guys do and everything you own. You're quite a badass, Mr. Worthington."

With Maya being her best friend, I wasn't surprised Emily was well versed in the Worthington family.

I also had a feeling she knew more than almost all the women I'd slept with.

"For the record, I've shared a bathroom before."

She laughed. "Yeah?"

"One with Jordan while we were growing up. Another in college when I lived in the dorms my first two years. And the final when I moved off campus and shared a house with some of my teammates."

She shook her head like she was recovering from a joke I'd just told. "You're cute."

"Tell me more, Emily." My eyes narrowed as I focused on her lips.

"You're cute because you're trying to compare what your life was like back then to what I'm experiencing now. Do you know what's not cute? Being thirty-one and having to wait to pee when you first wake up since one of your roommates is taking a shower."

I huffed out a mouthful of air. "Damn."

"I know. But it's fine. I'm saving and dreaming about when I'll be able to get my own place. In the meantime, aside from the bathroom situation, I'm honestly having the best time. I love both of my jobs, so I don't mind working so much. The rehab center is a much different speed than a hospital, and I appreciate the level of calmness, and my part-time gig with Dr. Kaplan puts me in the pediatric sector, and I love that more than anything."

"Is orthopedics—I figure that's the main focus at a rehab center—what you concentrated on in school?"

A swell of emotion came over her face before her expression turned stoic. "No."

"And that was?"

"Pediatrics." Her eyes may have changed, but the softness in her tone was telling me the emotion was still there.

"I can see why. You were so good with Ben." I traced the edge of the glass with my thumb. "Did you ever work in a hospital?"

She drew in a deep breath, which I never saw her exhale. Instead, she took a long drink, holding the liquor in her mouth, her throat bobbing as she swallowed. "I did. I worked in labor and delivery." She glanced at her lap. "Things didn't work out. It just became . . . far too much. And when Maya mentioned they were hiring at the rehab center, I jumped at the opportunity, and I've been there ever since. They're so good to me, and I'm surrounded by patients like Bettie, who I'm obsessed with." Her thumb went to her mouth, and she nibbled on her nail. "I was young when I lost my parents—my dad to cancer when I was in middle school and my mom to a heart attack my freshman year of college. So working at the rehab center, surrounded mostly by patients who would be around my parents' age and older, gives me this weird sense of family."

Both parents?

Fuck.

"Damn, Emily. I'm really sorry to hear that about your mom and dad."

"It's okay. Maya is a sister to me, and my colleagues are more immediate family. Everyone and their mother invites me for holidays—I'm rich in love, trust me."

"If Grandma finds that out, she's going to invite you too."

She laughed.

"You know, Grandma's not an easy woman to please. Every time I talk to her, she tells me how happy she is there, so you're not only treating her like family, you're giving her the best care." Since both of our drinks were nearly empty, I went to the bar and retrieved the bottle and brought it over to the couch, topping off her glass and mine. "Believe it or not, this is the first time a nurse has ever had to come over here." I was amused by the way her eyes were now lighting up. "Are you surprised to hear that?"

She unfolded her legs and crossed them, holding her glass with both hands. "A little."

"Why?"

"Your son is fearless. You should have seen the way he was speed skating me around that rink." She released one hand from the glass and raked her fingers through the ends of her hair. Ends that, even though her hair was up, were teasing the top of her tits, drawing my attention there and keeping it. "When they have that kind of determination, things like buttons up their nose and hurt limbs and gaping wounds are bound to happen."

Ben skating with Emily. That was something I wish I'd seen.

"I don't know if he's like that with all sports," she continued, "but on that ice, he was wild."

"He's just like his uncle was when Jordan played in the NHL. On the football field, Ben's just like I was."

She gave me a half smile. "Which is?"

"A fucking animal."

"Oh God." Her teeth skimmed across her bottom lip, and she briefly fanned her face, making me chuckle. "Tell me about it."

"Football?"

"Yes. I want to hear all about you, considering you just heard all about me."

I set my drink on the middle of my thigh and stretched my other arm over the back of the couch. "Where do I start . . . ?"

"The beginning." She released her hair and started to play with one of the hoops hanging from her ear. "Where did you go to school?"

"I was recruited by quite a few and chose the University of Alabama—mostly for football, but the weather didn't hurt either."

"You don't like the cold?"

"Fuck no. I hate it."

"But you live in Boston. I'm assuming you were born and raised here. You're not used to the temps by now?"

"Used to it, yes. Like it, no. Ben needs to be around family, and mine is here. That's the only reason I live in the north. But during college, I enjoyed every second of warmth in the South, and spending my entire NFL career in Tampa, I got even more of it."

"Tampa sounds dreamy."

"You haven't been?"

She shook her head. "Orlando and Miami—that's it." She shifted so she could lean her side into the back cushion. "What made you retire from football?"

"It's a layered answer."

"I'm sorry, you don't have to talk about it—"

"No, no, it's all right. You know, for a lot of the football season, I was on the road, and when you're a single dad, that makes things hard. I have an incredible nanny, and I wouldn't have been able to play ball had she not been with me. She even moved with us from Tampa to Boston, but being that Ben doesn't have his mother in his life, he needs me. My team also needed me. It was one hell of a mental battle."

She was quiet for a moment before she replied, "I can't even imagine."

"And then there's the body." I pushed up the sleeve to my long-sleeve T-shirt. "It can only handle so much, no matter how well I treated it off the field. I was lucky—unlike some of my teammates, I never got an injury that made me miss any games. I hurt like hell, but nothing that required surgery or time off. But, again, it all came down to Ben. I needed to be my best for him, and ultimately you can only be lucky for so long. Trying to care for a young kid with a torn Achilles or rotator cuff—I couldn't let that happen. So I made the decision to retire, and the timing happened to be perfect." I smiled. "My last game, we won the Super Bowl."

"Epic." She took a sip.

"It was."

She swiped her thumb over her lips like she was trying to dry them. "And what's cool is that you're still deeply involved with football. You're just coming at it from a different angle."

Worthington Enterprises was a company that began with Bettie's financial backing many, many years ago, my parents paying off every dollar they borrowed from her and, with the help of my brother and me, building it into the empire it was today. We owned every professional sports team in Massachusetts, and we had an extremely large portfolio of residential high-rise apartments.

We wanted to dominate Boston, and we were well on our way.

"An angle I really enjoy," I told her.

But what I was really enjoying was this view, an almost full shot of her front, a hint of her side, how her legs were now crossed, the material pulling tight so I could see the outline of her thighs.

It was more than just her beauty that was making my dick achingly hard. There was something about this one, and fuck, I didn't know what it was.

"Are you a go-into-the-office-every-day kind of guy? Or do you oversee things from home? And do you ever travel with the team?"

"I do it all." I pushed up my other sleeve and drained the rest of my scotch. "More office than home since home, sadly, doesn't allow me to get much work done. Although Ben is involved in things after school and my nanny is here, it's not easy keeping a seven-year-old from bursting in, given that he always wants to be around Dad."

She laughed. "The most adorable work nightmare ever."

"Exactly." I stretched my arm over my head, lowering it to grip the back of my neck. "As for the away games, I don't attend all of them but I attend enough. Same with baseball. Jordan focuses on basketball and hockey—we divided the sports between us. For the real estate part of our business, the two of us dabble. Decision-making, brand, concepts, acquisitions—those types of things, we're largely a part of. The rest, our team handles."

"Fascinating."

"It's just business."

"I wasn't talking about your job." She finished her drink too. "I was talking about you, Gavin." As soon as the words left her mouth, I could tell she was lured in as deep as I was.

"What about me do you find so fascinating?"

When her thumb left her lips, I couldn't look at anything but them. I wanted to know how they tasted. I wanted to know how hard they could suck.

I wanted to know how loud they could moan.

"I get the feeling—and maybe I'm wrong—that you could have easily stopped working after retiring from the NFL. But you didn't, and the job you have now doesn't sound easy at all."

"I thought you said this fascination wasn't about my job?"

She smiled. "You're right, I said that."

I chuckled.

"But we're going to keep talking about your job because that's my comfort place." She covered her face with her hands for a second.

Fuck, Emily. I see you and I hear you loud and clear.

When her hands dropped, the embarrassment leaving her expression, I went to give myself a refill, and she held out her glass. I added more to hers before I gave myself three fingers' worth.

I set the bottle down and leaned back into the couch. "Do you know what I find fascinating?" I paused. "That someone like you is single."

"Someone like me?" She let out a loud laugh. "What does that even mean?"

"You want the truth?"

She sighed. "Please."

My foot, crossed over the opposite knee, had been pumping the air, but now it stilled. "You're the most beautiful woman I've ever seen."

Her eyes widened. "Ever?"

"Yes. Ever."

"Wow." She went quiet. "I didn't expect that. I . . . don't even know what to say . . . and normally I have all the words." She glanced down at her body. "I mean, I'm not even in clothes. I'm . . . in scrubs."

"Clothes have nothing to do with what I'm looking at, nor would they make me change my mind." My arm had returned to the back of the couch, and I bent it, holding my cheek with my palm.

"But my hair's in a ponytail. At this point, I'm positive I don't have any makeup left on my face—in fact, I was seconds away from getting in the bathtub before Dr. Kaplan's office called."

I wish she hadn't put that vision in my fucking head.

Emily naked, stepping into a tub was something I wanted to see.

"I would much rather see you without makeup on than with. Why? Because masks aren't for me. I want to see what's underneath, and I want to see what I'm going to wake up next to."

She hid her smile as she said, "This is all me. Unmasked."

"Which brings me back to my previous question: Why are you single?"

She let out a long, loud breath. "It's not by choice, I can tell you that. I want to date."

"It's a bad-timing thing?"

"No, it's an every-guy-is-so-wrong-for-me kinda thing. It's frustrating, I'm not going to lie."

"Fuck."

She nodded. "So I've stopped trying. I don't do the dating apps, like Hooked, which a bunch of my friends are on. I don't put myself out there in the sense that I'm trying to attract men. I just let things happen. The same way I did tonight. Except I did return to your condo when I found out I was able to have a drink, so maybe I just contradicted myself—I don't know."

"Why did you come back?"

She laughed. "That's a big ask."

"Why?"

She set her glass down and wrapped her arms around her stomach. "I don't know how to bullshit, so my answer will be beyond truthful. It won't only be awkward to say it, but awkward for you to hear it."

"Try me."

Her stare intensified the longer she looked at me. "When I saw you that night at the arena, I couldn't believe what I was seeing. I thought then—and I still do—that you're the hottest man alive. That was why I was a little shell-shocked when the elevator door opened and you were standing there. That's why I could barely look at you the whole time I was helping Ben. And that's why I was blown the hell away when you asked me for a drink and completely gutted when I couldn't have one. But when I got that text from Dr. Kaplan's office telling me I was clocked out, there was literally no way I was going to let the opportunity pass."

Fucking Jordan. Not once had he mentioned that Maya's best friend was this hot. I needed to yell at him for that.

"It was a good decision to come back, Emily." My blinks were slow as I gazed at her through my lashes.

She glanced away as though she couldn't handle it. "Why are you single?"

"I choose to be. Ben plays a big factor in that. I don't want to bring a woman into his life unless she's the one I'm going to marry. And giving a woman that much time means hours away from my son, and I'm not about that."

She leaned forward. "Are you saying you're . . . completely woman-free?"

"You mean celibate?" I chuckled.

"Thank you for saying that so I didn't have to."

I cocked my head. "If I was celibate, would you have a hard time believing it?"

"Yes." Her face turned red again. "You're, what, mid-thirties? That's prime sex age. Plus, I've already told you how handsome I think you are, and I promise anyone who meets you feels the same way, so I'm sure the ladies come on strong." She released her stomach to play with her lip. "We all have needs, Gavin. I would have a hard time believing you don't. Or that you don't take care of those needs."

God, this was fun.

I placed my glass on the ottoman. "I'm struggling with something, Emily. Something I need you to tell me."

"Okay . . ."

I was mentally stripping off her scrubs and rubbing my mouth across her neck. "Are you asking me what those needs are? Or are you wanting to see just how I take care of them?"

CHAPTER THREE

Emily

Are you asking me what those needs are? Or are you wanting to see just how I take care of them?

Gavin had only said those words once in his deep, gritty, sexy voice, but I continued to hear them over and over as they repeated in my head. And when his cobalt gaze accompanied those two sentences, it felt as though I were sitting on this couch, buck-ass naked, panting, with my legs spread.

I was no prude. In fact, I was the complete opposite. Sexually, I was extremely in tune with my body and what I wanted.

But there was something about Gavin—the way he looked at me, the way he made me feel, the size of his body and how I found him so consumingly handsome—that made me realize I didn't have the sexual upper hand.

He did.

And I willingly gave it to him.

With each second of silence that passed, my nerves came on stronger, and a shyness was building—two things that normally didn't have a presence, but they'd been churning inside me since I took a seat in his living room, the two warring with one another.

"I . . ." My voice cut off. Why was I having such a hard time expressing myself? Because this whole night felt like a fantasy? Because I never envisioned getting a close-up of the man I'd been drooling over at the hockey game? Because I was so sex deprived, I was mentally humping his words? "Yes, I'm asking you what those needs are, and I'm also wanting to see just how you take care of them."

I felt his exhale even though there was a whole cushion between us.

Stillness followed.

Five seconds, ten. I didn't know how long we sat like that. It just seemed that nothing was moving aside from what was happening in me.

And then, suddenly, he got up from the couch and stood in front of me, holding out his hand for me to take. "Come with me."

Did this mean he was going to show me how he took care of his needs?

The tingles in my body weren't just igniting—they were exploding.

Even more so as my fingers landed within his grasp. A touch that made me breathless. That made my insides melt toward my outsides, the aching between my legs increasing to a throbbing.

Once I was on my feet, his palm pressed to mine, he lifted the bottle we'd been drinking from and walked me into the kitchen. The closeness was a heat I wasn't expecting. His stature and broadness, while still a pace ahead, made me feel the tiniest.

I couldn't imagine facing this man on a football field.

But facing him here, I wanted nothing more.

He set the bottle on the island and turned toward me, his hand landing on my upper arm, dragging higher to my shoulder and eventually stopping on my neck.

A touch so subtle, yet my back arched.

I heard myself intake some air, but I didn't feel it.

All I felt was him.

"God, you're fucking gorgeous."

My heart was pounding out of my chest, his statement only making it beat faster.

Things from there happened so quickly, I couldn't keep track of the steps, but the next thing I knew, I was sitting beside the bottle on the counter and he was standing in front of me.

Our faces were close.

His chest was goading me to touch it.

He lifted the scotch to his lips, taking several sips. "Are you hungry?"

It took a few moments before his question registered. "As in . . . food?"

He laughed. "Yes, Emily, as in food."

I'd been so fixated on him, none of my senses were picking up on anything else. But now I noticed the kitchen smelled incredible, a delicious combo of tomato sauce and meat.

My stomach growled.

"Ben eats early—too early for me. While he eats, I usually have a salad so I can do dinner with him, and I eat the main part of my meal later on. That was about to happen when he came bolting down the stairs with the button up his nose. So I shut off the oven, keeping the pizza in there. Are you up for having a slice?"

My brain wasn't anywhere near the thought of ingesting food. Neither was my stomach, but maybe putting something in my mouth would tame the thoughts that were running through my head. "Sure."

"It's either you or pizza, but I fucking need to eat something." He gave me a smile.

And when he turned around and went over to the oven, I completely lost it, dissolving into a pool of wetness on his counter.

He slipped his hand into a mitt, opening the door and removing a large pizza stone, placing it on top of the gas burners. "It's homemade." He looked at me over his shoulder. "Pepperoni, mushrooms, and jalapeños. You good with those toppings?"

I nodded. "Homemade—you're saying you cook?"

As he turned back toward the stove, taking a plate out of one of the cabinets and a pizza cutter from a drawer, he replied, "I can. I'm actually pretty decent at it." He placed a slice on the plate, put the rest of the pizza back in the oven, and brought the plate over to me. "I don't do it often. That's only because I don't have the time. If I didn't work as much, I'd probably cook every night. I enjoy it. This, though, I didn't make."

I balanced the plate in front of me and lifted the slice. "Who made it?"

"I have a chef."

My brain had immediately thought it was a woman in his life, even though he'd already confirmed he had no such thing. But of course he had a chef. The man was a billionaire.

"Goals." I released a long sigh. "Honestly, that's so dreamy."

"It's a time-saver. But you know, I'd rather do it myself. I love getting lost in tastes and smells and experimenting with different combinations."

He made everything sound like a sex song.

"Now that's a sight I'd like to see." I chewed on my lip.

His brows raised. "Me in the kitchen, you mean?"

"A man who can cook—I die over the thought of that."

"Don't die. He's right here." He brought the bottle up to his lips, his throat bobbing as he swallowed. "What do you think of the pizza?"

I'd taken a small bite, surprised that it wasn't dried out and still somewhat warm, the crust crispy like I preferred, the toppings a perfect mix. "Delicious."

"It's not too cold?"

"Cold doesn't bother me, but no, it's not." I nodded toward him. "Are you not having any?"

He bent his head and leaned his body in closer, causing me to instantly draw in some air, and he took a bite from the side of my slice.

I laughed as I watched him chew. "You're an animal off the field too."

He smirked. "I'd rather have some of yours."

"And what if I don't like to share?"

He swallowed and moved in again, holding eye contact as his mouth parted and he surrounded the crust. He paused right there, the smile no longer on his lips but in his eyes, and he eventually pulled back to chew what he'd bitten off. "I told you, it's either you or pizza—but I'm going to eat something."

"Do you want me to make that choice for you?"

"I want you to tell me what you want, Emily."

I set down the plate and took the bottle from his hand. There was something so sensual about putting my lips on the same place his had just been, letting the scotch pour into my mouth, burning my tongue before it went down my throat.

There was no such thing as liquid courage at this point.

I knew what I wanted. It was brewing within me, and saying it out loud was going to give me such relief.

I licked the wetness off my lips. "You."

"Me." His head did a solo nod, and he flattened his palms on either side of me. "I need to explain something to you." He positioned himself between my legs, his hands now on my neck, aiming my eyes up at his. "It's about the question you asked, the one I've yet to answer, so I will right now. Yes, I have needs, Emily. Needs that are strong, that are fucking hungry, that are feral. And how I take care of those needs is with women. I already told you that I don't have time for dating. My son gets all of me, and there are no exceptions to that. So when I'm with a woman, it's for one night and one night only. Tonight, I want that woman to be you." He stroked his thumb along the bottom of my jaw, goose bumps rising over every inch of my skin. "If I'm what you want, I need to know that you're okay with these parameters. That you understand exactly what I'm saying. That you won't be expecting any more from me."

If I was looking for honesty, I couldn't have possibly gotten any more than what he'd just voiced.

The guidelines had been defined.

Nothing would happen beyond tonight.

But what I would get out of this, more than likely, was the best sex of my life. Or, at the very least, I would be getting laid by the hottest man alive, with a body I was dying to see naked. And I would get to fulfill every thought that had run through my head since seeing Gavin on the ice at that game.

Plus, I would finally be out of this endless sex-deprived zone.

I didn't know whether he was someone I wanted to date. I didn't know whether we were even compatible. All I knew was that our sexual chemistry was scorching, I was beyond attracted to him, and if anyone was going to rock my world, I wanted it to be him.

"I accept." I finally touched his chest, my fingertips meeting muscle that was as hard as the counter beneath me. "But under one condition."

"I'm listening."

"The most I've ever gotten off in one night was twice. Gavin"—I tapped his pec, the feel of it causing me to let out a tiny moan—"you need to break that record."

He let out a chuckle, a sound that wrapped around my legs and dove between them. "I'm not just going to break it. I'm going to fucking destroy it."

CHAPTER FOUR

Gavin

Just when I thought Emily couldn't get any hotter, she blew that theory out of the park by agreeing to sleep with me under one condition: I would make her come more than twice tonight.

I could accomplish that with just my tongue.

Something I certainly planned to do.

But for now, my hands slid away from her neck and dropped to her waist, pulling her to the end of the counter, where her legs wrapped around me. "We have a deal."

Her arms circled my shoulders. "You have your work cut out for you, Mr. Worthington."

Was she really doubting my abilities?

Or challenging me?

Whatever the case was, I liked this side of Emily.

When she'd walked into my condo, I immediately picked up on her shyness. After a drink, that had started to diminish, a confidence coming through. Even more than that, an outwardness. She was sure of what she wanted and seemed sexually adventurous.

I liked that.

I didn't want to be with a woman who was going to hide her body or cower under the covers or turn out to be a boring participant, wanting things to be over as soon as they started.

I wanted a woman who craved sex as much as I did.

Who needed it to survive.

Who considered it a sport where there were two teams involved and both were willing to compete.

I pressed my forehead against hers. "You should know, I take my work seriously. Whatever the job is, I don't quit. And whatever the goal is, I crush it." I moved back to look at her face. She was grinning, just like I anticipated.

"Maybe. But I'll really believe it when you prove those words to me."

"Let it be known that if my son wasn't upstairs, I'd devour you on this counter. I just won't take the chance of him coming down and catching us." My hands lifted to the sides of her navel, my thumbs rubbing over her ribs.

I could already tell she had one hell of a fucking body, something I'd known a few seconds after she arrived, but feeling the tightness beneath these scrubs only confirmed it.

"How do you normally hide this kind of stuff from him?"

"I don't have to. I don't bring women to my condo."

"Not ever?" Her brows rose.

"Not ever," I confirmed. "This is Ben's home. That's something I take seriously. You are, and will be, the only exception to that rule."

"Are you sure you want to make the exception? I would understand if—"

I couldn't fucking wait another second, that was how badly I wanted her.

My lips landed on hers, and I cupped her face to hold her against me, my tongue sliding through to taste her at the same time I breathed her in. Her scent reminded me of warmth, a mix of coffee and vanilla, like the lattes I made during the cold winter nights.

She knew just how to take in my tongue, how to circle hers around it, her body bending into mine. But this was more than just a kiss. This was Emily showing me what she wanted. This was her giving me what I wanted.

I was out of patience.

I was out of air.

I forced myself back, separating our mouths but still holding her cheeks. With my eyes now locked with hers, I finally answered, "I'm sure I want to make you the exception," in case the kiss hadn't proved that to her.

Her chest heaved as though she couldn't catch her breath. "I love that for me." She smirked.

Besides, with the way my dick was fucking dying to be inside her, there was no way I could keep that rule tonight.

"We're going to have to be careful."

She smiled. "And quiet."

"Ben's room isn't above mine, and the boy could sleep through a fire alarm, but yes, I would prefer it if there wasn't any screaming." My hand moved up to her chin. "Are you a screamer, Emily?"

"Depends on how talented you are." Her eyes narrowed. "What kind of superpowers do you have, Mr. Worthington?"

"They're going to shock you." I chuckled. "And you're really going to have to hold it in."

"Sounds like someone is confident in his abilities."

She was a challenging one.

Fuck, that turned me on.

"I'm going to be the best fuck you've ever had."

She leaned in to my face but didn't put her lips on me. "Prove it to me, Gavin."

I couldn't stop myself from smiling. "Here's the deal. I'm going to have to lock my bedroom door. If Ben knocks, we're going to have to stop, and you're going to have to hide. The where-do-babies-come-from talk with my son isn't happening any time soon."

"Understandable."

"So if I send you into my closet, you'll be good with it?"

"It's like being in high school all over again and your parents come home unexpectedly—but kinda worse." Her front teeth teased her lower lip. "Of course I'm good with it." She fanned her fingers over the whiskers of my short beard. "Lock me up. Make me force myself not to scream." She rubbed those same lips together. "I'm ready."

Those words, in her voice, were painfully erotic.

So I wasted no time, lifting her off the counter and tossing her over my shoulder, her stomach the bending point, where her front half was hanging over my back and, from her waist down, she was folded across the front of me.

"Gavin!"

I held her thighs as I walked us out of the kitchen, through the living room to the other side of my condo to the primary bedroom wing.

"I already have you screaming and I've barely touched you." I was smiling, she just couldn't see it.

She banged my ass with her fists. "That wasn't a scream. That was me being surprised that you picked me up so easily."

"Emily, I squat double what you weigh. Maybe triple. You feel like nothing in my arms."

"Says no man ever—except you."

I shut my bedroom door and locked it, moving over to the bed, where I set her on the edge. She held on to the lip of the mattress with both hands, staring at me while I pulled off my shirt, tossing the long-sleeve on the floor.

She waved her hand in front of her face. "I'm not going to visually survive this."

"I'm not even naked yet."

"And I'm already dying and overheating."

I pulled at the drawstring of my sweatpants. "Do I need to cool you off?"

"As in a shower?" She nodded. "I'm already envisioning your skin all wet and bubbly and—I can't even. Yes, please. I want that."

My only worry was Ben. If he knocked on the door, I wouldn't hear him if we were in the shower. If he was going to wake up, I didn't think it would happen any time soon, but I just never knew. Which meant we had to be quick.

I lifted my chin toward her. "Are you going to wear that in the shower?"

She glanced down at her body. "No."

"Then take it off." I backed up until I reached the dresser, and I leaned my ass against the edge. "I want to see every inch of your fucking body so I can decide where I want to put my mouth first."

"Whoa." She shook her head and untucked her top, lifting it over her head, and once it was in her hand, she flung it toward me.

I caught it, laughing, and tossed it toward my shirt.

She stood, and while she lowered the bottom part of her scrubs, she slipped her feet out of the clogs, along with her socks, and faced me in just her bra and panties.

A set that was lace.

See-through.

And a light-pink color.

I ran my hand over the top of my head. "Fuck me." I gripped the longer hairs. "You're unbelievable, Emily."

"I'm not even naked yet."

She was using my words, so I was going to use hers. "I'm not going to visually survive this."

"How about this?" She reached behind her back, and the straps of the bra fell from her shoulders and the lace peeled away, her tits bouncing as they were set free. "Do you still feel the same way?"

I bit down and swore I tasted blood. "Worse."

She smiled, her eyes gleaming as she pulled at the strings on her hips, dragging them down until the lace dropped and she was stepping out.

"Emily . . ."

There was perfect, and then there was her. She exceeded that word. Fuck, she even doubled it.

A body full of curves and the right amount of thickness with arches of muscle and skin that I could tell was smooth even from all the way over here. This was a woman who hadn't had anything surgically added or tucked. She worked for this body. She was good to it too.

I didn't try to hide how hard I was staring, nor did I feel the need to apologize for it.

Even as she walked closer, I didn't make eye contact.

My gaze lifted to her neck and dove to her knees, and during one of the passes, I stalled in the middle where a small black mark was grabbing my attention.

"Is that a tattoo?" I finally met her eyes.

She laughed. "I was wondering when you were going to notice."

The ink, a spot that would be hidden by her panties, wasn't directly at the top of her pussy, more off to the side.

"A crown?" I asked.

"For my king. Once I find him. Obviously."

I shook my head. "The king of your pussy . . ."

"Of all of me, but yes, that too."

She came to a stop, within grasp, but neither of us touched.

I couldn't move yet. I could only keep looking. Admiring. Pre-cum leaked from my tip as my brain spiraled over all the different ways I wanted to fuck her.

"I'm going to tell you right now: I've never—not in my whole life—seen anything like you."

"I want to be able to say the same thing." She pointed at my sweats. Those and my boxer briefs were the only things I had on since I was barefoot. "Take them off. Or I'll be happy to take them off for you."

I pressed my hands into the top of the dresser. "Be my guest."

She closed the distance between us and gently traced down my chest, holding my gaze the entire time, and when she reached my sweatpants, she didn't pull straight down. She gripped the waist, along with the elastic of my boxer briefs, and held them out just wide enough to release my hard-on, and then the layers of fabric fell.

"Jesus Christ," she gasped as I lifted my feet from the holes. "I've officially seen a god." She took a step back, worshipping me the same way I'd done to her. "Ravish me. Please. Right now. I don't think I can wait another second."

My smile was coming on hard. "We think alike."

I lifted her into my arms, carrying her to the door. I unlocked it before I walked her into the en suite, where I set her on the bench inside the shower so I could turn on each of the showerheads. There were many—several overhead, some on the sides, one that even shot up from the floor. When they all reached the temperature I wanted, I led her toward the middle of the large walk-in. Once we were both wet, I squirted some soap into my hand, and I rubbed it across my chest and down my abs.

"I envisioned this all wrong." She gathered some of the bubbles from my pecs, so when she surrounded my cock, it felt like a cloud of warmth and pressure. A combination that made me hiss. "All I pictured was muscle. I had no idea what this"—she pumped me—"was going to look like. If I'd known, damn . . ."

I knew what hung between my legs was impressive as hell. I didn't need to be told.

But I was tempted to hear it in her voice.

"And?" I challenged.

"Don't take this the wrong way, but Gavin, I'm in love."

I laughed, pulling her closer, burying my face in her neck. "It's all yours tonight."

"Even in here? You unlocked the door. I wasn't sure how that was going to work . . ."

I added more soap to my palm, and while I kissed across her collarbone, I massaged her back, gradually moving to her ass, gripping it with both hands. The way her cheeks dipped, the way they rounded out—this part of her alone could own me.

My dick arched forward and pressed against her stomach.

I just wanted a taste.

But it wasn't time for that yet.

I slid around her hips and went to her tits, grazing my thumbs across her nipples, earning myself several moans before I lowered to her pussy. I clasped the back of her neck, tilting her face up at me, my lips hovering over hers, while I rubbed her clit.

"Gavin"—she drew in air, a noise that sounded like a gasp—"ah!"

"You wanted a shower to see me covered in soap. Which you got. But now it's my turn to get what I want."

Each pant ended in a small moan. "Which is?"

I gave her a hard, sharp kiss, and when I finally tore my mouth away, I got on my knees, spreading her legs to get her in a position where my mouth could fit. "Licking your cunt."

She gawked at me.

"You've got to keep an eye on the entrance of the bathroom. If you see Ben, you have to stop me."

"But the walls of the shower are already steaming up. It's going to be hard to see him if he walks in or . . . to concentrate on anything while you're down there."

"Then you better come. Fast."

Once the last word left my mouth, I focused solely on her pussy. For the first few moments, I rubbed my nose over her flesh, inhaling her warm, incredible scent, getting familiar and intimate with this part of her body. Something I could do all fucking night long. But given that time could possibly be against me, I dragged my tongue to her clit and flicked it from bottom to top.

"You feel . . . so good."

After every swipe, I could feel her moans. Not just in my ears—they were vibrating through her and landing on my tongue. Each one was getting louder.

"Whatever you do, don't stop."

She was diving into my hair, squeezing my strands into her palms.

She probably thought that was the only way to keep me here.

But I wasn't leaving, and I would never stop.

Because I dreamed about licking a pussy as beautiful as this one.

Because I loved this as much as she did.

And because I could already sense she was getting close. Her clit was hardening, the wetness surrounding my finger was getting thicker—an addition I sensed she liked, given that the deeper my finger went, the more she welcomed it in.

"Gavin, oh my God!"

Up to my farthest knuckle, I arched my hand, aiming for her G-spot, and I upped the speed on both—the way I lapped her with my tongue and the way I finger-fucked her.

And what that earned me was her first orgasm.

"Yes!" Her whole body tightened. "Agh!"

A quick glance toward her stomach showed it was shuddering, matching the sounds she semi-shouted, and by the way she was twisting my locks, that only confirmed what I already suspected.

Fuck, she tasted good.

I stayed on my knees until I was positive I'd licked out every quiver, and on my way up her body, I lifted her into my arms and held her against me, turning off the water before I carried her back into my bedroom.

"I'm sorry I doubted your abilities. Or questioned them. Or challenged them." Hair was clinging to her cheeks, and she pushed it away. "I don't know what I did . . . I can't even think straight."

I chuckled. "We're only getting started. You still need to get off a few more times." I locked the bedroom door and set her on the end of my bed.

"I'm soaked." She pushed herself up as though she was trying not to get the comforter wet. "We both are."

"I don't care. Don't move."

I went into my closet and grabbed a condom out of my wallet, and with my teeth, I tore off the corner of the foil as I returned to her.

But Emily had moved.

She was no longer on the end. She was kneeling in the center, hands holding her tits, thumbs on her nipples.

"Fuck . . ." I halted at my nightstand, watching her as I rolled the latex over me. "You are such a sight."

"Get over here."

As soon as the condom was locked in place, I crawled onto the bed, and she was on me immediately, encouraging me onto my back and straddling my waist. "Someone wants my dick."

And I wanted to give it to her, but it was even hotter that she was taking it. This was a sport to her, too, and damn it, she was in full competition mode.

"In ways you can't even imagine." She sat up, placing my tip in just the right spot, and she slowly sank down, moaning louder as she took in each inch.

"Emily—fuck!" I banged the back of my head against the mattress, blown away by how good she felt. But she wasn't taking it easy, letting herself get used to me—she was going straight at it, her tightness hugging me, her wetness sliding me right in.

Within a few strokes, she was already switching up her movements, gliding up and down my shaft, and after several plunges, she kept me fully snug inside and rocked back and forth.

"Ah hell," I groaned, my thumb now on her clit. "You're riding me like you want me to come."

"Isn't that what we both want?"

I sat up and gripped the back of her neck, forcing her lips to mine, wedging my thumb in a bit more to massage her harder. "But I have a goal to meet."

"Who says you can't? There's no reason I need to sleep tonight. Do you?"

I smiled. "You'll be sore."

"Gavin, I want to be sore." She wrapped her arms around my neck. "If I can't walk tomorrow, then tonight was the best night of my life." She bucked against me, her pussy closing in. "I've gotten everything I wanted this evening. Now, more than anything, I want to see you come."

She didn't pause. She didn't slow either. If anything, she was going faster, deeper.

I bit my lip as my balls contracted. "Why do you want it so soon?"

She spread her hands over my face. "In my opinion, there's nothing sexier. You covered in soap is a close second—and believe me, that was epic—but riding you and seeing you come, I'm positive nothing will ever beat that."

"Then fuck me."

Holy shit, she did.

She held nothing back, grinding like she had only one purpose, and since I kept my thumb between her legs, I knew we were reaching the same place at the same time.

"You have no idea what you're doing to me."

She leaned up even higher, balancing on her feet, using her thighs to drive her. "*Mmm.* I think I do."

I gripped her hips, nuzzling my face to hers. "Kiss me. I want to know what you taste like when you come."

"I think you already know what that tastes like."

She was smooth.

"On those lips, yes. Now I want these."

The moment our mouths collided, I let go of the little control I still had left, and with each sway of her hips, she worked the orgasm through me. The only reason I let it peak was because it was also happening in her.

I could hear it.

Feel it.

Hell, I could fucking taste it.

And when that familiar moaning sound erupted from her throat, I fully fucking lost it. I pulled my face back, thrusting upward at the same time I growled, "Emily!"

Her breath heaved, her chest inflated, and her hands bore down on my face. "Yes! Gavin, yes!" I was shocked she still had speed and power left, but both increased, even more so as I reared up, drew back, and met her in the middle. "Just like that, do not stop!"

"Fuuuck." My head fell back, overwhelmed by the sensations running through my body. She was taking me all in—my cock, the cum-filled condom, the way I looked when I became completely vulnerable.

What continued to send me over that edge was the feel of her milking my dick, the softness of her body against mine, and the sound of her in my ears.

"I can't even," she cried.

I looked up, catching her eyes as the final drip left my tip. "Neither can I."

Her shudders eventually stopped, so did her movements, and she hugged her arms around me, panting in my neck. She didn't give me her face until I pulled my thumb off her clit.

But when she did, I wasn't prepared for how beautiful she was.

"Emily . . ." My voice was soft and whispery.

"In case you're wondering, you also look like a god when you're coming."

I chuckled.

"I'm not kidding, Gavin. That was hotter than hot."

I needed a second—to collect it all, to get my body and thoughts straight. "Sounds like you want to see it again . . ."

She nodded. "Again and again and again."

CHAPTER FIVE

Emily

In Gavin's en suite, I finished getting dressed and putting myself together, and I walked into his bedroom, expecting to find him in there. But it was empty, the room exactly the way I had left it a few minutes ago—the comforter, a ball of mess in the center of the bed, the sheets pulled up from each corner, the smell of sex thick in the air.

We'd done damage.

And God, I loved it.

But given that it was past four in the morning and I couldn't be here when Ben woke up, it was time to go home.

I made my way out of his bedroom, and as soon as I went into the kitchen, I swore I got wet again. He was standing at the island in the sweatpants he'd been wearing earlier, and no shirt, facing away from me, the muscles in his back tight and flexed as he did something on his phone.

After five orgasms, getting wet was something I didn't think was possible. Tonight gave *satiated* a whole new meaning. But Gavin's presence had the power to make everything tingle, even the spots that were beyond sore.

"Hi." I halted several feet behind him, my stare leaving his back to admire all the other parts I'd gripped and straddled and dug my nails into.

He turned around, a smile growing across his features as he took me in. "There isn't a spot on your body that hasn't been fucked tonight—I'm pretty sure I covered every inch of you with my tongue. Yet you look like you're ready to go out."

I laughed. "Yes to the fucking, you definitely gave me plenty of that. But no to the going out. The only place I'm going is home for a nap before I need to head to work." I touched my hair, the long strands weaved into a messy bun after the two showers we'd ended up taking together.

"What time do you have to be at the rehab center?"

I looked at the clock on the microwave and sighed. "Eight."

"Ouch. That's going to be rough."

I slowly nodded. "But worth it." I reached into the pocket of my scrubs, my phone miraculously still in there. "I'm going to order an Uber so I can—"

"Your ride is already waiting for you downstairs."

I glanced up from the screen. "You ordered me an Uber?"

"My personal driver is going to take you home." He crossed his arms over his delicious chest.

"You have your own driver?" I didn't know why I asked that, it wasn't relevant. I also shouldn't be surprised he had a driver. "Anyway, you didn't have to do that."

"Did you think I was going to let you get in some stranger's car? At this hour? Fuck no. If Ben wasn't asleep, I'd take you home myself. Since I can't, this is the next best thing." He came over to me, his hands surrounding my face as he stood in front of me.

His height wasn't new to me, nor was his build—I was well acquainted with both after spending hours connected to him. But they were strangely taking me by surprise.

"I had a really good time tonight, Emily."

I touched his sides, my fingers slipping toward his abs, immediately regretting the move because, once again, I was lost and swoony and on the verge of wanting him to bend me over the kitchen island.

"Same."

"I hope you're able to get some sleep before work." His mouth was getting closer to mine.

This was the awkward "after" phase. When I was on borrowed time, the possibility of Ben coming down at any second combined with the realization that I wouldn't be seeing Gavin again, at least not in the way I'd experienced here. He was trying to be cordial. He was a nice guy, but ultimately, this was just sex for him. There were no feelings involved. I'd satisfied his needs, nothing else. And when I'd agreed to tonight, his purpose was solely for my needs.

But I'd be lying if I said I felt nothing.

I felt something before. I felt something during.

And I certainly felt something now.

"I'm a professional napper. I just need enough space where I can curl into a ball with a set of earbuds, and I can fall asleep anywhere." Although I was staying still, his lips were getting so close to mine. "After an hour and a shot or two of espresso, I'll be good to go."

"That makes me feel a little better about keeping you here so late."

I attempted a smile even though the placement of his hands was making that hard. "Do you really feel bad about it?"

His grip lowered to my ass, squeezing my cheeks.

For someone who wanted nothing, he sure was grabbing everything.

And, oh God, I liked it.

"Not even a little." He moved in closer, and I swore there were only hairs between us. "Kiss me, Emily."

Reluctantly, I left his abs and circled my arms around his neck, my forearms grazing the tops of his shoulders, my hands clasping behind his neck. I was sure he thought I was getting in a position to give him what he asked for. Really, I was just delaying things, making him want my mouth even more. Which I did again as I dove into his hair, holding the longer strands the same way I had when he'd been eating me out in the shower. And instead of leaning my face in to his, I moved back, scanning his eyes.

Right to left, left to right.

With each second that passed, he clenched me tighter, and eventually, when I could feel his hard-on through the sweatpants, pressing against my stomach, I caved.

But what I got was far more than a kiss.

It was an answer.

This man wanted me. There was no question about it.

When I felt like I'd given him enough, I wiggled out of his hold and pulled our mouths apart. As I was dragging my arms away, I stopped on his face, cupping it, giving him the briefest of grins before I fully separated us. "Your driver is downstairs? In front of your building?"

He nodded.

I pointed toward the living room. "I'm going to grab my bag." I felt his eyes on me as I turned my back to him, and I made my way over to the couch. The bag was on the floor, the same place I'd left it when I'd been treating Ben. I placed the strap over my shoulder and gave Gavin a quick glance. "See you around." I followed that up with a smile, and I headed for the elevator.

"Long night?" Maya asked, standing in front of the nurses' station while I sat behind the desk, on the computer, yawning, doing everything I could to keep my eyes open. Neither the nap nor the damn espresso had worked. "Girl, you have bags under your eyes." She was in the process of putting her long coffee-colored hair into a high ponytail.

I wiped the bottom of my eyelids as though that would make the bags disappear. "I didn't get much sleep."

"You didn't text me when you got home. I woke up this morning, checked my messages, and panicked. So I immediately tracked your location."

Shit.

I'd completely forgotten. But I couldn't exactly text her at four-something in the morning. All that would do was trigger her to ask questions.

Questions I wanted to avoid since I wasn't sure I was going to tell her about my evening with Gavin.

But then another thought hit me. My best friend was a runner. Whether she stayed at our apartment or Jordan's, she got up long before the sun rose and put in multiple miles, so her wake-up time varied based on when she went to sleep.

When she'd checked on me, had I been on my way home? At home? Or at Gavin's?

I needed to proceed with caution.

"Were you relieved when you saw I was at the apartment?" I held my breath as I waited for her response.

"Big-time." She leaned over the top of the desk and pulled a strand of hair off my lip. "I swear, you need a bodyguard or something. Being on call, so late, I don't like it. I worry about you."

The guilt was setting in. I told Maya absolutely everything. So why was I having a hard time telling her about this? She never judged me for any of my decisions, she never gave me shit for sleeping with a man. Gavin just felt different from anyone I'd been with in the past. Mostly because he was Jordan's brother, and we'd had a one-night stand. And things between Jordan and Maya had finally reached a good place after a very rocky start, and I didn't want to make anything awkward by creating weird or unnecessary drama.

So, for now, I was keeping this to myself, despite there being a chance that Gavin could tell Jordan, and Jordan could then tell Maya. But I had a feeling Gavin wouldn't do that. He just didn't seem like the kind of guy who kissed and told everyone about it.

I crossed my legs, pulling down the top of my lime-green scrubs. "You know, the day shift isn't any safer than the night shift. Someone could steal me at any hour, regardless of it being light or dark outside."

"Let's not put those thoughts into the universe. Nothing—and I mean nothing—can happen to my best friend during the day or at night."

"Aw, I love you, too, but really, don't worry, no one would want to take me. I'm far too spicy." I winked at her and exited out of the patient file I'd been looking at before she came over and reclined into the chair. "How was last night and this morning? Did Jordan do anything extra dreamy that I need to be jealous of?"

"That man, Em." She fanned her face, which instantly flushed the moment I mentioned him. "Seriously, things are great. But he's so slammed, him and Gavin are working on all the things, and they really have their hands full. Gavin called him at least twice before dinner, and that's after being at work together all day."

I'd heard Gavin's name come out of her mouth many times. But this time set off every alarm.

I crossed my arms over my chest. "Seems, from what you've told me, they're involved in so much."

"There's just many facets of their business, and the two of them run the show even though their dad's still technically present in the company."

I set my elbows on the desk. "Does that mean by the end of the day, they can't stand each other? Or are they just as close outside of work as they are inside of work?"

She ran her finger over her eyelashes, her brown eyes still as big as ever, even without any mascara on. "They're super close. Like us, but brothers. And you know Jordan is obsessed with Ben, you saw that when we went ice-skating."

Everything changed when she spoke about Jordan—her tone, her expression, the hearts that appeared in her eyes.

I was so incredibly happy for my best friend. She deserved this, and Jordan was perfect for her.

So I had to say, "And now you know he's going to be the best dad," because I knew it would make her smile.

She waved the air. "My brain can't even go there. Not yet, at least."

I snorted. "Babe, it's already gone there. Over and over and over again."

She rolled her eyes at me, but she knew I was right.

"I don't think I've ever seen a kid as cute as Ben," I added.

"I know! And those big bright-blue eyes of his . . . I die."

I wanted to ask about Ben's mom, but was that weird? Was I just sleep deprived and too far into my own head, or was that a completely normal question to ask my bestie?

I drew in a deep breath. "I meant to ask you this after we went skating and I forgot . . . is Ben's mom in the picture? Ben never mentioned her—I just wasn't sure what the situation is."

She tilted her head, a few seconds of silence passing. "You know, that's a good question. Honestly, I don't know. I haven't asked. But it seems like Ben is with Gavin whenever Jordan is talking to him on the phone, at least when Gavin is home and not at work. So whatever the situation is, Gavin has him most, if not all, of the time."

That was a question I'd wanted to inquire about last night, I just didn't want to push Gavin for information, considering it was really none of my business. He'd made it clear that he was single, and that was all that mattered.

"Whatever the case is, Ben's incredible, and that means he's had the best parenting."

"Agreed." She checked her watch. "I have to go check on Bettie." She held out her hand. "Come with me."

Gavin's grandmother. Just another reminder of him.

"I would love to." I got up from the desk and looped arms with her, and we entered the room at the end of the hall. "Bettie, my darling, your favorite girls are here," I announced from the doorway.

"Now that's one way to make my morning." She set down her book of crossword puzzles. "How are my gals doing?"

Maya and I had completely fallen for this eighty-four-year-old woman. I wasn't bullshitting Gavin when I told him we wanted to take her out. That was how much we enjoyed spending time with her.

"We came in to ask you that question." Maya stood near the head of Bettie's bed, smiling at her. "How's the knee feeling?"

"As good as it can be." She took a drink from her plastic water cup. Even her upper half was moving gingerly.

"Still a little stiff?" Maya asked.

"I'm afraid so." Bettie set down her water. "I'm really feeling yesterday's PT."

Knee replacements were tough, especially for someone of Bettie's age. Not only were they dealing with the pain from surgery, but also the aftereffects of the anesthesia could last for weeks, and that wasn't kind on someone's system.

"You're doing amazing—I hope you know that." I tightened the bottom of the bedding, knowing she preferred a perfectly made bed. "And despite how you're feeling, you're looking mighty fine in that hot burgundy lip color." Lipstick, she never went without, no matter what time it was.

"Gals, I've always lived by two rules." She patted her silver curls like she was checking to make sure they were in place, and they were. "You smile regardless of how you're feeling. It hides just how good the good is and just how bad the bad is. And while you're smiling, wear lipstick. But the lipstick is for you, because whether your smile is lying or telling the truth, your lips should look fabulous."

I held on to the foot of her bed, grinning. "I love that."

"My new motto," Maya said.

Bettie waved the air, but I could tell she was flattered by our responses. "How'd my blood work look this morning? A sweet gal came in and took it at around four. I swear, they just don't want you to sleep in this facility. It's as bad as a hospital."

"When I started my shift a little bit ago, the results weren't in yet," Maya explained.

"I think the results just posted," I told Maya, which was what I'd been looking at when she came to speak to me at the nurses' station. "Do you want me to go get the results?"

"I'll do it." Maya pointed at the two of us. "You guys don't have too much fun or get into any trouble while I'm gone."

As Maya left the room, I grabbed an extra pillow and carefully lifted Bettie's leg to slip it beneath her knee. "The higher elevation will improve the blood flow, and that'll help with the pain and stiffness and mobility." I gave her a soft smile. "You're doing great. Just a little bit longer and you're going to feel up to your old self."

I sensed her eyes on me while I moved up the bed, giving the pillow under her head a little extra fluff.

"My girl"—she put her hand on my arm—"is everything all right?"

I finally looked at her.

I'd been avoiding her gaze since Maya walked out. A part of me felt guilty that her grandson and I had done all those naughty things last night.

But why?

We hadn't done anything wrong. We were single. Careful. We had mostly taken all precautions to prevent Ben from seeing or hearing us.

I shouldn't feel anything.

But I did.

"I'm just tired," I admitted.

Her thumb stroked my skin. "You're not wearing any lipstick."

Her way of saying she was seeing right through my grin.

So I felt the need to reveal: "I work two jobs. Sometimes the hours get to be a lot—not the work, I love the work. Just the amount of time

I put in. I think it's caught up to me this week. But I have tonight off, and I'll be able to catch up on my sleep."

Her fingers lowered to my hand, holding me in a similar way that Ben had when we'd been skating. "What's your other job?"

"I'm an on-call nurse for Dr. Kaplan. You probably haven't heard of him, he's a pediatrician."

She was still wearing her bright-red framed reading glasses even though she was no longer doing a crossword puzzle, and she slid them halfway down her nose, looking at me over the lenses. "Dr. Kaplan, of course I've heard of him. He's a dear friend of the family, and he's Ben's doctor."

I didn't confirm—I couldn't, by law. I just smiled at her. And what that earned me was a gaze so intense, I felt it move right through me.

Was I surprised to hear she knew he was Ben's doctor? Or was I silly to think Bettie wouldn't know that he was Ben's doctor?

I really needed more sleep.

"You must work evenings for him, given that you're here during the day."

"I do."

"Were you working last night?" When I nodded, she continued, "It must have been a daunting case. I hope that little girl or boy is okay." She put her hand on her chest.

I gave her fingers a shake. "Everything worked out the way it was supposed to."

That wasn't a lie.

"Glad to hear it."

I waited a few seconds before I asked, "Do you need anything? Anything at all? Takeout"—I batted my lashes at her—"an extra blanket, lotion, mouthwash? Just say the word and I'll make it happen."

She smiled. "Everything is perfect at the moment."

"I'll check on you in a little while."

She released me, and as I was walking out of her room, she said, "My gal, I know how those long hours can weigh on you. I can't tell you how many days I ate all three meals at my desk and slept on the couch in my office only to wake up and do it all over again." She pushed her glasses to the highest peak of her nose. "The hard work will pay off. Whatever it is that you want, you're going to get it. Mark my words."

CHAPTER SIX

Gavin

I slid into the back seat of my Range Rover, my driver looking at me through the rearview mirror as I shut the door behind me. I knew that look, I knew just what it meant, and I immediately huffed out a mouthful of air. "What's up, Denis?"

"Get comfortable." His silver eyebrows, at least an inch thick, rimmed his dark stare. "The traffic isn't pretty this evening."

I sighed, my patience already nonexistent from a night of no sleep and a day at work that wouldn't fucking end, so this news made my nerves spark like goddamn lightning bolts. "Do the best you can."

Just when I thought things couldn't get any worse, my phone rang from my pocket. I checked the screen, swiped my finger across it, placing the call on speaker mode before I groaned, "Jordan, I'm in the car. If you tell me you need me to come back up to the office, the answer is no. I'm going home."

Denis was waiting for my signal to start driving, since he knew a call from my brother could result in many things. Tonight, the only thing it was triggering was how badly I needed to get out of here. I gave Denis a circling of my finger, telling him to do just that.

"I'm headed home too," Jordan replied. "I called to talk to you about the Deers."

Our NFL team.

Even though the season hadn't begun, we were deep in the planning stages.

I rested my head against the cushion behind me and closed my eyes. "What about them?"

"I was walking to the elevator, on my way to the parking garage, and an idea hit me."

"I can't fucking wait to hear this."

He let out a loud chuckle. "You okay, brother?"

"What's your idea?"

"You've been short-tempered all day. As in a straight-up asshole. Do you want to talk about what's eating at you?"

"Nothing is eating at me."

Except for the fact that I'd never be eating Emily's pussy again. Or that my hands would never roam her body. Or that I'd never get to watch her come.

From my experience, women didn't know how to keep things light. If you hooked up more than once, feelings would sprout, and I didn't need feelings in my life. I needed one-night stands where my needs were met and there was zero commitment.

Assuming Emily was like the others, there could never be a repeat of last night.

And that made me angry as hell.

"I don't believe you," my brother shot back.

"Believe whatever you want."

He laughed harder. "It must be a woman . . . That's the reason you don't want to talk about it."

My eyes flicked open, my head lifting from the cushion, and I glanced out the window at the bumper-to-bumper traffic. "Fuck that."

"Point proven." He paused. "Who is she?"

"There's no woman."

"Are you sure about that?"

Was he testing me? Had Emily said something to Maya, and Jordan already knew what had gone down between his girl's best friend and me? I couldn't tell, only because I couldn't see his face. One look at Jordan's eyes and I always saw the truth and what he was hiding behind them. But on the phone, I had no way of knowing.

"I'm sure," I answered.

"Because there's only two things in this world that can set you off. Ben and a woman—and I don't get the sense it's Ben, since you didn't bring him up once during any of the times I saw you today. Which leaves the other option. A woman."

I watched Denis shake his head while I said, "You're wrong. There are three things that set me off."

"What's the third?"

"When my brother harps on something I don't want to fucking talk about." I ended the call and shoved the phone in my pocket.

I didn't normally hold back from telling Jordan about the women I slept with. There were times I brought it up and times when the topic went there, and I offered the information.

So why the hell was I such a vault about Emily?

Why didn't I want to admit that she'd been at my place and things had taken a turn? And that it was one of the best nights I'd had in, shit, I couldn't even remember how long?

And why the fuck wasn't I able to get her out of my head?

There hadn't been a single mention of her today—no one I encountered at the office, over the phone, or through email had the same name as her. Jordan didn't even bring up Maya, so my mind should have been clear.

But it wasn't.

I thought of her when I got into the shower, remembering the two times I'd carried her in there, the memories hitting me again when I came into my room and my bedding was twisted like a knot. Ben and I spoke about her and the button and the consequences of his actions over breakfast. When Ben's nanny took him to school, the two of them left me alone in the kitchen and, out of nowhere, I got a whiff of pizza, realizing it was still in the oven. I reached in, taking out the stone, and set the cold pie in the sink. But my mind wasn't on my movements, it was taking me straight back to Emily as she was sitting on my island, holding a slice, locking eyes with me as I took a bite of the crust.

What was it about that bite that was so fucking hot?

I adjusted my dick in my suit pants and caught a glimpse of the rearview mirror, Denis's stare on mine. "I know you were listening to that conversation with my brother . . . Don't look at me like that."

"Mr. Worthington, if I may, in all the years I've driven for you, never once have you ever had me take a woman home."

I hissed, "And?"

"When I dropped her off, you gave me specific instructions to message you and let you know she got home safely."

I chuckled, running my hand over the top of my head. "What are you getting at, Denis?"

"I'm just pointing out my observations. That's all."

First Jordan, now him.

I didn't like even the thought of getting double-teamed, never mind it actually happening.

"And what exactly are you observing?" I pushed.

"When I took you to work this morning, you were in the same mood as you are now."

"Quite the detective work . . ." I slipped off my suit coat and set it beside me. "I didn't get any sleep. That would put anyone in a pissed-off mood."

"Should I point out that you're not much of a sleeper, Mr. Worthington? For the last few weeks, you've been averaging only three or four hours a night."

He drove me to the office, back, and everywhere in between. That was a lot of hours, and instead of silence, there were times I'd confessed my thoughts and actions. Driver-slash-therapist, but now I regretted ever saying a word to the man.

"You think I'm acting this way because of her. You've taken a side, Denis, I get the point."

"Is Jordan's side such a bad one to take?"

I went quiet for a moment. "There's nothing there. The well's dry. Don't try to pump it. There's not a single drip left in that hole."

Ben's mother had once filled it. It had sat empty ever since.

"That's not what her expression told me at four this morning," he offered.

I pulled at my tie, loosening it from my neck. "You and my brother, forever trying to get me to settle down. I'll tell you the same thing I've been saying for years: Things are good. Ben needs all of me. And that's not going to change, regardless of who I sleep with."

"That boy wants his father happy." He glanced at me through the rearview mirror. "And despite the attitude that's been steaming off you since this morning, there's a look in your eyes. I saw it the second you got into the car, and I've never seen it before."

"Daddy!" Ben shouted from his seat at the island as I walked into the kitchen, lugging my briefcase and suit jacket and tie, setting them on top of a barstool. "Want a cupcake?"

There were two vanilla cupcakes, one in front of Ben, the other by his nanny, the icing at least four inches high. Jenny was using a fork to eat hers, but my son was hands-deep, his mouth covered with frosting as well as his shirt.

I held my breath as I took the remaining steps toward Ben and pressed my lips to the top of his head, releasing the air only to ask, "Where did you get those?"

"Emily! The pretty nurse, Dad!"

My eyes squeezed shut, the word I'd been afraid of hearing echoing in my ears. "How did Emily get you cupcakes?"

"She delivered them," Jenny explained, wiping her mouth first and then pushing up her thick, oversize glasses, the same pair she'd been wearing since I hired her when Ben was only a month old. "She brought them about an hour ago. Since Ben finished his whole dinner, I allowed him to have one for dessert."

At least twice a week, I worked late, and on those evenings, Jenny made sure Ben was fed, and she took care of all the nightly duties until I got home.

"Gavin, you have to have one. They might be the best things I've ever tasted, and I don't normally even like vanilla. There's a whole box of them over there." She pointed to the section of counter near the coffee machine.

Just as I was about to ask how they knew the cupcakes were from Emily, Ben shouted, "Daddy, she gave me a card too! With dinosaurs on it! And she called Fenway my friend—that doggy was so cute. We need a dog just like Fenway!"

Jenny pushed the card over to me, and I lifted it off the island.

Ben, you were the bravest boy last night, and I'm so, so proud of how well you handled the removal of the button. (We won't talk about why it was in your nose, we'll leave that for your dad to discuss with you.) I was walking by a bakery this morning and saw these and knew someone very special who would love them.
Triple frosting, just like I promised, enjoy!
Your friend,
Emily & Fenway (he says "woof")

I set the card down, breathing through whatever the hell was happening in my chest, and said, "Did Emily bring them up here?"

"She left them downstairs with security." Jenny used a napkin to wipe a chunk of cake out of Ben's hair. "I wasn't sure who she was, but security confirmed her identification and assured me she was the same nurse who came here last night and treated Ben. Don't worry, without their confirmation, I never would have allowed Ben to eat them."

Had that thought even crossed my mind?

Shit, I was so all over the place, I didn't know what the fuck I was concentrating on.

"It's all good." I gave Ben's head another kiss. "I've got to make a phone call. I'll be back in a few minutes."

As I was making my way out of the kitchen, Ben said, "Daddy, hurry, you need to have a cupcake, and we need to finish the puzzle we started last night before it's bath time and you make me go to sleep."

"I won't be long." I pulled my phone out of my pocket and walked into my office, shutting the door behind me. As I took a seat at my desk, I found the number I was looking for and held my phone to my ear, listening to it ring.

"My darling grandson, how are you?"

I rocked in the chair, staring at the framed NFL jerseys on the opposite wall. None were mine. They belonged to the players I grew up watching, ones who served as role models for my career as I tried to play even a tenth of how well they did. "Grandma, how are you?"

"I'm hanging in there quite well. I can't complain. The rehab center is doing everything they possibly can to keep me happy."

"And your recovery?"

"I miss walking around my townhome, boogying to the beat, and making cookies for my boys. I have faith that I'll be dancing in no time. But speaking of my boys, how's my Ben?"

I released some air. "Grandma, he's trying to give me a heart attack."

"You know, you and your brother did the same to your mother. My phone would ring almost every day with her telling me the trouble you two got into. Little menaces, that's what you were. It's only fitting you're getting a taste of your own medicine."

I chuckled. "I think Jordan and I were worse than Ben."

"Probably so." She paused. "Is Ben all right?"

I picked up a pen, constantly pressing the top to extend and retract the tip. "He put a button up his nose last night. He wouldn't let me take it out, so I called Dr. Kaplan, and he sent over a nurse."

"I see."

"Ironically, the nurse was Emily, who's also your nurse."

"Oh yes. Lovely, lovely gal."

My thumb paused on the button, and as the room turned silent, the back of my head rested against the seat, my eyes closing. "She isn't working right now, is she? I want to . . . thank her. For . . . everything."

"No, darling. Emily only works during the day."

I looked at my watch. It was almost seven.

That explained the timing of the cupcakes. She probably left work, came here, and went home.

"You should come visit your grandmother, and then whatever you have to say to Emily, you can say it to her in person."

"I was just there a few evenings ago to visit you."

"If it were up to me, you'd visit every day."

Emily, in nursing scrubs, smiling at me as I thanked her for the cupcakes.

Those gorgeous eyes.

Lips.

That goddamn body.

Fuck.

But if Maya and Jordan went on the path I suspected, making Maya my soon-to-be sister-in-law, then I would be seeing more of Emily. And each time, I'd just have to control myself. I'd have to keep my dick in my pants. I'd have to keep my thoughts tame.

I could do that.

No fucking problem.

"I'll try to swing by in the next couple of days," I told her.

"Good. Now go give that boy a big kiss for me."

I shook my head and exhaled. "I will, Grandma."

I dropped the pen on the desk and got up from the chair, my cock so hard, I had to adjust it. That was all it had taken—those brief thoughts of Emily and I immediately started to ache.

Two days. That was how long it had been since Emily was in my bed, yet every time I walked in my room, I saw her.

Us.

Our bodies intertwined somewhere near the center of the mattress, naked and sweaty. I could still feel her skin. I could smell her in the air. I could taste her on my tongue.

Who was this goddamn woman, and how did she have this hold on me?

All I wanted was to walk in here, like I'd just done, to take a shower before I went to bed, and I stood frozen, halfway between the archway and my bed, staring at the flat comforter and puffy pillows—the way my housekeeper had left things when she cleaned this morning.

What the hell are you doing to me?

I shook my head, forcing myself to look away.

But that only lasted a second before my gaze returned to the mattress, my head filled with memories of that night.

Of each position.

Of every orgasm.

I clenched my fists, knowing the second I got into the shower and the wetness hit my skin and the soap squirted into my hand, I was going to grip those fingers around my cock and pump until I came. And while I worked myself toward that, I would see her behind my closed eyelids. The same way I had last night when I'd done the same exact thing.

Her eyes.

Mouth.

Tits.

Pussy.

Details as vivid as though she were here now.

Emily was haunting me in a way I'd never experienced, goading me without even trying to.

What the fuck did that mean?

And how could I make it stop?

CHAPTER SEVEN

Emily

"Are you sure you don't need anything?" I asked Bettie, who was perched extra high in her bed today, wearing a smile bigger than normal. Since I knew her philosophy on smiling, I really hoped that didn't mean she was in extra pain or beyond miserable, or this facility—or worse, me—was failing her in some way and she refused to say anything about it. When it came to all things medical, there needed to be full transparency between patients and the staff, and I hoped I had that with her. "You know I'm here for whatever you need, right? You just have to say the word."

She grabbed her reading glasses and phone from the table beside her, the phone going to her lap, the glasses on her face. "I know, my lovely gal." She glanced at her screen. "Everything is just glorious."

"Glad to hear it." I moved to the doorway of her room, and before I walked through it, I decided to turn toward her and add, "And the stiffness is still the same, right? You have no additional pain that you haven't mentioned?"

"Actually, it's a little better today."

Maybe the smile really was a smile.

"Exactly what I want to hear." I paused. "Remember, hit the button if you need me and I'll get here as fast as I can."

She gave me a nod and focused on her phone, and I went into the hallway, stopping at the portable computer station to enter some notes for a previous patient. Just as my hands hit the keyboard, something made me glance up from the monitor.

A feeling.

One I couldn't explain, but when I saw Gavin making his way toward me, it all made sense.

Or maybe it didn't make any sense at all.

He certainly wasn't coming here to speak to me. He was headed for Bettie's room, which was only two doors behind me.

But still, the sight of him was doing everything to me. My blood pressure skyrocketed, the tingles, starting between my legs, exploded through my body, and the anxiousness peaked.

Was that because he looked so different from the last time I'd seen him? Instead of the sweatpants-and-shirtless look he'd had going on during the early hours of that morning, here he was dressed in a suit. One that was extremely sharp, black, and a level of sexy I couldn't even fathom. He'd paired it with a light-blue shirt and a tie that had the two colors mixed in smooth, small stripes. His black hair was gelled toward the center, his scruff just as long and thick as it had been when we'd kissed.

Oh God, that first kiss.

I didn't think I'd ever get over it.

But that didn't mean I was going to throw myself at him or act like I was dying to see him. That would have zero effect on a man who only wanted a one-night stand.

So I gave him a wave, and as he approached, I said, "Hi, Gavin," and I entered my password so I could work on the notes.

"Emily . . ." He stopped near the back of the computer, the movement sending me a wave of his cologne. That spicy ginger-cinnamon scent was enough to make me weak, and it was absolutely enough to make me glance up and lock eyes with him. "Just the person I came to see."

He came to see . . . me?

Even though his eyes were on mine, I felt them on every part of my body, even the parts that were covered by my scrubs.

I'd never been so thankful that Maya had the day off.

"And why is that?" I asked. "Why aren't you here for Bettie?"

"I wanted to thank you."

Now, this was interesting.

I let my brows raise, my teeth finding my lip before I said, "For what?"

"What you did for Ben. Since he saw you, you're all he's talked about. Well, you and Fenway." His head dropped, and he looked at me through his lashes. A gaze so charming and provocative, it should be on the cover of a romance novel.

"When I took the job with Dr. Kaplan, I learned very quickly I needed to provide a distraction for my patients. Fenway comes in handy during almost every visit."

"Most kids love a cute dog." He pursed his lips in a masculine way. "Good choice."

I ran my hand around the edge of my V-neck top. "I'm just happy it worked out and you didn't find yourself at the ER. How's he feeling now? Any soreness? I imagine things must be okay since some time has passed."

"The next morning, he didn't even bring it up, which means he felt nothing, since that kid doesn't hold anything back."

"Most don't." My head tilted while I stared at him. "You've got the most adorable kid, Gavin. Truly. Ben is really something special."

"I got lucky."

"Well, yes, but luck has nothing to do with how great he is. That's because of the way you're raising him. You've turned him into such a little gentleman. Thoughtful. Caring. Kind. Kids aren't born with those traits—they're taught those traits, and you've done an incredible job with him."

God, that grin was so delicious. It didn't even come with teeth, just a small pulling of his lips, and that was all it took to melt me.

He reached into the pocket of his suit jacket, removing a piece of folded paper that he handed to me.

"What's this?"

"Open it."

I unfolded the paper, and inside was a drawing. Two exaggerated stick figures, the first a self-portrait of Ben semi-sitting on a couch, the other, me, kneeling in front of him, an oversize Fenway beside us. He even signed his name at the bottom. But it was the detail that captured me the most—the color of my hair, the design of my scrubs, the way he'd even remembered Fenway's red collar.

I held the art against my chest. "I love it so much. Please thank him for me." I refolded the drawing and carefully placed it into my scrubs pocket.

"He drew it this morning before school when I told him I was coming to see you. All on his own, I didn't even tell him to. And he gave me strict instructions to make sure you got the drawing." He laughed.

My eyes closed for a moment while I took this all in. "Best kid ever."

"It's his thank-you note for the cupcakes. You didn't have to do that, but that gesture made my son so happy."

"It's no problem." I shrugged. "Giving gifts is kinda my thing."

"But it is a problem. After dinner wasn't enough—he was asking to have one for breakfast too." He smiled.

I laughed. "Did you let him have one?"

"Hell no." He lifted his head, looking at me dead-on rather than through his lashes. "The last thing I need is his teacher calling, saying he's on a sugar high and disrupting the whole class. My kid has enough energy he needs to get out. A cupcake for breakfast, he'd be bouncing from the floor to the ceiling."

"Believe it or not, I can actually envision that." My brow furrowed. "But did you have one? That's the real question."

"A cupcake?" When I nodded, he continued, "The night you delivered them I did, yeah."

"Time for you to confess." I grinned. "Are you a vanilla guy? Like your son?"

His chuckle was deep and breathy. "No. The cupcake was good . . . but no."

"If you're not vanilla, what are you, then?"

He licked his lips. Very slowly. "We are talking about flavors, aren't we?"

I wanted to strip this man naked and hurtle into his arms.

I drew in some air instead. "Of course."

"Caramel, Oreo, chocolate, even peanut butter or coffee. I need a kick. Vanilla's too plain for me."

"Same."

He nodded like he was listening to music. "I know you like a kick."

With his gaze growing more intense, I was sure my face was getting redder by the second.

"Ha! You know nothing about me aside from the type of pizza I'll eat—and that I'll even eat pizza and that I'm not a fussy drinker."

"Oh, I know a lot more than that."

"Like what?"

"You really want to hear this?"

I didn't need to think about his question, but I acted as though I did and finally responded, "I believe I do."

"What you probably want to hear is that I know what you look like while you're working, the attention and focus you give a patient and how you ease them." He glanced to either side of us as though he was making sure no one was within ear range, and then he took a step closer. "But what I'd rather say is that I know what you taste like. I know how tight your pussy gets right before you're going to come. How wet. How your nails dig into my skin and they don't release until you stop shuddering. Or how about the way you look in the morning. Not after sleep, but after five orgasms. That amount of coming should wreck you. But you didn't look that way at all. You were fucking beautiful."

And I was internally dying from every word he just spoke.

I filled my lungs and breathed, "Gavin . . ."

"It only took one night, but I know things, Emily. More than you think I do."

"I don't even know what to say." I shook my head, but my smile didn't fade at all. "I . . . like strawberry." I laughed, realizing how ridiculous that sounded following everything he'd just said, but if I commented on the sexy stuff, I feared the two of us would be locked in the supply closet in less than a minute.

His expression transitioned from feral to amused. "Strawberry?" He sounded shocked. "No."

"What do you mean, no?"

"Fruity desserts don't make any sense. I'm all for liking fruit—I like it, too, as part of my breakfast or for a snack. But if I'm going to indulge, it's not the kind of ending I'm looking for. I want something rich and promising." He slipped his hands into his pockets, the position causing his jacket to open, revealing more of his chest. The muscles beneath, the ones his shirt were hugging, were as hard as stone and had the ability to toss me on a bed—a counter, a bench in his shower—as though I weighed nothing.

I didn't know what was making me wetter: his presence, his sexual knowledge of me, or remembering his strength and talents.

I leaned against the wall beside me, breathless, and crossed my arms. "Define *promising* . . ."

"Something that's going to leave a lasting effect."

He was good.

But so was I.

"Such as?"

He scratched his short beard, the sound of bristles reminding me of the noise they'd made when he scraped them against my inner thighs. "A satisfaction. A memory. A craving for more."

"And strawberry doesn't do that for you?"

"Not even close."

Breathless . . . no. I couldn't even breathe anymore.

"Okay, Mr. Worthington. I'll have to remember that. And next time—although hopefully there won't be a next time—I'll send half vanilla and half of a promising flavor, whatever that is. I wouldn't want you to have to indulge in something so plain and unmemorable." I flicked my teeth over my lip.

"A next time . . ."

"That would mean another button or something worse, and we're not going to manifest that, so let's hope your future of desserts are ones you purchase and not ones I send."

He didn't respond, but his eyes did. They were savoring me, taking me in like I was wine, and he was swirling it around his mouth several times before he swallowed.

"Gavin . . . you can't convince me you came all the way here just to thank me. Not when you could have called the rehab center and asked for me or your grandmother's cell and had her give me the phone."

He nodded toward me. "I tried that the night you delivered the cupcakes. You weren't here."

"I only work the day shift."

"I know that now."

With his attention on my mouth, I couldn't help but play with my lips, rubbing them together before biting them. "So if you now know that, why didn't you call? Why are you here?"

"I had to give you Ben's drawing." He shifted his weight. "Plus, I thought it would be more personal if I gave you my appreciation face-to-face."

"Your appreciation . . . It was only cupcakes. You didn't have to make the trip just to thank me. Unless you came in to see your grandmother too. In that case, it makes perfect sense."

"She's part of it, yes, but you're most of it."

Silence grew between us. It was so thick, even if I could have breathed, I wouldn't be able to find the air.

"You're welcome." I waited. "That is what you wanted to hear, isn't it?"

He let out a short laugh. "I suppose it is."

I loved this conversation more than anything. The fact that he had come here for me, that I was getting his attention, that he was looking at me this way.

But I also loved the idea of ending this chat on my terms. Of being the first one to walk away. Of making him look over his shoulder to stare at my ass.

I moved out from the computer to a spot that was only a few feet from him. If I thought I was a dripping mess before, the closeness was nearing me toward an edge I wasn't prepared for. "It was good to see you, Gavin. I know Bettie is going to be thrilled that you're here." I gave him a smile, gently running my finger down his chest, and once it grazed his belt buckle, I stepped away.

Rather than walk to the nurses' station to enter the notes I'd attempted to do just minutes ago, I went into the nearest patient's room and stopped at the side of his bed.

I didn't know why, but keeping myself occupied with a patient felt easier on my brain than going to the desk and forcing myself not to stare at the doorway of Bettie's room.

"Henry, how's everything going?" My hands went to my hips.

He adjusted the oxygen tubes in his nose. They never sat right as they lay on top of his mustache. "Just dandy. When, my dear Emily, are you going to kick this old geezer out? This hip is ready to enter the world."

I laughed. "Is that so?"

"Mmm-hm."

"And what does your wife say about that?"

He rolled his eyes. "After sixty years of marriage, wouldn't you want me here too?"

"Aww, not the case at all, Henry. But your wife also has a bad hip, and she wants to make sure you're strong and healthy so when you return home, you'll be able to take care of her."

"She just likes the time off from cooking."

I grinned. "I bet she's counting down the days until your return." I pulled his blanket up, knowing he was always cold. "PT will be in soon. Can I get you anything in the meantime?"

"Yes, you can tell the chef I'd like more mayo on my tuna salad. There was hardly any in my sandwich last night. I could barely eat it. And he needs to add a lot less onion. I thought the night nurse was going to pass out from my breath."

I laughed even harder. "I guess I'm happy I work the day shifts." I put my hand on his arm. "I'll deliver the message, don't you worry."

Henry didn't remember, but he'd checked off the box for onion because I'd helped him with his dinner order.

"If you need me, you know how to reach me," I said.

"Sure do!"

I gave him a smile, and as I was leaving his room, Gavin was standing right outside, leaning against the wall, staring at me. Between not expecting him and his nearness, I gasped.

"I didn't mean to scare you."

I separated us, taking a few steps back.

This wasn't where I'd left him.

He had relocated.

To here.

But why?

"Is Bettie not in her room? Or something?"

Several seconds passed before he replied, "I don't know. I haven't checked."

"I'm confused . . . What are you doing?"

His cobalt eyes were smoldering. "Talking to you."

"I know that, duh." I smirked. "But you already thanked me. Isn't it time to go see her?"

"I should, yes. But that would mean leaving you . . . and I'm not ready to do that."

CHAPTER EIGHT

Gavin

Emily stood not far from where I was leaning against the wall, staring at me like a deer in fucking headlights, especially since I'd told her I didn't want to go see my grandmother yet, because doing that meant leaving her and I wasn't ready for that.

"If you're not ready to leave . . . then what do you want with me, Gavin?"

Fuck.

That was a dangerous question.

The truth was, I wanted her naked.

I wanted her legs wrapped around me.

I wanted to thrust inside her pussy.

Those thoughts, along with this raging hard-on, were the reason I hadn't left the hallway, that I'd moved outside the doorway of this patient's room, waiting for her to come out.

"Are you sure you want to know the answer to that?" I bent my knee, pressing the bottom of my foot against the wall, keeping my arms crossed to stop myself from reaching for her.

"It's either that or go to my next patient's room so I can check on them." Her eyes narrowed as she looked at me. "But would you follow me there?"

I let out a short laugh. "Probably."

"Why?"

Wasn't that obvious? Couldn't she tell I was on the verge of fucking eating her?

I'd done everything I could to get her body out of my head.

All that made me do was think about it more.

"I think you know why," I offered.

She shook her head. "Just the opposite, Gavin. I know nothing that's going through your mind right now. All I know is that the other night was a one-time thing. A way to fill your needs. And a way to fill mine. We had that conversation and agreed to it. So I think you can understand why all of this"—she traced the air between us—"goes against everything we talked about."

She was either being honest, or she could see right through me and wanted to hear my confession. Regardless, she deserved an explanation.

"You're right, I didn't have to come here to thank you. I could have called the rehab center or my grandmother's phone and spoken to you that way. And giving you my appreciation face-to-face is certainly more personal . . . but it goes beyond that."

"How?"

I released a loud breath. "I wanted to see you."

"You're seeing me."

When I exhaled again, my cheeks puffed out. "Oh, I am."

"Gavin—"

"Do you know why my arms are crossed? So I don't reach for you and put you against the wall and strip your clothes off. I don't care that we're in public and this is your place of work—it's taking that much restraint to keep my hands away from you." My gaze dipped down her body, a body I hadn't stopped dreaming about, and I banged the back of my head into the drywall. "All I can smell is you. All I can see is you. All I can fucking feel . . . is you."

"I thought we had an understanding." Her tone was teasing me.

I nodded. "We did."

"And you're telling me you want to break that one-night commitment?"

"I'm telling you . . . I want a taste of you." I gripped the back of my neck, the need so strong, the crossing of my arms wasn't enough. "I fucking need a taste."

She moved against the wall beside me, the position of her tongue at the corner of her lip taunting me in a way I couldn't fucking handle. "I'm not a drug, Gavin."

"Tell my dick that."

She laughed. "I'm serious."

"So am I. I haven't been able to get you out of my head, Emily, and I've tried. Fuck, I've tried. So I'm back for more, and I hope to hell you want the same."

A smile came across her mouth. One I hadn't seen on her before. "How will I know that after this, you won't come back a third time? Or a fourth? Because even though I told you I want to date, I don't know if hooking up with my best friend's soon-to-be brother-in-law is really the best move." She held her chin. "The last thing I need is for things to be messy in even the slightest way. You and I need to be able to be in the same room together. I can't avoid their wedding or baby shower or holiday party or whatever because I don't want to see you . . ."

"I don't want that either."

She put her shoulders back, her tits automatically sticking out, and every fucking part of me noticed.

"So we're both on the same page?" she questioned.

"I've already told you, I don't do this. Ever. I can't even believe I'm fucking here right now. So yes, we're on the same page."

Her smile turned into a laugh.

"What's so funny?"

"You."

My dick was making my patience even thinner than normal. "What about me?"

"You're expecting me to fuck you right now."

"That's exactly what I'm expecting."

She glanced behind her before she said, "Gavin, I'm at work. I can't do that."

"How is work a problem? Aren't there any unoccupied rooms here? An office? Or just say the word and I'll kick my driver out of the car and we can go in there."

She sighed. "Denis, that poor man, would never mentally recover knowing what had just gone down in his office."

She was wrong. Based on the conversation I'd had with Denis several days ago, he would be pleased to know I'd gone back for more and that all his observations were correct.

"Offer a solution." I glanced at my watch. "You have less than a minute, or I swear, you're going over my shoulder and right into the back seat of the Rover."

She bit her lip before she hissed, "Relentless."

I focused on her mouth, the way she'd roughed it up with her teeth, and I wanted to do the same to it. "I know you find it hot that I'll do absolutely anything to have you."

"I never said I didn't."

I didn't want to stop looking at her, but I did to glance at my watch. "Fifty seconds, Emily."

"My shift ends in a couple of hours. You could come to my apartment and—"

"No." I couldn't live with this hard-on for another minute, never mind a few hours. "I want you now."

CHAPTER NINE

Emily

Gavin Worthington.

What has gotten into you?

I wouldn't admit that I wanted him as badly as he said he wanted me. That would give him way too much insider knowledge and control when things were perfect just the way they were. Never did I think he was going to show up here, practically panting, with a stare that hadn't stopped undressing me. I also didn't think I was going to see him this soon, not with how much he worked and how busy he was with Ben. I assumed that run-in would happen when I was with Maya and Jordan, Gavin and I having to pretend that we didn't know each other. A situation, I figured, that would either be fun or extremely painful.

But less than a week from our initial meet-up and here he was.

Wanting.

Needing.

"Forty seconds," was his next countdown reminder, and as his statement hit the air, I couldn't get over how sexy he looked while saying it.

He had turned down my offer to come to my apartment later.

I didn't want him to kick Denis out of his SUV.

That left one option.

"There are going to be rules," I informed him.

"Rules?"

I nodded.

"All right, I'm listening."

I mashed my lips together, enjoying every second of the suspense I was keeping him in, especially as he lifted his arm up the wall, knowing he was doing everything he possibly could not to wrap it around me. "No loud noises. No loud talking. No loud *anything*."

"I'm not the loud one."

I playfully slapped his other arm. "And we have to be quick."

"Fuck. That's a problem."

"Gavin, I'm serious. I can't just leave my wing for thirty minutes. My supervisor would start looking for me. And if a patient hits their call button and I don't respond, that will raise even more concern and make her search for me." I tapped his chest. "You cannot get me in trouble." I paused. "Understand?"

"No trouble. Got it."

"You're sure?"

He growled, "Five seconds, Emily."

He hadn't even looked at his watch. He had no way of knowing how much time was left. He was just the most impatient man in the universe at the moment.

"Follow me." I led him toward the nurses' station, where I briefly stopped to let one of my coworkers know I needed her to cover my wing for a few minutes. I then took him down the opposite hallway, slowing as I neared the supply closet. I looked to my left and right, and when I was sure the coast was clear, I waved my badge in front of the reader and unlocked the door. Once we were inside and the door was shut behind us, I flipped on the light and faced him. "I can't lock us in. Anyone with a badge has access to this room. But no one uses this supply closet—they use the one next to the nurses' station." He towered over me, his hands going to my waist, pulling me against him. "What that means is, anyone can walk in at any time."

The room was divided into rows, the separation due to floor-to-ceiling racks that stored and organized the unit's supplies. Gavin took a quick inventory of the space and lifted me into his arms, bringing me to the farthest row, positioning my back against the wall, his mouth immediately going to my neck.

"And if someone walks in and sees me"—it was getting harder to talk as he was kissing up to my ear and across my collarbone—"they'll most likely rat me out and I'll get fired." I moaned as he raised the bottom of my shirt, cupping my breast, rubbing my nipple back and forth. "Don't let me get fired, Gavin. I really love this job and need it." As soon as my plea was out, I was groaning.

Aching.

Desiring this man like I needed air.

I slid my fingers into the back of his hair, holding on even though I didn't need to—he had me, and I knew, without any doubt, he wouldn't let me go.

"Do you know how badly I want to eat your pussy right now?" He breathed each word across my skin, covering me in goose bumps. "I want to go back to work and taste you on my lips all fucking day."

He ravaged my mouth as though he was starved. As if the days we'd been apart had torn him in half.

And I was the only thing that could put him back together.

A hasty melding of lips and tongues while our hands desperately clutched, squeezed, dragged across each other's bodies.

Out of nowhere, the hard ground was beneath the soles of my shoes and my pants dropped to my ankles. I gasped from the coldness of the room hitting my skin. The same sound came out of me again as he lowered my thong.

Gavin was now kneeling in front of me, the hard, stiff points of his whiskers roughing up my thighs and pussy before his tongue licked between me and flicked my clit.

Whatever was building in my throat, I couldn't hold it in, a mix of mumbled words and breathy exhales coming out.

"*Mmm.* I missed this." He gazed up at me, his eyes reinforcing what he'd just said.

My head pressed into the wall, my fingers twisting his hair as the wetness of his tongue took me even farther away. His words, his admission, things I never anticipated he'd say, only added to this feeling.

"I missed"—I sucked in a deep inhale—"your tongue."

He pulled me closer, molding his mouth to me. I could barely handle it. He felt too amazing.

I reached for the rack next to me, gripping the hard pole with all my strength. When I eventually glanced down, trying to bring myself back to the present, our eyes locked again.

"You fucking taste so good."

I was positive there was no one in this world who was as beautiful as this man.

And in this position, I could not only admire how hot he was physically but also the steaminess of his desire as he ate me with this fierce passion, demanding only one thing from me.

For me to come.

It only took a few more swipes of his tongue before I completely lost it. As I shuddered against the wall, humming, *"Ohhh, yesss,"* I cupped his face. Not because I needed to hold him there—I knew he wasn't going anywhere—but to show him through my fingers just what he was doing to me.

The tingles swept through me, a wave that started in that throbbing spot between my legs and sped through my entire body. "Gavin!" I couldn't process whether I was screaming or whispering. I just knew that his name had been spoken from my lips. "Oh my God!"

He sensed the moment I turned sensitive, when I was past the peak and quickly coming down, and he rose from the floor, his hands going to his belt, unbuckling the clasp, followed by his button and zipper. He lowered his pants to the middle of his thighs, his boxer briefs next, a drip of pre-cum bubbling from the tip of his dick as it sprang free.

I'd given him a blowjob during the very early hours of our night together, but I couldn't leave that sexy bead of white just sitting there, glistening. So I put my lips around his tip, sucking the end, remembering how perfect he tasted, and I grasped the bottom of his shaft with both hands since my mouth could never reach that far.

"Fuck me," he quietly roared as I bobbed.

There was something so incredibly fulfilling about having this man's dick in my mouth. About possessing this level of control while giving him pleasure the same way he'd given it to me.

But within a few dips, he was pulling out. "I need to fuck you." He stared down my body. "Take your pants off so you can spread your legs around me."

I did as I was instructed, and once I stepped out of both, he grabbed his wallet from his back pocket and removed a condom from inside one of the flaps. He had the corner of the foil torn off and the latex rolled over him in what felt like only a few blinks.

"Get over here," he demanded once his hands were free, lifting me into the air, my legs straddling him with the wall giving my back support.

Now in position, my arms resting on his shoulders, his mouth hovering in front of mine, he thrust in.

"Gavin!" The fullness, the thickness, the length—I hadn't forgotten, it was just a fast, hard reminder as he reared back and stroked in. "Ah!"

"You're so fucking tight."

He devoured my mouth, and the harder he kissed me, the deeper he went and the more power he used.

I didn't know what to grip. I wanted to pierce every surface with my nails, that was how amazing he felt.

I moved with him, bouncing upward to help separate us and sliding down to meet him. Of course, I had no idea if this was my doing or if his strength was what forced the motion, but it was added friction, and that only increased the intensity building inside me.

I pulled my lips back and cried, "Oh! Fuck!"

"Someone's close."

The short, trimmed hairs above his dick were grazing my clit, giving me even more pressure.

"It's your fault. This is what you do to me. The second you're inside me, I no longer have control over my body." My palms went to his cheeks.

"That's what I want. To own your pussy."

He owned it, inside and outside this room.

But I didn't want to admit that.

So I begged, "Harder," instead.

Each of his breaths were bellowed into my face, combined with a moan. "You're trying to make me come."

I squeezed my walls around him, pulsing against his girth, and I bit his lip, holding it between my teeth, releasing it to say, "I don't think I need to try."

He groaned, a sound that told me he felt the way I was contracting. "But we're running out of time, goddamn it."

"Then you better make this as memorable as possible."

It was as though a switch had gone off. His movements were suddenly unhinged, his hips bucking forward and back with an urgency I didn't remember feeling from him before. But it wasn't just the way he was rocking into me that made this fire move through me—it was also the way his hands were locked on my body, the way his deep, guttural breaths were exhaled into my face, the way the passion and heat was so thick between us, my skin was blazing.

"Agh!" I couldn't contain my sounds, but I did everything I could to keep them several octaves below screaming. "Yes!"

The orgasm was already sparking, the rest of my body turning completely numb, and at this point, all I could do was hold on and take it.

So I did.

"Kiss me," he ordered.

I mashed our lips together, moaning into his mouth, and by the noises he was making and how his pumps had turned even wilder, I knew that what was happening in me was also happening in him.

"Fuck," he panted against my lips. "Your pussy is fucking milking me."

Because I was coming.

Peaking.

Everything completely dissolving except for the pleasure spreading through me, and with each drive of his cock, I got closer to that edge.

"Emily!"

When I reached the summit, when there wasn't a spot in or on my body that wasn't lit and blazing, the shudders took over.

"Gavin!"

My nails stabbed whatever they were touching, my legs tightened around him, and I did everything I could not to scream.

"Yesss." He aligned his face to mine. "You make this feel so fucking good."

He held us together, slowing a little more with each stroke until we were still, our arms hugging one another.

It took a few breaths and a smile before he said, "Do you think the entire floor just heard us?"

I laughed, rubbing my cheek along his scruff. "If they did, I think someone would have come in." I flattened my hand on his chest, the softness of his tie and the starchiness of his shirt a combo I enjoyed. "But you know what's the worst thing ever?"

"Tell me."

That I had to stop gazing into his gorgeous cobalt eyes. That I had to stop smelling his delectable cologne. That I had to unwrap my arms and legs, my pussy no longer full of him.

Rather than saying any of that, I said, "That I have to go."

"I know . . ."

He set me down, and I reached for the bottom half of my scrubs, along with my thong, and I pulled them up, trying to put myself together.

"Is there a restroom on your floor?" He stared at the condom still on his dick.

I giggled. "There is. By the elevator. You can take care of that in there"—I nodded toward the latex as he looked up at me—"along with the foil, wherever that went."

He lifted his pants, tucked himself into his boxer briefs, and buckled up. When his hands were finally free, they went to my face, and he pulled me toward him. "I came here with a long list of reasons to thank you. Add this to it."

"You don't need to thank me for having sex with you. What you got out of this, so did I."

But I got so much more.

There were things I wanted to say. Questions I wanted to ask.

I couldn't.

Gavin was here for his needs. I wasn't going to put him on the spot and start a conversation that would have an ending I probably wouldn't want to hear. Not from a man who was all physical take and no emotional give.

If he wanted more, he knew where to find me.

Just like last time, I had to leave on my terms. There was no way I was going to let him walk out the door while I sat here in silence and memories.

So I tapped his chest first and then wiggled out of his grip. "You be good, Mr. Worthington. Whatever you do, don't let anyone see you when you leave."

I gave him a smile and I was gone.

CHAPTER TEN

Gavin

The moment I walked into her room, my grandmother glanced up from the book she was reading, took off her glasses, closed the hardback, and set it on the table beside her. Her smile was so large, it reached her eyes. "My darling grandson. It's about time you paid me a visit."

Because I knew I was coming in here, I'd left the supply closet and gone into the restroom, ditched the condom and wrapper, and washed my face. The thought of kissing my grandmother with lips that had just been on Emily's cunt didn't sit right.

But that also meant I wouldn't get to taste Emily for the rest of the day, like I'd intended, and that didn't sit right with me either. I didn't know why, but the idea of getting to smell her, lick her—I liked that.

I wanted it.

And now she was gone.

I stopped at the side of my grandmother's bed and leaned down to kiss her cheek. "But I'm here now. How are you feeling?"

"Better and better each day."

"How's your mobility?" I pulled up a chair and sat beside her. "I'm assuming they're getting you up as much as possible? Having you walk longer lengths? Working on your balance?" My grandmother didn't do vulnerable well. She was a woman who had built an empire entirely on her own during a time when that was impossibly difficult and almost unheard of. There was no weakness—she was all strength. Therefore, I knew this conversation wasn't easy for her, so I added, "You know, given my sports background, I've been through this many times with my teammates. Blown-out shoulders, torn knees, ruptured Achilles. I'm extremely familiar with this process. I've seen even the toughest—like you—have to endure some of the hardest surgeries and comebacks."

The head of her bed was mostly upright, putting her in a slightly reclined position where she was fully dressed, sitting on top of her bedding with a blanket over her. A blanket that was normally on her couch at home. She pulled it back and lifted her loose pant leg well past her knee. "She looks good, doesn't she?" She rubbed her thigh. "I have many, many miles to put on her, and I'm almost ready to test her out."

This was the first time, out of all the times I'd visited her here, that she had shown me her knee. "Wow, it looks great. Minimal swelling. And your incision—whoever stitched you did a fantastic job. I've seen some gnarly scars, and it looks like yours is going to be mild."

"That's because Dr. Coffey, my plastic surgeon, stitched me. I requested him to close me up after surgery. I've seen some of the scars that knee replacements leave." She wiggled her finger at me. "I refuse to let my body look like that."

"Grandma, I don't think I've ever even seen you in shorts."

She then waved her hand. "My dear boy, having a modest scar is for me, not anyone else."

At eighty-four, with more money than she could ever spend in ten lifetimes, she could have anything she wanted.

I chuckled. "All right, that's fair."

"I'm surprised you didn't come here after school so you could bring my Ben. How is he?" She held her chest.

Had I brought Ben, nothing would have gone down in the supply room, and I had a motive when I walked through the door of this rehab center.

A motive I wasn't going to share with my grandmother.

"He has something after school today, it wouldn't have worked," I told her. "Not if I was going to make it here during Emily's shift. But he's doing well, recovered from the button incident, and an endless ball of energy."

"Ah, yes, my lovely Emily. Have you had a chance to speak to her?" Her brows raised, her head tilting down as though she were looking at me over the frame of her glasses, but she no longer had them on.

"I have."

She silently stared at me for a few moments. "Wonderful." She reached for something beside her and continued, "Your brother is quite smitten with Maya. Something tells me those two are in it for the long haul."

"Long haul, yes, I'd say so." I ran my hand over the top of my head, not remembering if I'd checked my hair in the restroom, since I was positive Emily had grabbed it more than once. "Jordan doesn't get this way about women. To hear the things he's been saying about Maya, I'm impressed with how much he's changed. She's good for him."

"And you'd be good for someone, too, you know."

My head dropped. "Grandma . . . come on."

"I can't help myself." Her hand moved to mine, causing me to look up. "I just hate to see you single for this long. Ben is seven, Gavin."

I took a deep breath.

I wasn't getting into this with her.

Grandma and my mother were the same. They openly voiced their desire for me to settle down and get married. As a parent, I understood why they thought this way. You wanted your child happy. You wanted them to have every dream come true.

But I was fucking happy.

I'd just gotten off in the supply room two wings over from here.

There was no reason to change anything about my life.

"I don't need to be dating or married. Between you, my mother, and Jenny, Ben has three women who are incredible role models. Please don't worry, my son wants for nothing. He's the happiest boy."

"But are you the happiest father, given that you're not sharing your life with someone?" She squeezed my wrist. "I'm your grandmother. It's my job to ask these kinds of questions."

She didn't ask every time I visited—whether it be here or at her town house or a family gathering—but she asked enough.

My patience regarding this conversation was thin as hell, so I offered, "I'm sharing my life with Ben, that's more than enough," and I didn't plan on saying another word about it.

She stroked her thumb over my skin. "I hope someday very soon there's more than one name listed in that sentence."

As I was on the verge of changing the subject, there was a noise in the doorway, and I turned just in time to see Emily walk through. Her eyes immediately landed on mine, showing a brief moment of surprise before that faded and she fully concentrated on Bettie, halting a few steps past the entrance.

Where did the surprise come from? Did she think I was already gone? Or was she remembering what I'd just done to her pussy and that was her reaction to me?

"Your call button was on," Emily said. "Do you want me to come back since you have company . . . or . . . ?"

"Come in, my darling." Bettie motioned her in farther. "I was hoping you could get me a little more situated."

"Of course." Emily's eyes didn't land on me even once as she went to the other side of Grandma's bed. "Are you feeling too stiff in this position?"

"Extremely." Grandma made a face. "Maybe lifting my legs a little higher will help." When Emily grabbed the remote that would adjust the bed, Grandma added, "I think the position of the bed is fine. Let's try an extra pillow."

"No problem." Emily went to the closet on the far side of the room.

While she opened the closet, getting on her tiptoes to reach the pillow on the upper shelf, Grandma said, "I can't get over the kind of care I receive here. Between Emily and Maya, I'm treated like a queen. They're the most caring, attentive, doting nurses."

I nodded as I took in Emily, studying that perfect heart-shaped ass and those delicious thighs and her narrow waist. My dick fucking throbbed as if I hadn't just come inside her. "She was the same way with Ben."

As Emily headed our way, I still couldn't take my eyes off her. Maybe it was how her scrubs didn't just hang on her body but molded to my favorite parts of her. Maybe it was the light pink of those scrubs that brought out the blond in her hair and the blue of her eyes and the smoothness of her skin, a beauty like she was marching on a goddamn runway. Maybe it was that my cock was full of need again, dying to feel the snugness and wetness of her pussy.

Whatever the case was, I was fucking mesmerized, and once she smiled at Bettie, I was done—blown the hell away by her, wishing more than anything she'd come straddle me and put me out of my misery.

"I appreciate you saying that." Emily carefully lifted my grandmother's legs to put the additional pillow beneath them. "But that's what Maya and I are here for. To make sure you're your most fabulous self, so when you return home, you don't, for any reason, find yourself back here."

"Which will be a sad day, my lovely, knowing I won't get to see you as often as I do here." Grandma reached out her hand and as Emily stepped closer, those fingers went to Emily's cheek.

"But you'll still see plenty of Maya, I'm sure." She let out a small laugh. "And you'll see me when Maya and I take you out." Emily adjusted the pillow behind my grandmother's head.

Grandma pulled her hand back and looked at me. "Can you believe these gals want to spend their free time with me?"

"Why wouldn't they?" I crossed my arms and legs, hoping to hide my hard-on. "When you're not in full-on lecture mode, laying it on extra thick, you're a pleasure to be with."

"Gavin"—Grandma playfully slapped my arm—"my motive is and always will be love. That's why I say those things to you."

"But you still say them." I chuckled.

Emily put her hands on her hips. "Bettie, I like this spicy side of you." She nodded at me, her eyelids narrowed, her expression extra sexy. "Slap him harder."

"Back in the day, I would have washed his mouth out with a bar of soap." My grandmother sighed. "I've softened in my old age."

Emily rubbed Bettie's shoulder. "I can understand that, but at my age, I thrive off spice, and that man deserves a spanking for speaking to you that way."

Yes, you do thrive off spice.

I leaned to the side, exposing an ass cheek. "Go ahead, ladies. I'm giving access and full permission."

Grandma pushed the air, like it was trying to bite her. "I can't with you young ones."

"Oh, Bettie, what an opportunity!" Emily laughed, moving the blanket and tucking the sheets down. "Anyway, how's the new position? Any better?"

"I'm much more comfortable, thank you," Bettie admitted.

"If you're feeling good, I'm going to run—"

"How about some fresh water?" My grandmother picked up her cup from the table and looked inside. "This isn't cold anymore, and it's been here since early this morning."

"I'm sure Emily has aides to help with things like that," I interjected before Emily could respond. "How about you let her get back to work, and she can send in someone to get you water?"

Emily lifted the cup and pitcher off the table. "I'm happy to do it. I'll be back in a minute."

As soon as she was gone, my grandmother said, "My gosh, she's beautiful. Charming. Sassy. Boy, do I like her."

I didn't realize I was still staring at the doorway, and turned my head toward my grandmother. "I have to get back to work, Grandma. I'll bring Ben in a few days to see you." I got up from the chair and kissed her cheek. "I'm glad you're doing so much better."

"Gavin," she said as I neared the door, and I turned around as she added, "I won't apologize for wanting you to find love. It's one of the best things I've ever experienced in my life."

"I know. I found love once, Grandma, and that was enough . . ." I didn't need to say another word, so I walked out of the room, and after passing a few doorways, Emily was making her way back, heading right for me. "I can't seem to stop running into you."

How was she more gorgeous than she had been less than a minute ago?

How was that smile making my hard-on rage?

How was her power so strong that it forced me to grin?

She nudged me with her shoulder as she reached me and then winked. "Then stop following me."

I waited a couple of paces and peeked over my shoulder. She was just about to go into Grandma's room, which gave me a final view of her ass.

An ass I needed to fuck . . .

Goddamn it.

CHAPTER ELEVEN

Emily

Maya flopped down on my bed next to me, moving onto her back, the same way I was positioned, staring at the white popcorned ceiling. She nestled her head into one of my fluffy pillows and released a long, deep breath. "What day is it?"

We were still in our scrubs, neither of us apparently having the energy to shower and change even though we'd gotten home from work a half hour ago. I hadn't even moved from my bed during that time. I'd been sucked into the mattress, and it had no intention of letting me go.

"Friday, I think."

She laughed. "You *think*?"

"Yep." I rolled toward her and used the pillow to prop up my head. "All day yesterday, I thought it was Wednesday. Until I was chatting with Bettie and I happened to mention that it was Wednesday, and she told me it was Thursday. At least, I'm pretty sure that went down yesterday, and if so, that would make today Friday. I think . . ."

That conversation with Bettie had taken place several hours after I'd had sex with her grandson in the supply room. A move that was pretty reckless on my part, but I had no regrets. I couldn't get enough of that man.

Which meant if today really was Friday, then I'd spent the last two days aching for him.

Wanting him.

Yearning for him.

But did he feel the same?

Did his thoughts go beyond his needs?

Last night, while I was in bed, I wanted so desperately to look at the spot where Maya was now lying and have Gavin there. I wanted to smell him in the air. I wanted his fingers to be crawling down my body, stopping between my legs, rather than my own hand. When I got off, I wanted it to be from his tongue. And when the shudders finally stilled in my stomach, I wanted to be surrounded by his arms and not the cool emptiness of my room.

What did he do when he got into bed last night? What did he think about?

If he wrapped his fingers around his dick, was it me he saw behind his eyelids?

Or was he already sleeping with someone else?

Ugh, I couldn't even put my brain there without feeling sick.

"How funny that the eighty-four-year-old can keep the days straight," Maya said. "Meanwhile, we're less than half her age, and we're a hot mess." She groaned.

"I feel like 'a hot mess' is a compliment." I snorted. "We're like the front wheel on the med cart. You know, the one that squeaks and rolls sideways instead of forward and back and you have to constantly reroute the cart so you don't run into doors and people? We're *that*."

Her mouth hung open. "Yes! We're the wheel. The wheel that needs to be replaced!"

"How about *retired*." I adjusted my arm to prop my head up a little higher. "That sounds better than *replaced*. But yeah . . . that wheel—she's a tired girl and we're *lots* of that." I paused. "Did that even make sense? Because it did in my head."

Maya laughed. It was one of those carefree, let-it-all-out kind of laughs. But it didn't stop—it got louder, and she covered her mouth and tucked her knees up to her chest, and tears started rolling out the sides of her eyes.

Delirious stage.

We were both in it, that was what this was, and her sound was so contagious, I began laughing and couldn't stop. I didn't even know what was so funny. It just felt good to be here, in this place with my best friend, whom I missed so much, and to have moments like this one since they weren't happening as often anymore.

"Oh my God, I can't breathe." Maya held her stomach. "I haven't laughed this hard in a long time."

"Same, girl, same."

"The wheel, I'll never get over that, and I'll never look at the med cart the same ever again." As she faced me, I pushed several of her dark locks out of her eyes. Her giggles eventually died down when she said, "Do you have to work for Dr. Kaplan tonight?"

"Nope." I smiled, exhaling loudly. "I'm off tonight and I couldn't be happier about it."

"*Ohhh.* What are you going to do?"

I hadn't given that much thought. The idea of having zero responsibility this evening was what had kept me going through my shift at the rehab center. The only thing on my agenda from now until morning was a very long, very hot shower.

"I don't know," I admitted.

"Well, I do."

I rubbed my lips together to hide my smile. "Yeah? And what's that?"

"You're coming to Jordan's for dinner." She raised her hand, preventing me from saying anything. "Do not even fight me on this. The last time I invited you, you didn't come, so this time you're coming no matter what, even if I have to carry you there myself." She winked. "How long until you'll be ready? I need to let Jordan know what time to send his driver."

"His driver . . ." I rolled my eyes.

"He won't let me take the bus or the T. Given that it's a battle I'd never win, I don't even try to negotiate."

I curled my legs in and hugged the long pillow to my chest. "What if I don't have the energy to get dressed?"

"Girl, I'm putting on yoga pants and a sweatshirt. I know you have enough energy for *that*."

"And makeup?" I sighed. "Because I can't even fathom putting on eyeliner—"

"Chapstick is the only thing I'm putting on. That, and moisturizer once I get out of the shower."

She was making this far too easy on me.

Regardless, my tank was empty.

"Ugh." I rolled onto my back. "It still sounds like so much."

Maya got up, walked around to my side of the bed, and looked down at me. "Please, Em. I want to spend time with you, and I know Jordan does too. Come to his place for me."

"Damn." I tucked my hands under my head. "Is that really the card you're going to play?"

Her brows rose. "Did it work?"

I exhaled. "Of course it worked. You know I could never say no to that."

"Good." She playfully slapped my knee. "Now, go get your ass in the shower."

"What can I get you ladies?" Jordan asked as he walked into the living room, where Maya and I were lounging on his couch.

One of our favorite cuisines was Thai, and Jordan had ordered enough for his entire building. He'd insisted we eat in the living room, and had covered the oversize ottoman with all the to-go containers. While I lay across two cushions, I stared at the lone fresh spring roll in the center, the last of the food I'd plated. But I couldn't possibly take another bite. Capacity had been hit several mouthfuls ago when I finished the papaya salad.

"Nothing. I'm so full, I feel like I'm about to burst." I rubbed my stomach as I spoke. "Thank God these yoga pants don't have buttons."

Maya laughed. "Right? Because I'd have to take mine off if they did, or if they didn't stretch." She reached for my plate, and I let her have it. "I'm going to take these into the kitchen, and I'll be right—"

"You're not taking them anywhere." Jordan pushed up his glasses and removed the plates from her hands, his green eyes focused solely on his girl. "I've got this. You two just relax." He smiled at her. "How about some more wine?"

Maya cocked her head and blew him a kiss. "I'm good."

I was relieved the brothers didn't really look alike. Height, stature, body type—yes. But facial features and hair color were different. It seemed everywhere I went, I was reminded of Gavin. I didn't want to look at Jordan and see Gavin's twin—or almost twin.

"Emily, how about you? More wine?"

I shook my head. "I'm beyond good."

Maya picked up her almost-full glass of wine and said, "Heart you," as Jordan carried the plates and a few of the to-go containers into the kitchen.

"Heart *you*," he echoed.

As I held my wineglass, I was almost too full to take a sip, but the cab—probably a bottle that cost as much as my rent—was so delicious. "Just so you know, you have the best man ever." She was less than a couch cushion away, and I turned my head toward her. "I mean it, you guys are everything together. The way he looks at you. The way he takes care of you. You have something so remarkably special, Maya."

I wanted my own version of that, which was why it was still so hard to say anything to her about Gavin. I didn't even have the man's number, yet I'd slept with him twice. Not that I felt bad about it—I certainly didn't. And even though I knew how he was, and he'd promised nothing, I wasn't working my way toward a relationship, and that stung.

It stung so badly, I couldn't admit it to someone who was in love with Gavin's brother.

"I don't know how I got this lucky," she whispered. "Seriously, Em. He's everything I've ever wanted."

I slung my arm toward her. "He's just as lucky, you know. The man may be perfect, but so are you. In every way."

She put her hand on mine, her expression showing her gratitude. "Now it needs to be your turn."

"No." I faced forward. "Stop."

"You've had your fair share of giant assholes just like I did before I met Jordan. You deserve someone spectacular. Someone who's going to love you so hard—"

"I'm too tired for 'spectacular.'" I took a deep breath, emphasizing my exhaustion, when really it was because I wanted to run from this conversation. "Me, myself, and I is plenty at the moment."

"Jordan," Maya said the moment he returned to collect more of the food, "don't you have any single-slash-spectacular friends you can hook Emily up with?"

I pulled my hand away from her and pointed at him. "Don't listen to her. It's the Thai food talking. It's her love language, so it makes her want crowns and castles and happily ever afters for everyone and their mother."

Jordan chuckled.

"Don't listen to her," Maya countered. "I need you to play matchmaker, Jordan. My girl needs a prince."

"See?" I mocked. "The girl is far too extra."

"I'm not nearly extra enough." She held her hand toward Jordan, and he grabbed it and sat under her stretched-out legs. "You must know plenty of single dudes, right?"

I guzzled half my glass and groaned. "Like I said, things are good just the way they are. I'm not looking for a man. I work two jobs. I wouldn't even have time for a relationship. Or to date. Or whatever it would all entail."

Maya smiled and looked at Jordan. "She's not convincing me. Is she convincing you?"

"Sorry, Em." Jordan grinned. "But I'm on Maya's side with this one."

I tossed a pillow at them.

"Brainstorm, Jordan." Maya took a drink. "Who do you know that's positively fabulous?"

"Positively fabulous"—he laughed again—"I'm not sure. I really need to think long and hard about this one."

"Please don't." I pretended to dry-heave. "The whole setting-me-up thing makes me gaggy, and it feels like a train wreck waiting to happen." My hand went to my heart. I didn't like the way it was pounding beneath my fingers.

"That doesn't have to be the case," Jordan offered. "I'm sure I can come up with someone good."

"How about someone you work with or a business associate?" Maya encouraged, crossing her legs over Jordan's while he held her thighs. "Or someone you played hockey with. Or—"

"Jordan, where you at?" a voice yelled from what I assumed was the entrance of Jordan's condo.

A voice, even though I'd only heard it a few times, I already knew far too well.

The sexiness and grittiness in Gavin's tone made me sit up a little higher and bring my wine much closer to my mouth.

"In the living room!" Jordan yelled back.

What was Gavin doing here?

And why, out of all evenings, did he decide to come over tonight?

I sucked in as much air as I could hold and waited. The music Jordan had playing in the background made it impossible to hear Gavin's footsteps, but I swore I could feel him getting closer, my body reacting to the anticipation of seeing him.

And when I did, when he crossed into the living room, wearing a pair of dark jeans and a cobalt-blue button-down, a color identical to his eyes so that they popped even more than normal, there wasn't a spot in my body that wasn't tingling.

Especially when his gaze locked with mine.

When his eyes narrowed and he took me in as if he were seeing me for the first time all over again.

I couldn't read his expression. I couldn't make sense of his posture. He had stopped at the base of the ottoman, his arms crossed over his chest, the material of his shirt tight against each muscle. With his height towering over me and his strength apparent in his size, I was dissolving into the couch, melting a little more every second. What didn't help was my nose sensing a subtle hint of his cologne, and after each inhale, I found myself breathing deeper so I could get more of his scent.

Why does he have this effect on me?

And why can't I shut it off?

"You know, your brother's single," Maya said out of nowhere. "I wonder if he could be an option?"

I couldn't speak. For so many reasons, the main one being that I was sure no words would come out—it would only be breaths that would sound like a moan.

"What do you think, Jordan?" Maya continued.

Gavin dragged his stare away from me and said to Maya, "What about me being single?"

"Gavin, my girl here needs a happily ever after. In other words, she needs a Jordan. So I asked Jordan if he had any single friends we could hook her up with, and you, being single yourself, just so happened to walk in." Maya smiled.

And I wanted to die.

CHAPTER TWELVE

Gavin

Ben was at my parents' for the night, which gave me the option to either go out or sit in a quiet house with thoughts dominating my mind. Thoughts that somehow constantly traced back to Emily. Since there was no way in hell I was going to spend my evening doing the latter, I reached out to Jordan, and he told me to come over. When Denis dropped me off and I walked into my brother's pad, never did I think Emily would be sitting on his couch.

She was a woman I simply couldn't escape, no matter how hard I tried.

Her expression, when her eyes locked with mine, confirmed she was just as surprised to see me.

But was her cunt throbbing like my dick was now doing in my jeans? Was her skin on fucking fire, desperate for me to touch it?

And if I did, something I ached to do, I wondered what the temperature of her flesh would be. If my fingers went to her pussy, would it be wet?

Would she buck her hips forward, forcing that finger to slip in? Would she continue to dive her pussy down my finger until it was fully inside her?

Those were the questions I wanted answered as I took her in.

Fuck me, she was sexy in anything she wore. Tonight happened to be workout clothes: black leggings that clung to her gorgeous legs, a Bears T-shirt that she'd tied and knotted at her waist, showing off the flatness of her stomach and the curves of her hips. Her long blond hair was in a ponytail on top of her head, her bright-blue eyes wide, aware, and on me.

And while I stared at her best friend, Maya spoke about me, the sound of my name causing my attention to shift to her.

"Gavin, my girl here needs a happily ever after. In other words, she needs a Jordan. So I asked Jordan if he had any single friends we could hook her up with, and you, being single yourself, just so happened to walk in." Maya smiled.

I got the sense she still didn't know about Emily and me. I assumed that meant Jordan didn't either, or he would have mentioned it. Therefore, Maya's statement was completely innocent.

But I didn't know how to respond, so I dropped my head, shaking it a few times before I gripped the back of my neck.

"Please . . . you guys seriously need to stop." As I looked at Emily, she was putting her hand over her eyes, like a visor. "I don't need you to set me up with anyone."

"Hold on a second. Jordan, we're being so rude." Maya pointed at Emily and me. "Do you guys even know each other?" She paused, and neither of us responded. "Em, this is Gavin, Jordan's brother—"

"We've met." Emily removed her hand from her eyes and slowly glanced up at me.

"I didn't realize that." Maya pulled her legs off Jordan's lap and positioned herself directly next to him, cuddling into his side. "When did you meet?"

"She was in Grandma's room when I came to visit her the other day." While holding my neck, my other hand slipped into my pocket. "She told me who she was and connected all the dots."

I could tell Emily was waiting for me to say more. Perhaps that she had come over to treat Ben, but I wasn't going there. The second I said anything about her coming to my place, my brother would take that story and fucking run with it and fill in every blank.

"Ah, perfect," Maya said. "Glad we're all acquainted."

Jordan grabbed Maya's glass of wine and took a drink. "Since you guys know each other, who do you think would be good for her? We must know someone." His brow furrowed, telling me he was really thinking about this. "How about Mitch Childers?"

Jesus Christ.

Out of all conversations, why did I have to walk into this one?

"Mitch Childers?" I chuckled as I walked over to his bar to pour several fingers of scotch into a tumbler. I refused to picture Emily with the quarterback's coach of the Deers. "That motherfucker doesn't know his ass from his elbow."

"But he's a nice guy," Jordan countered.

I filled the glass higher than I'd planned and returned the bottle to the shelf before I took a seat at the end of the sectional, putting at least five spots between Emily and me. "Who the fuck cares if he's nice or not. The dude speaks football, nothing else. She'd be asleep within five minutes of their conversation."

"You're being a little rough on the guy, aren't you?"

I stared at my brother like he had six fucking heads. "He's not right for her. Move on."

"I just want to make sure . . . you do want a nice guy, don't you, Emily?" Jordan inquired.

Emily tucked her legs to her chest. "As opposed to an asshole? For sure." She was rubbing her hand over the front of her head, then stilled. "But remember, we're not setting me up."

"She doesn't mean that—the not-setting-up part, I'm talking about." Maya winked at her friend. "Keep brainstorming, Jordan."

"Oh shit, I know." My brother nodded toward me. "Mike Wilson. He's perfect for her."

"Why does that name sound familiar?" Maya asked.

Jordan pointed at Emily's shirt. "She's already a fan." He laughed, even though not a single word of this was fucking funny. "He's the head coach of the Bears."

I drained a third of my glass. "And someone who wouldn't be perfect for her."

"I beg to differ." Jordan put his arm around Maya's shoulders and turned toward Emily. "Mike's in his mid-thirties. Divorced. He has an adorable little girl. And he's a nice guy, not the playboy type or someone who's going to treat you like shit."

But he was too nice.

He wasn't going to hold her against a wall and pound her pussy just the way she liked. He wasn't going to show up at her work and have her straddle his face until her cum was on the whiskers of his beard.

Maya gave Jordan's cheek a kiss. "Why is he divorced?"

"His wife cheated on him." Jordan gave Maya her wine back. "He came home from a stint of away games and found her with another guy. He was fucking wrecked—I know because I went to the arena and talked to him about it."

"That type of traveling schedule has to be tough on a family. Poor Mike." Maya's tone had softened. "But Em, with how much you work, that schedule would totally jibe with you. You wouldn't feel guilty for being so busy all the time. And you love kids—the single-dad thing is *so* your jam."

Why the hell were they encouraging this?

Because they didn't know I'd tasted Emily, or that she'd been on my mind every waking second since I'd met her.

My jaws clenched, my teeth now grinding together.

"Do you have a picture of him?" Emily asked.

I looked up from the floor, not realizing I'd been staring at it, and squeezed the thick glass between my fingers.

Did she just say what I think she did?

She's fucking interested in Mike?

"I'm sure I can find one." Jordan pulled out his phone, his thumb swiping the screen. "Here you go."

The phone didn't make it past Maya's hands. As she studied the photo, her expression was full of too much goddamn excitement. "Oh yes, we need to make this happen. You're right, he's perfect for her."

"Why do you say that?" Emily was now hugging her legs.

"Because I'm literally staring at your type."

Emily laughed.

"Tall. Athletic. Extra handsome. Facial hair galore." She handed Emily the phone. "Meet your future husband."

"Let's not get ahead of ourselves." She finally glanced at the screen. "But you're right, he's definitely my type."

I was surprised I hadn't cracked a tooth yet.

"Do you want me to make this happen?" Jordan questioned.

Emily's chest rose. "I don't know. Maybe?"

Maybe?

There was more conversation between the three of them, but I didn't listen. I'd heard more than enough. I left my drink on the floor and returned to the bar, grabbing the bottle this time and bringing it to the couch.

"Thirsty, brother?"

I hadn't noticed they were watching me as I refilled my glass, the last bit drained when Emily admitted Mike was her type. "It's been a long day."

"You want something to eat? There's a shit-ton of leftovers." He pointed at the ottoman, where multiple to-go boxes were sitting. "I can get you a plate—"

"I'm good." I wiggled the full glass in the air. "This is my dinner."

"Gavin, you can't have that for dinner." Maya slid to the end of the couch as if she were on the verge of getting up. "Please let me get you a plate."

"No, really, I'm fine." When the scotch hit my tongue, it no longer burned. And the more I drank, which I planned to do, the less I would taste it.

I hoped to hell that meant the less I would think about her too.

"If you're not going to have any, I'm going to clean up the rest of this and pack it into the fridge." Jordan got up and collected some of the boxes.

"I'll help." Maya picked up what Jordan hadn't, and the two of them disappeared into the kitchen.

Once their backs were facing us, Emily's gaze slid over to me. She rubbed her lips together, her body staying folded. The only thing moving was her hand, bringing the wine to her mouth. "I didn't know you were coming here tonight."

"I didn't either. But Ben's at his grandparents', and when I called Jordan, he told me to come over." I swirled the scotch inside the tumbler. "My plan was to drag him out with me."

"Didn't you think Maya would be here?"

"That wouldn't stop me from trying to convince him."

She smiled but didn't show any teeth. "Of course. The asshole type." She winked.

God, why was she so fucking hot?

"How well do you know Mike?"

My brows rose, staying high as I replied, "Wilson?"

She nodded.

I huffed out the air in my mouth. "Well enough. Why?"

"Jordan and Maya are Team Mike. I'd like to know what you think since you know both of us."

For some reason, sitting here was nagging the shit out of me. I was too still. Too confined. That was one of my favorite parts about my old job—I was always moving on that field. "Didn't you tell me you don't want to date?"

She shrugged. "I also told you I want to date. I've just stopped putting myself out there, and I let things happen on their own. Clearly, I'm a bunch of mixed signals."

When I looked up her Instagram account last night, what I saw wasn't a mixed signal at all. There wasn't a dude in any of her photos. Emily came across very single. But she wasn't one of those girls who posted half-naked shots of herself or only selfies. What she shared instead was a collage of her life. Her friends, places she went, things she found beautiful. One of my favorites was a picture of her and Maya at the Bears game, the first night she'd seen me, which I knew because I cross-referenced the date. Right by the glass, in Bettie's seats, and wearing the same T-shirt she was in now.

But now I knew what was underneath that cotton.

I knew the scent of her skin.

I knew just how she tasted.

"So are you going to give me your opinion?" She stretched her legs across the couch in my direction, but she wasn't tall enough to reach me. Still, what that did was send me the faintest hint of her perfume.

Coffee and vanilla.

I wasn't going to survive this fucking night.

There was suddenly nothing left in my glass, and I immediately took care of that. "Why does it matter what I think? Why don't you just take my brother's word?"

"Because you know me better than he does."

More air came through my lips, and just as I was about to respond—words I hadn't prepared at all—Maya and Jordan returned to the living room. Maya was holding a bottle of tequila, and my brother was carrying four small glasses.

"Shots?" Maya inquired.

"Oh, it's that kinda night?" Emily laughed.

Maya sat next to her best friend and rubbed their shoulders together. "Why not. We don't have anywhere to be."

Emily set her wine down. "I just wasn't planning on getting *that* drunk."

"Well, I am." I finally pushed back against the cushion, making myself comfortable. A few shots of tequila mixed with this scotch was exactly what I needed. "I'll take two."

CHAPTER THIRTEEN

Emily

A furry blanket was spread over Maya and me as we lay next to each other on the couch. The fireplace across from us was roaring with flames, making the mood extra cozy, and the music—a mix of country, rock, and rap—was just loud enough to hear the words, but not overpowering so I couldn't make out anything her, Jordan, or Gavin had been saying throughout the night.

Tonight had been absolute perfection, including Gavin's surprise appearance, something I still hadn't gotten over.

But there was one problem.

The tequila and wine and the second helping of Thai takeout had made me so sleepy. I lifted my phone from the cushion beside me, hit the icon for my Uber app, and rolled my head toward my best friend. "I love you more than life itself, but I need to go home."

"Nooo."

"I have to go to bed, Maya. I'm fading so fast. And since I'm off from both jobs tomorrow, I have a crapload of stuff I need to get done."

She moved onto her side to face me. "How about a sleepover? I'll order us breakfast in the morning, and then you can attack all the things."

That would only lead to mimosas, and then I'd really get nothing done.

"I can't." I twirled one of her locks around my finger. "I'm going to call an Uber and—"

"You're absolutely not calling an Uber." She leaned up and looked at Jordan, who was sitting at the end of the couch, deep in conversation with Gavin. "Jordan, Emily needs to get home. Will you call your driver and have him—"

"I'll take her."

Gavin's voice shot through the room like a bullet, landing straight in my heart. As he stared at me, his expression turned that bullet so that it made the hole even larger.

The man couldn't look hotter if he tried. He was leaning forward on the couch, his arms resting on his thighs, his glass of whatever-alcohol-he-was-on-at-this-point dangling between his legs. With his chin positioned over his shoulder, the light from the fire showed the thickness of his scruff and the darkness of his gaze. Heat was blazing from his eyes and wrapping right around me.

I pulled the blanket up to my neck even though I was suddenly sweaty. "No, you don't have to go out of your way. I'll call an Uber."

"Em, it's wicked late. You're not calling an Uber at this hour."

I knew my best friend wouldn't bend, but I still tried to convince her. "I call one all the time when I'm on call for Dr. Kaplan—"

"I'm headed out too." Gavin got up from the couch, emptied his glass with one gulp, and set it on a nearby table. "My driver's right outside. There's no reason he can't take you home."

"Problem solved." Maya linked her fingers with mine. "And I didn't even have to pull the mom card."

The booze made me laugh at her. But my nerves about getting in a car with Gavin cut that laughter short. "Who says I'm not going to jump in an Uber the second I step outside."

"I do."

There was that voice again. The one so incredibly sexy, I could barely breathe.

"See, Gavin has my back." Maya threw her arms around my neck. "I'd say text me when you get home, but I know Gavin won't let anything happen to you. So text me in the morning, okay?"

Gavin wouldn't let anything happen to me. Ugh, the most seductive words I'd ever heard.

I hugged Maya back. "I had the most fun tonight, babe."

"That's why you need to come over more often." She squeezed me with more strength. "*Ohhh*, and we need to talk about Mike. That's on tomorrow's agenda. Do not forget, lady."

I pulled back, still holding her arms. "I've agreed to nothing."

"But you will." She smiled. "It's so going to happen."

I rolled my eyes, wiggling my arms away. "You're so extra."

"I know." She giggled.

I crawled out from under the blanket, slipping on my white Birkenstocks that were on the floor next to me, and I went over to where Jordan was sitting to give him a hug. "Thank you for everything. Tonight was amazing."

"I'm glad you came over."

As I stepped out of his hold, I glanced from him to Gavin, the brothers only a few feet apart. Football and hockey were literally towering over me, their bodies like brick, but their gazes so different as they looked at me.

I could feel Gavin's penetrating my skin.

Did he have any idea what he was doing to me?

Could he see right through me?

"Are you ready?" he asked.

I nodded. "Yep."

He man-hugged his brother and gave Maya a quick kiss on the cheek before he joined me in the back of the living room, and we walked to the elevator. Jordan's setup was similar to Gavin's condo, where the door opened directly inside his foyer.

"You don't have to do this," I whispered as he hit the button for the elevator.

"I know."

Why was he standing so close?

Why did it feel like his hands were all over me even though they weren't?

"I can still take an Uber home. Maya will never know."

"You're not taking a fucking Uber." The blue of his eyes was more intense than ever. "I'm getting you home safely. End of story." The door opened, and he put his hand on my lower back, leading me inside, the warmth from his fingers reaching well past my skin.

I moved to the far wall, away from his grip, and leaned my back against it. I then tucked my phone into the waist of my leggings so I could hold the thin-lipped railing with both hands.

Gavin pressed the lobby button and stayed toward the side, the door finally closing. Even though my focus was on the door, I could feel his eyes on me.

I could feel them moving down me.

I could feel the wetness they were causing.

How dare he have this effect on me. This control. This ability to trigger such a demanding need.

There was only one way to make it stop.

I finally looked at him, ignoring the chemistry exploding between our gazes and the scent of him in the air and the way my body was internally pounding, and said, "You never answered me. What's your opinion on Mike?"

The muscle in his cheek contracted, telling me his jaws tightened. "That's what you want to talk to me about? Now?"

If I thought my heart was pounding before, the speed had upped, and I could feel it all the way in my head. "Yes."

He pointed his chin upward. "Fuck Mike."

"Why would you say that?"

"Because I don't give a fuck about him."

"I do."

"You . . . *do*? You don't even know the dude. Why do you care about him?"

"That's not what I meant. I meant—"

My voice cut off as he closed the distance between us, his arms going above my head, his palms flattening on the wall, putting me in a Gavin prison.

I loved every second of it, but I wouldn't show him that.

"I don't *ever* want you to ask me about Mike again."

I drew in some air, his face so close, every bit I took in only smelled of him. "Why?"

He exhaled several times, each one hitting me. "Because I don't want to hear about you being interested in him." His voice was getting deeper and louder. "I don't want to hear about you being interested in anyone."

"What is it that you want to hear, Gavin?"

He released the wall, his fingers going to my chin, which he lifted until my lips were aligned with his. "Your moans."

I shook my head, a smile dragging across my lips.

He had it as bad as I did—the tingling, the throbbing, the needing.

"That's the only fucking thing I want to hear right now."

Wait.

Now?

I found my voice and uttered, "Now—"

His movement cut me off as he reached toward the front of the elevator, opening the small box below the display screen. Whatever he hit caused the elevator to come to a sharp stop.

"Yes. Now." His hands cupped my face. "I can't leave this elevator without having your taste on my lips."

"But—"

"Are you saying you don't want me to taste you, Emily? That the entire time you were sitting on Jordan's couch, you weren't fantasizing about what you wanted me to do to you. And what you know I'm capable of." His teeth flicked his bottom lip. "I saw you staring at me. I saw that look come across your face more than once—the one where you bite your lip and get lost in your thoughts after I tell you what I want to do to you." I felt his fingers on my stomach. "Let's see if I'm right." I felt them move beneath the waist of my leggings, heard the sound of my phone falling to the floor before his hand sank between my legs. "Soaking wet. Just like I thought you'd be."

I was caught red-handed.

But I didn't care.

This was what he did to me, and he already knew that.

"Do you have another 'but' for me, Emily?"

Had I said *but*? I was so lost, I remembered nothing before my phone dropped.

"No."

The moment the one syllable was released in my voice, he pressed his mouth to mine. His kiss was rough. Dominant. It started with his tongue, the flavor of scotch thick and perfect, and ended with a bite from his teeth. His scruff scraped my cheek, and even that made me moan.

"Do you know what you've been doing to *me* all night?"

I drove the back of my head into the wall as he slipped a finger inside me, gasping, shaking in pleasure before I ordered, "Tell me."

"I thought of every possible way to get you alone in that condo so I could put my mouth right here"—he tapped my clit—"and every time I came up with an idea, someone would fuck that up."

My hands went to his shoulders, my nails digging into the thin fabric. "But you have me now."

That smile.

My God.

It could make me agree to anything and everything.

"I do and I'm going to make it mine." I hadn't even blinked and he was already kneeling on the floor, tearing my leggings to my ankles, his nose on my clit. "No panties." He breathed me in, filling the elevator with sounds of satisfaction. "Were you planning on being naughty tonight?"

My hands left his shoulders and slid through his hair, my eyes closing as he grazed his nose over me. "I don't wear them with leggings. It feels like a traffic jam."

He let out a short, huffy chuckle and glanced up at me as my eyelids opened. "I would prefer you not wearing them, so there's less to take off and I can touch this"—he licked me—"whenever I want."

"Don't phrase sentences like there's going to be a next time. We both know what this is."

It was another occasion for my feelings to grow even stronger.

But were his?

He held my gaze, his tongue working its way between me, and it flicked the very top.

I quivered. *"Ahhh."* And within a few swishes, I was smiling. "You on your knees for me . . . there's nothing hotter."

He sucked me into his mouth, holding the end with his teeth, the pressure causing my lips to part, my breathing to come out in waves.

"Fuck!" I clenched his hair and held on despite the weakness that was already moving through my legs.

He released me, and "Now I'm going to make you come" seemed to echo through the elevator.

Before I could even fill my lungs, he started to live up to his promise.

Licking.

Fingering.

Achieving.

I couldn't look at him anymore, the movement, the build, the hunger and desire in his eyes—it was all too much. So I tilted my head back, the overhead light shining in my face, and I rocked against him.

"Gavin!" I gulped air into my mouth as everything started to increase. Not just the orgasm that was sparking inside me but the speed he was using. With each thrust of his hand, he was adding more friction, and with his tongue, the combination was accelerating the tingles. They lifted from the base of my pussy and shot through my stomach and up toward my chest. "Oh! Yes!"

I didn't know what I was holding, squeezing, stabbing, but I was on this ride, and I couldn't let go.

The peak came hard, and with it a surge of shudders completely took over my body. It felt as though I were melting into his mouth, giving him exactly what he wanted. "Oh God! Agh!"

As lost as I was, my chin still dropped, my eyes opened, and what I met was his stare. One that was hard, determined, and more sensual than I'd ever seen.

This time, when I screamed, "Gavin," it was because I'd reached the end. His mouth had brought me to this breathless, satiated place, and the only thing I had left was stillness.

A smile of triumph reached his gaze, and he kissed the sides of me and down to my inner thighs, his finger slipping out before he pulled up my leggings and rose from the floor.

His palm returned to the wall above my head, his lips now in front of mine. I was all over him, the wetness glistening from the light.

My hand went to his chest, immediately meeting the hardness of his muscles. "Looks like you got what you wanted."

"A taste of it, yes. But I'm hardly done." He focused on my eyes, lips, chest, and then roamed back up. "It's time to get out of here."

CHAPTER FOURTEEN

Gavin

Once I slid into the back seat of my SUV, pulling Emily against me, my arm went around her shoulders, and I said to Denis, "We're going to my place." My face dove into her neck, kissing the soft spot below her ear and the one above her collarbone and another right in the middle of her throat.

I could still taste her on my lips.

I could still feel her on my tongue.

But I wanted more.

What had gone down in the elevator wasn't nearly enough.

As I pulled my mouth away, she looked at me for several seconds. "Denis, I'll be going to my apartment, not Gavin's place. Thank you."

Denis had already driven away from the curb, and because of Emily's instruction, he turned at the light instead of going straight.

"Your apartment, huh?" I nuzzled my nose against her cheek.

She smiled, the headlights of the passing cars showing off her gorgeous grin, but I wished there was better light so I could see every detail of it.

She wanted to switch things up by taking me to her home. I just knew, based on what she'd previously said, that her roommates limited things, like a joint bathroom could hinder my ability to fuck her in the shower and we'd have to watch our noise.

But that was all right. As long as I got to have her, I didn't care.

My arm drew back and I held the side of her face. "I was a little shocked to hear you haven't said anything to Maya about us . . ."

"'Us'?"

"You know what I mean."

Her chest rose a few times. "I haven't. I don't plan to either. Unless you say something to Jordan and I have no choice, since I know he'll tell her—that would be too juicy for him to keep in."

"I'm not going to tell him."

Her eyes stayed on mine. "Is it easy for you to keep it from him?"

"I don't tell him everything."

"But this is different. He knows me, I'm . . . in his life."

"Which is even more of a reason not to say anything."

She slowly nodded. "Right."

My fingers dragged across her skin until they reached the back of her head, buried in her nest of blond. "It's funny, I thought tonight was just going to be a regular evening. Jordan, me, in a bar somewhere. You were the perfect surprise."

"Seems like that happens every time I see you. The perfect surprise, over and over."

"Over and over—I like that." My lips went to her ear, and I breathed her in. "That's going to be the pattern I take once I get you inside your bedroom."

Her head leaned back, and she laughed. A sound so beautiful, I ached. When her neck straightened, her finger crossed my lips like she was silencing me. "I don't think I've ever met anyone as confident as you, Mr. Worthington."

I held her wrist. "I know what I want, Emily, and I always get what I want."

"You were devising an agenda with each sip of scotch that went down your throat tonight, waiting to pounce."

"Like I said, the elevator was my first opportunity."

Her hand lowered to my chest. "And while you sit here in this back seat, you're thinking of all the things you're going to do to me once you get me in my room."

"You're not wrong."

"There's only one problem with your plan." She glanced out her window, her stare gradually returning to mine.

"And that is?"

As the SUV came to a stop in front of a building that I assumed was hers, she smiled, her top lip lifting enough to show her teeth. Her tongue then gradually came out, and she ran it over the inside of her bottom lip before she bit it. "You're not coming home with me."

I blinked, hard, trying to understand what she was saying. "I'm . . . *what?*"

She opened the door, slipping out, and as she held the side of it, she looked at me while she stood on the sidewalk. "Have yourself a good evening, Gavin." She winked.

"You're kidding."

She shook her head. "I need my beauty sleep."

"You're really not going to invite me in?"

This time, she grinned without giving me any teeth. "Nope."

"Then how about you give me your number."

Something I'd never asked any other woman. Something I hadn't planned on asking her.

But Jesus fuck, the words came right out of me.

And now that they were off my tongue, they felt right.

The next time I saw her, I didn't want it to be a surprise.

I wanted it to be chosen.

Controlled.

I wanted the anticipation to be like foreplay.

She leaned into the doorway. "You want *my* number?"

My jaws ground together, my patience completely gone at this point as my hard-on fucking raged. "Yes." I took out my phone, pulled up my contacts, my thumbs hovering, waiting for her response.

"You know . . . I don't think I'm going to give that to you."

I looked up from the screen. "What? Why?"

"If you want to talk to me, you're just going to have to make that happen on your own." Her smile grew. "Catch you later, Gavin." The door shut, and she hurried toward the entrance of her building.

Was this a goddamn joke?

I tossed the phone onto the spot where she'd been sitting, my hands balled into fists.

I could feel Denis's eyes on me from the rearview mirror.

"What the fuck just happened?" I spit out.

He released a long chuckle. "Do you really want to know?"

"No."

"Well, I'm going to tell you anyway. That girl knows exactly how to handle you, and she just proved that to the both of us."

I ran my hand over the top of my head. "What does that even mean?"

"She's given you what you want. Now she wants what she wants."

"Denis"—I banged my head on the cushion behind it—"I've given her more than I've given anyone."

"Have you considered her side of things?"

"I did tonight. In the fucking elevator." I realized he had no idea what that meant, but the man wasn't stupid—he knew me better than anyone. He could put the pieces together.

He turned at the light, heading toward my high-rise. "Perhaps you should look at things from a view that isn't physical. I'm talking about the kind of 'more' that you haven't given to anyone since Ben's mother."

He triggered a brief silence from me. "Asking for her number, that was more."

"And in order to achieve that, it sounds like she's going to make you work for it."

◆ ◆ ◆

The pounding on my office door caused me to glance up from my phone and shout, "Come in." There was only one motherfucker who dared to hit my door that hard, and within a second, his face appeared in the now-open entryway.

A face much too excited for my liking.

"What's got you smiling so hard?" I asked Jordan.

"I was just passing our assistant's desk, and she was about to bring you this." He pointed at the mug he was carrying and set it directly next to the one I'd just finished drinking. "I thought I'd bring it instead so I could check in with my older brother and see what's making you cranky."

"What would make you think I was cranky?"

"Because I know you." He laughed.

The annoyance made me shake my head. "Why are you so chipper?"

He took a seat in one of the chairs and crossed his legs, adjusting his suit jacket and then his tie. "I had an excellent weekend with Maya." He nodded toward me. "What's crawled up your ass this fine morning?"

"It's fucking Monday. It's not even nine and I have over four hundred emails in my inbox and a full day of meetings I have no desire to attend."

"Doesn't look like you're working that hard on clearing your inbox." He pointed at the phone in my hands.

He was right.

I'd been making my way through Emily's goddamn Instagram account.

Again.

But instead of admitting that, I replied, "I'm reading the emails from my phone."

"When you have a desktop in front of you? That, with a quick highlight of your mouse, could delete the four hundred emails much faster?"

I set the phone down and leaned back in my chair, holding the armrests with fingertips that were turning white. "Did you come in to pick? Because if that's the case"—I nodded toward the exit—"there's the door."

"You're not getting rid of me that easy." He smiled. "How was your weekend?"

I rocked in the chair, my cup of patience still not refilled from when Emily had left me in the back seat of the SUV. "Ben came home from Mom and Dad's late Saturday morning. From there on, it was nonstop. Park. Skating. Food. Movies. More food. We slept and did it all again on Sunday."

"What about Friday night?"

I made sure to keep my expression steady as I asked, "What about Friday night?"

"When you took Emily home."

My hands left the armrests and folded in my lap. "What are you asking?"

"I'm assuming it went all right?"

"You would have heard if it didn't." Jordan was goading me, I was sure of it. But in any normal circumstance, when it came to a woman other than Maya, I would make a comment. If I didn't now, my brother would find it suspicious. "By the way, you never fucking told me Maya's best friend is such a smokeshow." I set my arms on top of my desk.

He smiled. "That was on purpose."

"Why?"

"Because Maya would come at you with knives if you ever hurt Emily, and you have the kind of reputation that would make her believe you'd try to sleep with Emily." He licked his lips. "You and women don't exactly have the best track record, brother."

He was preaching the truth, but I still responded, "What are you saying?"

"I'm saying, before I found my girl, you and I were the same. Different chicks every weekend—or even sometimes during the week. Forever bachelors, not giving a fuck about anyone's feelings." He pulled at the sleeves of his jacket. "Maya changed me. You, well . . . you're still rocking the single life."

"So you didn't tell me Emily was hot in fear that I would try to fuck her? That's deep."

His smile got even larger. "Did you?"

I blew out a mouthful of air. "Go to hell."

He laughed and got up from his chair. As he was heading for the door, he looked at me over his shoulder. "Remember, Maya's a nurse and trained on the human body. If anyone knows how to physically torture you in the worst possible way, it's her."

"She can keep her knives in the kitchen."

He laughed once more before he walked out.

CHAPTER FIFTEEN

Emily

"Bettie's last week here," Maya said as she approached me in the hallway of the rehab center where I was parked behind the portable computer station, inputting the info for each of my patients' charts. "Sob."

"Ugh. Girl, I know. Don't get me wrong, I'm so happy she gets to go home. I'm sure she's dying for some decent food and a bed much larger than the twin she has here, and her bougie bedding and pillows. But selfishly, I'm really going to miss her."

A braid hung over my shoulder, and Maya pulled at the elastic and reworked each weave to tighten them. "She asked me first thing this morning if we'd finalized the plans for our night out together."

I snorted. "Of course she did. The woman is a planner." I put my hands on my hips. "What did you say to her?"

"She mentioned dinner and a hockey game. I told her that sounded perfect. I didn't think you'd mind." Every time Maya moved her hands through my hair, I got a strong whiff of antibacterial gel, our signature scent while we were at work.

"I don't mind at all. I love both ideas."

She finished the braid and showed me her phone. There was a text from Bettie with a screenshot of the Bears' schedule. "While we were talking about the plans—or, her plans, I should say—she sent me this and told me to talk with you about which game would work best for us."

"That lady." I shook my head. "I can only hope to be as sharp as her at eighty-four."

"Ditto." She turned the screen toward her. "I'm forwarding you her text. Check out the games and pick a night you're off. I don't care if it's a weekend or a weekday. I'm sure she doesn't either. Although, knowing her, her social calendar is probably busier than ours."

There was a vibration in my pocket that I assumed was Maya's text. I took out my phone and saw her notification on the screen, but that wasn't the only one that had come in. There was one from Instagram, too, a message request from an account I didn't follow with a name that made it impossibly difficult not to smile.

Still holding my phone, I slowly glanced at her. "I'll check my schedule during lunch, and I'll let you know."

She set her elbow on the corner of the computer stand. "What are you doing for lunch?"

I shrugged. "You know, I even went grocery shopping. Who forgets to pack something to eat when they have food in the fridge?"

Someone whose brain is solely focused on Gavin.

That was who.

"How about we run away for sushi? We can go to that restaurant that's a few blocks from here and has incredible lunch specials."

"I want that."

She squeezed my shoulder, and as she was walking toward the opposite end of the hall, I noticed the color of her outfit. A super-pretty lavender I'd never seen her wear before. And I knew Maya's wardrobe as well as I knew my own, since I raided hers at least once a week.

"Hey, are those new scrubs?"

She turned around and laughed. "I was waiting for you to notice. Jordan bought them for me."

I grinned at my best friend. "Does he need a sister wife? Because I'm available."

"We're going to talk about Mike over lunch. Girl, don't think I forgot."

My chest tightened as she turned away. I didn't know how I was going to get out of that, but instead of dwelling on it now, I opened my Instagram app and leaned against the wall while I read Gavin's message.

Gavin: I found you.

Me: I hope you had to work hard to do that.

Just as I was putting my phone back into my pocket, it vibrated again.

Gavin: Can we upgrade to text? I'd say I earned your number.

Me: I don't know . . . it took you a few days to reach out. I'd say that earned you a couple more days of Instagram DM torture.

Gavin: I was going to message you Friday night.

Me: And describe in detail how blue your balls were?

Gavin: You're wicked.

Me: I told you, I needed beauty sleep.

Gavin: You still haven't given me your number.

Me: You still haven't earned it. 😊

There was another vibration as I was putting my phone in my pocket, but I ignored it, smiling to myself as my hands returned to the keyboard to finish up the patient charting.

"Hey, will you be able to leave in about ten minutes?" Maya asked as she looked over the high bar top where I was sitting behind the computer at the nurses' station, an oversize wall that separated our area from the hallway.

"Ten minutes is perfect." I exited out of a chart and pulled up my email. "I just have to finish reading these notes from a doctor and then I'll be ready."

"I'm going to check on Bettie one last time. I'll be back."

While she took off for Bettie's room, I skimmed the last few lines of the email the doctor had just sent me, double-checking the medications for our newest intake, and forwarded the scripts to our in-house pharmacy. Once I exited my inbox, I took out my phone for the first time since this morning. I knew there was a message from Gavin waiting for me. I just didn't realize a few of the other vibrations I'd felt over the last several hours had also been from him.

Gavin: You're a tough one, Emily. I'd hate to be opposite you on the football field.

Gavin: Maybe that's where I should take you. Or the ice since Ben taught you how to skate.

Gavin: How about you start with a yes, and I'll surprise you.

Me: Are you asking me out?

Gavin: It sounds that way, doesn't it?

Me: You know . . . it kinda does.

Gavin: But I need one thing first to make that happen.

Me: What's that?

Gavin: Your number.

I laughed and messaged him the digits, knowing within a few seconds, there would be a text from him.

And there was.

Unknown: So much easier.

Me: How is it that you get everything you want? You have some serious luck on your side, Gavin.

Gavin: Luck? I've been messaging you for hours. This has been work.

Me: Ha!

Gavin: And I don't get everything I want. If I did, you would have come home with me. Or invited me into your apartment. Instead, I got a door in my face.

Me: But I didn't slam the door.

Gavin: You might as well have.

Me: Not true. I closed it with love. And look what it did, it inspired you to reach out to me. Which I'm honestly shocked about.

Me: So shocked that it has me thinking . . . this is you, isn't it? An alien hasn't taken over your body? Because for someone who only wants his needs taken care of, "working" and texting isn't exactly your thing.

Gavin: It's me.

Me: Oh, a new version of Gavin. It's nice to meet you.

Gavin: How about we make that introduction in person?

"Ready?"

I jumped at the sound of Maya's voice and shoved my phone into the pocket of my apricot-colored scrubs. "Yep. I'm starving."

"Same."

I stood from the desk and joined my best friend, our arms looped as we headed for the elevator. "How's Bettie?"

"Great." We broke apart as Maya stepped into the elevator first, hitting the button for the lobby, and I followed behind her. "She's all excited because Gavin is supposed to come in sometime today."

The mere mention of his name made my heart beat like a drum solo.

"Is he bringing Ben?" My question was purely innocent, something I would certainly ask, given that I had a history with Ben and I knew Maya would take it that way. "I'd love to see that little nugget."

"She didn't say anything about Ben coming, just Gavin. Ben's probably at school."

If he was coming solely for Bettie, he would bring Ben with him. Did that mean he was mostly coming to see me? I wasn't going to focus on that too hard. He'd made the effort to reach out. He was texting me nonstop. He was even waiting for a response on his date invite.

Things were good. That didn't mean I should start doing brain-cartwheels.

"Oh my God, I can't believe I never asked you how things went when he gave you a ride home the other night." She pulled a clip out of her pocket and used it to hold up her hair after she twisted her dark locks into a knot.

"There isn't much to say about it. I rode with him to our building, and he dropped me off. It was pretty uneventful."

If she only knew the way I was overheating in these clothes . . . or could feel my pulse.

Her eyes narrowed, a devilish grin spreading across her lips. "But you find him delicious, don't you?"

I laughed. "Why would you say that?"

"It's funny, when Jordan showed us Mike's photo and I was saying he was your type, I realized the description I gave was basically Gavin's description too. The two guys look nothing alike, but the characteristics are almost exact. Which means Gavin's also your type, I just didn't mention it—I figured I'd save us both the embarrassment."

I fanned my face, something I'd do regardless of who she was talking about. "Gavin is everyone's type. The man is drop-dead sexy."

"It's too bad he's such a player." She groaned. "Don't get me wrong, so was Jordan before we met. But Gavin isn't going to bring just anyone around his son—Jordan told me that once. So he'll end up being this forever bachelor and never settle down. Or he'll at least wait until Ben is older and won't get attached in the meantime."

I wondered what she'd think of the texts that were currently sitting on my phone. Would she still agree with her statement? Would Gavin's effort soften her opinion?

It didn't matter. I wasn't going to show her my cell.

Still, I wanted to push this conversation a little further. "But you changed Jordan. You made him want to only be with you."

She smiled. "I think he wanted to change. He was ready."

"Gavin's not?"

She shrugged. "I don't know." The door opened, and she moved beside me while we exited. "But what I do know is Mike is supposedly this awesome guy. He has an incredible career. I mean, he's the head freaking coach of the Bears, Em." Her voice was growing more excited with each box she checked off. "He's good-looking. And Jordan says he's super sweet. I think you should let Jordan make the connection for you."

I stuck my hands in my pockets. The urge to pull out my phone and reply to Gavin was almost unbearable. "Jordan called him super sweet?"

"He might not have used those exact words."

I gently hit her shoulder at the start of the crosswalk and laughed. "I didn't think so." I paused for a moment. "But I really want to think about this, okay?"

She looked at me, staring straight into my eyes. "Babe, why?"

I needed a reason. And I needed one quickly.

Because on paper, Mike was everything I wanted.

"Hockey's a very long season. I can only imagine, as the head coach, he basically lives at the arena, and I know their travel schedule is bananas. Plus, he's a dad and that takes precedence. There's nowhere for me to fit in."

I was impressed with myself, despite every word being the truth.

The only thing I hadn't mentioned was that Mike wasn't a man I was interested in.

Because bits of my heart already belonged to someone else.

"But he would become obsessed with you, and he'd fit you in."

"I know I'm fabulous, but fitting me into a tiny window isn't enough. I want more, Maya." I let the emotion in so she could hear it. "I want all of it. Like you have."

"And that's what you deserve." She put her arm around my shoulders as we approached the restaurant. "I'm going to drill Jordan tonight. Back to the drawing board we go."

"I love you. More than anything and anyone in this world. But when the perfect guy for me comes along, it's going to happen for all the right reasons, and when it does, I'll be ready."

She put her hand on top of my head, turning it until I looked at her. "You're saying you don't want me to play matchmaker, aren't you?" She sighed when I nodded. "Womp, womp." She opened the door to the restaurant.

Before I walked in, I said, "Don't hate me."

"Are you kidding, I could never." She stood next to me in the entrance and hugged my arm. "I'm going to run to the ladies' room. Will you grab us a table?"

"Of course." As she headed for the back of the restaurant, the hostess nowhere in sight, I pulled out my phone to reply to Gavin's last text.

Me: I heard that introduction might happen today at the rehab center.

Gavin: Look at Grandma blowing up all my surprises.

Me: She told Maya who told me. Blame Maya, I guess.

Gavin: Are you hungry? I was going to bring a late lunch.

Me: I'm at a sushi restaurant right now with Maya. So, yes, I am, but in about thirty minutes I'll be stuffed and ready for a nap.

Gavin: She likes sushi . . . noted.

Me: I also like dessert.

Me: Don't let your brain go there, I'm talking about the food kind.

Gavin: When it comes to you, my brain always goes there.

CHAPTER SIXTEEN

Gavin

Me: Tell Maya you're going to grab some coffee and come inside the shop across from your building.

Emily: How do you know I'm still with Maya?

Me: Because I'm sitting by the window of the coffee shop, and I can see the two of you walking toward the rehab center.

Emily: What if she wants to come with me?

Me: Convince her not to.

Emily: I only have about ten minutes before I have to get back to work.

Me: I won't keep you any longer.

Light orange wasn't a color I'd ever pick for Emily, but the woman looked fucking breathtaking. The top of her scrubs was tucked into her waistband, giving me a view of that perfect body. And because of the way I was sitting, I could also see the conversation she was having with Maya, working an angle to get herself alone. I couldn't hear the words, I could barely see her lips moving, but I knew the result once she hurried across the street, the bell above the glass door chiming, signaling she'd come inside.

She skimmed the small room, her eyes quickly landing on mine. I could tell she was trying to fight her smile. She was flattered I was here and didn't want to admit it. But as she walked over to my table, she gave in, and one hell of a grin covered her face as she took the seat across from me.

"Hello, gorgeous."

"What are you doing here?" She glanced at the small high top, holding the end of her braid. "And what is all this?"

I lifted my coffee and held it near my chest. "I didn't know if I'd be able to get you alone while you were at work, especially with Maya there. So I had to create my own alone time. And this"—I nodded toward the table—"is every dessert the coffee shop makes. Aside from strawberry cupcakes, I had no idea what your favorite is."

"So you ordered everything?" She laughed.

It was my turn to hide a smile. "It isn't that much."

"There's enough dessert here for my entire wing."

This was the only available table, and I'd had to overlap most of the desserts just so they'd fit. There were probably twenty total, ranging from cinnamon buns to doughnuts. There was even some kind of tart thing that I would fucking hate, but maybe she'd dig it.

"You can box up whatever you don't eat and take it to the nurses. I'm sure they'll love something sweet."

She sucked her lips in as she inventoried the buffet. "And I'm just supposed to tell Maya that an urge came over me and I bought the entire dessert-display case?"

I took a drink of my coffee and set it back down. "You said you like to give gifts, didn't you?"

Her eyes narrowed. "You remember . . ."

"Just like I remember not getting an answer about making that introduction in person."

She broke one of the doughnuts in half and took a bite. "It's strawberry." Her eyes acknowledged that she was still avoiding a response.

"That's why I got you two of them."

"You're so interesting, Mr. Worthington." She shook her head as though she couldn't believe what she was seeing. "Question: Why didn't you bring Ben when you knew Bettie would love to see him?"

I set my shoe on the footrest of the tall barstool. "If I brought my son, I wouldn't be able to do this."

"Which is?"

"Spend time with you."

She took another bite. I swore it was to mask whatever expression wanted to burst through her face. "And why do you want to do that?"

"You have a lot of questions, Emily."

She turned silent for several seconds, but her stare told me that nothing was quiet in her head. "I've been with you—if that's what you want to call it—three times. And now, suddenly, you want my number and you want to ask me out." She fisted a napkin, wiping the sides of her mouth with it. "This doesn't seem like you, Gavin. I want to know what brought on the change."

"You."

She immediately looked away, taking the last bite of the doughnut half, holding her hand, balled in a fist, in front of her mouth while she chewed. When her eyes returned to me, I could see the pleasure inside them.

I could even see the smile that her hand was blocking.

"What, you don't have more questions for me?"

She swallowed and her hand stayed. "Oh, I have no less than a million."

"Let me see if I can answer them all at once." I rubbed my palms over my suit pants before I crossed my arms. There had been sweat on them. This wasn't my specialty—the kind of talk I wanted to have with her—but I was trying like hell. "Here's the deal: I've been thinking about you. A lot. At night. In the morning. When I'm with Ben. When I'm without him. And our meetups have been random." I paused. "I don't want them to be random anymore. I want to see more of you."

"Meetups." She moved some of the desserts so she could rest her arms on the edge of the table. "As in this is just sex?"

"No." My reply came out faster than I anticipated. "Do I love having sex with you, fuck yeah." My eyes dropped to her chest, and I let out a small chuckle as I thought about what I wanted to do to her nipples, my dick part of every thought, always. "But that's not why I asked for your number and it's not why I want to see more of you."

"This is . . . wild."

"Why do you say that?"

She dragged her thumb over her lips before her hand returned to its original spot on the table. "I just had a conversation about you with Maya on our way to lunch. She asked how it went when you dropped me off, and I was pretty bland at responding. You know, as a precaution. But the topic stayed on you, and she called you a forever bachelor and mentioned how you don't want to bring a woman into Ben's life."

"I'm sure she learned that from Jordan."

She nodded. "She did."

"She wasn't misinformed. You know that—you and I have had the same conversation."

"But what I'm hearing is that your opinion has changed." She looked at her hands. "Am I right?"

"Yes."

She eventually gazed up, her eyes wide and emotional. "And that's what I find wild. Mind-blowing, in fact."

"Emily, you're the one who changed my opinion." I smiled, and it caused her to do the same. "You know Ben is my priority and always will be. You know my dedication to him and the time involved as a single parent. That's why I'm being up front and honest and talking to you about this rather than just letting things unfold. Football may not be part of my day-to-day anymore, but I still follow a playbook in many ways."

"Communication is the sexiest thing alive, in my opinion. I'm literally eating up every second of this." She turned her finger in the air. "Give me more."

I loosened my tie a little and chuckled even though we were entering the most serious part of the conversation. "About Ben. I don't want to go there until I know. Until I'm absolutely sure." I tried my best to soften my voice. "I need you to understand that, and I need to know you're going to respect that."

"Gavin, of course. I know your life is different than mine. I know how seriously you take Ben's feelings, and you and I are going to be separate from him and I until you're ready to merge the three of us together."

"And until *you're* ready."

She smiled. "I appreciate that." She let out a short giggle. "I'm not going to lie, this might be the most mature conversation I've ever had."

"I'm right there with you." She was way too far away. "I'd reach for your hand if the sleeves of my suit wouldn't get coated in every type of dessert."

She laughed.

"Come here, Emily."

As she got up from her chair, I turned in mine, separating my legs so she could stand between them, my hands going to her waist as soon as she was within reach. "It's been a long time since I've done anything like this. Since I've ever wanted something like this. It's just been Ben and me since he was born. No one else. But this sexy nurse with the most beautiful blue eyes has fucking owned my thoughts, and I can't seem to let her go." I tightened my grip, moving my face closer to hers. "I'm rusty, Emily. You're going to have to bear with me."

"Rusty is hot. It means I can oil you up any way I want you." Her head fell back, and when she looked at me again, she had the biggest grin I'd ever seen on her. "What am I going to tell my coworkers when they ask why I'm smiling this hard?"

"That you just ate the best doughnut of your life."

"Which is somewhat true." She linked her hands behind my head. "Do you want to still keep this from Maya and Jordan?"

She nodded and her shoulders lifted. "I like this bubble. I like that it's just us. I like that we're learning and seeing and exploring and figuring out without any questions or pressure." She took a deep breath. "I don't want to step outside that bubble yet. At least not until things either really work . . . or don't."

"I have no problem with that."

She inhaled again and nodded. "Good."

My hands moved up her sides, across her shoulders, and stopped on her cheeks. "I need to kiss you. Right now."

"Inside this coffee shop? That's packed full of people?"

There was a smile etched across every part of my face. "Fuck yes."

CHAPTER SEVENTEEN

Emily

Me: I'm currently surrounded by a team of extremely happy nurses who are on quite the sugar high. If they could, they'd say thank you. However, I'm Miss Popular instead, lol.

Me: Also, not kissing you in the hallway before you left the rehab center = excruciating.

Gavin: I could tell. You were biting your lip when you waved goodbye.

Me: That's how you know I want to kiss you?

Gavin: That's one way, yes. Your eyes also tell me by the way they look at me and your body by the way you can't sit still.

Me: You're more observant than I mentally give you credit for.

Gavin: I'm learning you . . . and believe me, I wanted to take care of you before I left.

Me: As in, drag me into the supply closet?

Gavin: And get on my fucking knees.

Me: Gavin, you're torturing me.

◆ ◆ ◆

Gavin: You have a fan.

Me: A what?

Gavin: My grandmother, she just texted me about you. You must have just left her room. She felt the need to remind me of how well she's being taken care of there and how much she's going to miss you.

Me: Awww. She's the sweetest.

Gavin: Do you think she's trying to send me a message?

Me: She couldn't be. She knows nothing.

Gavin: My grandmother? That woman knows fucking everything.

Me: You're saying she saw you eye fucking me when we were last in her room together?

Gavin: And drooling. Probably.

Me: Is that a problem? Do I need to worry?

Gavin: A feisty eighty-four-year-old is now going to do everything in her power to make sure we're together. Do you see that as a problem?

Me: Go, Bettie, go!

Gavin: You know, as my brother's girl, I adore Maya. But when it comes to you, she's a real cockblock. I can't send anything to your work, she'll see it, I'm sure. I can't send anything to your apartment, she lives with you. I don't like it . . .

Me: She's barely home, she's always at Jordan's. My gut tells me they're going to be moving in together soon.

Me: You also don't have to send me anything.

Gavin: I want to.

Me: Do you know what the best gift was?

Gavin: Tell me.

Me: When you called me last night to say good night.

Gavin: I need to see you. Even if it's only for 10 minutes. Are you working for Dr. Kaplan tonight?

Me: Yep.

Me: And don't even think about putting a Lego up Ben's nose.

Gavin: I would never . . . but I wouldn't put it past me to say he's spiking a high fever.

Me: Lol. I'm at the rehab center until 4. Does that help?

Gavin: What time can you escape to the coffee shop?

Me: 12? 1? I'm sure your day is wild, what time can you get away?

Gavin: I'll see you there at 1:00.

Me: Oh . . . and don't try to kiss me. I've decided I'm no longer doing that in public places after you ravaged me the last time we were there, having me so worked up, I was panting when I returned to work.

Gavin: You're not letting me kiss you? Are you trying to fucking torture me?

Me: Nothing makes me happier.

Gavin: I know . . . my fucking balls are still blue.

Me: Ha!

◆ ◆ ◆

Me: Panting. Again. What the hell are you doing to me, Mr. Worthington?

Gavin: You're the one who kissed me.

Me: That's not what happened. You pulled me against you, lifted me into the air, and laid one on me.

Gavin: Is that how it went down?

Me: I left out a few details, like the way you looked at me right before you kissed me.

Gavin: I can't help it. You're fucking gorgeous.

Me: ♥

Me: So this weekend . . . I know you mentioned getting together while we were at the coffee shop, but are you sure you want to send Ben to your parents' house? I could always sneak over while he's asleep. I don't want to take away any of your time with him.

Gavin: I don't want to wait until this weekend to see you.

Me: Good thing this weekend isn't that far away.

Gavin: My mother is begging for Ben to come over and spend the night. I'll take him there at 4. I'll pick you up right after.

Me: Where are we going?

Gavin: You're not getting that out of me.

Me: You're the worst.

Gavin: Because I want to surprise you?

Me: A girl needs to plan, like what to wear, how to do my hair—all the things.

Gavin: That outfit you wore to Jordan's, those tight workout pants and the Bears T-shirt you tied at your waist, I want you in that. But I want it to be a Deers T-shirt.

Me: How do you even remember that outfit?

Gavin: I see your curves in those pants and how your stomach was peeking out every goddamn day in my head.

Me: Ahhh. The outfit that made you get on your knees.

Gavin: Here's the other thing, if I need you to be in something dressy or something specific or even something for overnight, I've got you.

Me: What does that even mean?

Gavin: When you come to my place on Saturday, you'll be spending the night, and you don't need to bring anything with you.

My stomach practically shuddered as I held my phone, rereading Gavin's last message. Clothes, he would get for me. Spending-the-night essentials, he had covered. A man with money and power and knew how to use both.

My insides completely turned to liquid.

But it was the way he made me feel that mattered far more than what he could give me or what he could do for me.

A warmth that lived in my chest, a smile that permanently marked my lips.

Somehow I had to hide it, because Bettie's discharge papers had been processed and she was leaving in the next few hours, which meant it was time to say goodbye. According to Gavin, she was on to us, so my mask needed to be thick.

I tucked the phone into my scrubs pocket and walked down the hallway, expecting to see her daughter in her room, who I was told would be picking her up, or Maya doing a final round of doting.

But Bettie was alone, lying on top of the bed, with her cell in her hands.

"My darling. Come in." Her deep-burgundy-painted lips pulled wide.

I stopped at the side of the bed and held the railing that framed the top of her mattress. "Before things get busy, I wanted to come in and say goodbye. Not *goodbye* goodbye, I know I'll be seeing lots more of you. Just goodbye for now."

Her hand went to my cheek, her thumb grazing my skin. "My gal, that smile . . ."

"I forgot lipstick. It's somewhere in my bag—"

"You don't need it. If I had your lips, I wouldn't cover them in anything." She removed her red glasses and set them on her lap, her stare never leaving mine in the process.

I put my hand on top of hers. "Thank you."

She was silent for a few seconds, her head tilting, her gaze deepening. "Happiness looks beautiful on you."

"How do you know my smile isn't a lie?"

"My dear girl . . ." She patted my cheek before linking her fingers with mine. "I've seen the lie, and right now I'm witnessing the truth."

CHAPTER EIGHTEEN

Gavin

A couple of months ago, I never would have thought I would drop my son off at his grandparents' to pick up a woman I was seeing, standing outside her apartment building, waiting for her to come down so I could take her to my place for the night. I never would have thought I'd spend two days planning an evening she wouldn't ever forget.

But here I fucking was.

And as Emily walked through the door and stepped onto the sidewalk, the first thing I noticed was that she had a surprise for me. It wasn't in a box, wrapped in paper with a bow.

It was on her body.

Goddamn it, this woman was fucking perfect.

The moment she was within reach, I pulled her against me, my lips pressing to hers before she could even get a word out. Even though the taste wasn't enough, I pulled my face back so my eyes could take another dip down the front of her.

"Where did you get that T-shirt?"

Instead of the Deers T-shirt I'd asked her to wear, she had on Tampa's logo and colors.

"I went shopping." That smile, it was fucking beautiful. She locked her hands behind my head. "I know the Bears is your team, owner-wise, but since you played for Tampa, I figured this would be a little more special." She rubbed her palms down my chest.

"The only thing better would be if my name and number were on the back."

She pushed against my pecs. "You're saying you'd love that?"

The thought alone had me grabbing her ass. "I would."

She wiggled out of my grip and turned around, lifting her long blond hair to show me my name at the top of the T-shirt, spanning across her shoulders, and my number below in the center.

"Emily . . ." I pulled her back against me, my arms crossing her chest, and in her ear, I whispered, "What are you trying to do to me?"

"I just went in for a shirt. When I saw this one, I couldn't help myself. I wanted to wear you . . . that's all."

"I like that. I like that a whole lot." I kissed her neck, her warm scent so heavy in that spot. "I cannot wait to take it off you." I released her to turn her toward me. "But that isn't going to happen until much later."

She bit her bottom lip. "What do you have planned?"

"You're still not getting that answer out of me." I opened the door to the back seat and climbed in after her.

"Miss Wren, it's nice to see you again," Denis said to her.

"It's lovely to see you, too, Denis."

I slipped my arm around her shoulders and pulled her toward the center of the back seat, my mouth going to the top of her head, breathing in more of her warmth.

"Denis, do you know what Gavin has planned for this evening?"

He looked at me from the rearview mirror. "I don't, Miss Wren."

"And if he did, he wouldn't tell you," I added.

She twisted, craning her neck back, a smirk covering her face. "You're saying I can't drag Denis to my side?"

I laughed. "No. And legally—also no."

She waved me away. "Jerk."

Denis chuckled.

That smart mouth made my dick hard.

I held her chin. "It'll be worth the wait." As she set her phone on the seat beside her, I continued, "You brought nothing with you. You listened. I'm impressed."

"Not an easy task, but yes, I listened."

When she'd eventually go into my bedroom later tonight, she would see that my assistant had gotten everything she would need. I didn't know what half the shit was—there were bottles of all different colors. But when my assistant was dropping the things off and I was putting them in my en suite, I didn't let my mind really think about what I was looking at. Or what this meant. Or that anytime Emily spent the night, she would have the necessities at my place.

Those thoughts were a lot to take in.

What I knew was that I liked having her in my SUV. I liked the thought of her spending the night. I couldn't take my hands off her. And I was already thinking about the next time she could stay at my condo, and it wasn't even the morning yet.

"I was with a patient when your mom came in and got Bettie, but I heard everything went well. Is she adjusting at home all right?" She dragged her fingers across the scruff on my cheek.

"Things are good. In fact, my mom is bringing Ben over there"—I glanced at my watch—"right about now. I'm sure Grandma has already put together a batch of cookies for him. She loves to bake."

"And I'm sure she loves to have Ben over."

"She does. So much so, she'll convince my mom to stay for dinner to spend more time with him. My dad will end up over there, the three of them sold on multiple games of UNO. Ben's a master convincer. The boy is far too slick for his own good. He knows how to charm."

"Like his dad." She winked. "He wouldn't have to charm me. I love UNO."

"No one over twelve likes that game."

She laughed. "Well, I do, so you're wrong."

"Do you know how many rounds of that game I've played?" I groaned, letting out a loud breath. "It's Ben's favorite."

"But you play."

I nodded. "I'll always play."

Her hand went to the back of my neck. "You're such a good dad, Gavin."

"He's the best dad," Denis chimed in.

"I don't know about that, but I'm ready to up the difficulty count. I'm going to teach Ben how to play chess."

"Chess? That's a tough game," she said.

"He's a natural-born athlete, but he doesn't have the mental strength—not at his age and not at the level he's able to play. That's where chess comes in. A game that'll toughen up his brain a little."

Her brows rose. "Prepping him for the NFL?"

The SUV slowed in front of my building, and I looked at her and replied, "I'm prepping him for life. Which is hard as fuck. I don't care what he wants to do or play, I just want my son to be happy."

She smiled. "I adore you."

"Ah. So the asshole type softens . . ."

"I did call you that, didn't I?" She laughed and pinched her fingers together. "He softens slightly."

When we came to a stop, I opened my door, getting out first, and I helped Emily to the ground. Before I shut the door, I thanked Denis, and I led her inside my building and into the private elevator.

She tried to lower the bottom of her T-shirt, lessening the amount of her stomach that peeked out. "I feel very underdressed."

My stare took a dive down her body. "Why? You look amazing."

"But you're not nearly as casual as me." She crossed her arms over her chest.

"Nothing special, just jeans and a button-down."

"And ridiculously hot."

I laughed. "Well, I can't help that." I held her ass, spanking the bottom a few times. "Stop worrying. One of my favorite outfits on you is scrubs. This is tied with that. I don't need you to get dressed up for me, Emily. I'm all about the athletic look, and you've got quite a handle on that."

"You have this hidden talent where almost everything that comes out of your mouth is so unbelievably sexy." She unwrapped her arms and looped them around my waist. "I want to eat the words you just said."

"Mmm." I leaned down and kissed her, and when the door opened and I immediately smelled dinner, I moaned again.

So did Emily. She closed her eyes and groaned, "Oh my God, what is that?"

"It's your surprise." I led her through the foyer and past the living room, stopping at the base of the kitchen, which was occupied by a chef and two helpers.

The chef was drying his hands with a towel hanging from his shoulder. "Gavin, it's good to see you, my man."

"And you, Walker." As he came over to me, I shook his hand. "Walker Weston, meet Emily Wren. Emily, Walker is the chef and founder of multiple restaurant brands. Horned is one he recently opened nearby in Portsmouth, Toro—a restaurant I'm begging him to open in Boston—and Charred, the world-renowned steak house that we have here in the Back Bay."

"I know it well. Charred is one of my favorites." She clasped hands with him. "It's wonderful to meet you, Walker."

"Good to meet you," Walker replied.

"How long has it been since you've been to Boston? When your book tour brought you through?"

He let out a long, winded exhale and nodded. "I believe so. But if I knew you had a kitchen like this"—his green gaze left mine to glance at his helpers—"I would have come more often."

Walker was the same age as me, but the light in the kitchen was picking up some of his gray hairs. With the speed his company was moving and building, I knew the motherfucker had to be stressed. But it had taken only a phone call and he'd agreed to come in for the night.

I chuckled. "You have an open invite."

"You're not based in Boston?" Emily asked him.

"LA." He rolled up a sleeve of his chef's whites.

"No one cooks like Walker," I told her. "My family has been a fan since the very beginning of his career, stumbling upon his father's restaurant during a trip to LA. That was many years ago, before the Weston brand exploded. You know, his cookbook is the only cookbook my mom keeps permanently on her kitchen counter."

"You came all the way here for Gavin?" Emily's voice was soft.

"And you." My hand briefly went to her cheek. "I wanted you to experience the best." I left her face to clasp my friend's arm. "And this here is the absolute best."

Walker returned the gesture, his hand going to my shoulder. "The first course will be ready in a few minutes. Why don't you get comfortable. My staff will be up to pour you wine and get you anything you need."

"I appreciate you." My hand went to Emily's lower back.

Emily thanked him, and I brought her outside and up the short staircase to the roof of the building. The space had a small pool and hot tub, and several seating areas, one of which had been converted into a dining room for tonight. Strings of lights hung above the table, and there were candles across every surface, music playing through the outdoor speakers.

"Is all of this . . . for me?" She gazed around, a look of awe on her breathtaking face.

"Yes."

Her stare finally landed on me. "Gavin, I think you like me."

I laughed. "You think so?"

She nodded.

"You might be right."

She cupped my shoulders. "I cannot get over this. I don't even have words to express what this is . . . and how much I love it."

"You haven't tasted anything yet."

"I don't need to. The effort, the gesture, this table, the view"—she looked at the city, the scenery easily taken in by how high up we were—"flying Walker in. I mean, my God. I'm . . . blown away."

"Good."

Her head tilted, her lips pulling wide before they rubbed together. "If we weren't about to be fed, this T-shirt would be on the floor and I'd be straddling you right now."

"I'll remember that for after dinner."

Her nails dug into my skin. "Which is when I'd like you to fuck me so hard."

"Done."

She smiled. "That's not my only request."

"I'll fulfill every one." I nodded toward the table. "But right now, go sit."

I helped her into her chair and slid it toward the table, and once she was positioned, I took the seat across from her.

One of Walker's helpers immediately appeared with a bottle of red that he poured in our glasses.

The moment we were alone again, Emily lifted her wine in the air. "To probably the best dinner of my life."

"And to the beginning." My eyes narrowed. "Our beginning."

She took a deep breath, her shoulders rising at the same time. "A much better toast than mine." She sipped the heavy-bodied wine. "You told me you were rusty. Yet this is technically date one, minus the coffee shop meetups that I don't know if you can really call dates, and you've nailed it out of the park. For the record, I searched for a football reference and couldn't come up with one."

I smiled. "I like good food. When you know the best, it's not hard to make that happen."

"You mean, it wasn't hard for *you*. There's nothing normal about flying in the best chef in the country. At least, not in my world."

"I don't like boundaries." I gripped the stem of my glass. "You're going to realize that the more you're with me."

"Ya think?" She snorted. "But seriously, it's hard to believe you're not an expert at this dating thing."

"I'm really not." I shook my head. "I weighed a lot of different options. But I thought, given that this is Ben's home, we won't be able to spend a ton of time here unless he's gone or asleep. So I figured why not just bring my favorite here."

"It's perfect." She went quiet for a moment. "While we're on the topic of Ben, can I ask you something? And once I ask you, if you don't want to talk about it, I understand." She took a breath. "But I need to ask . . ."

"Okay."

"Ben's mom . . ."

I filled my cheeks with air and slowly blew it out. "What about her?"

"You've said Ben doesn't have a mother in his life. Is she just not in the picture? Does she live far away? Did she abandon him?" She flattened her hand on the table. "I don't want to assume anything, but I'm very curious about the whole situation."

Seven years. In many ways, that felt like an eternity. It also felt like those years had passed in seconds. But every time I glanced at my son, I saw what that amount of time looked like.

It didn't make it easier to talk about.

It didn't make it hurt less.

When I filled my lungs, I felt the burn. "Ben's mom passed away."

Her hand shot across the table and reached for mine. "I'm sorry, Gavin. I didn't know. Oh God, I'm positively gutted for Ben. And for you."

"It's okay." I nodded. "Ben never got the chance to know her . . . so he doesn't know what he's missing."

CHAPTER NINETEEN

Emily

Me: I need to thank you again for the best night ever. I swear I haven't stopped smiling since I got home.

Gavin: I want to see that smile.

Me: You can. Soon, I hope.

Gavin: How soon?

Me: Lol. You tell me.

Gavin: I think I can peel myself away from work tomorrow. Lunch?

Me: I would love that. See you tomorrow then.

Gavin: Good morning, gorgeous. How did you sleep?

Me: Not as good as when I'm in your bed. You?

Gavin: I much prefer waking up to you.

Me: You just like the way I wake you up . . .

Gavin: Did I love opening my eyes to you blowing me, fuck yes. But that's not the only reason I like you in my bed. Just like having my mouth on your pussy before you fall asleep isn't the only reason you sleep well when you're with me.

Me: You may have a point.

Me: I get to see you today . . . it's going to be very difficult to keep my hands off you at lunch.

Gavin: There's always the backseat of the SUV.

Me: You have a better chance of that happening in the restroom at the restaurant than getting me to agree to kick Denis out of the driver's seat.

Gavin: Don't put that idea in my head, Emily. We'll be in a stall for the whole hour of your lunch.

Me: I'm surprised you wouldn't just shut down the entire restaurant. 😉

Gavin: I would.

Me: I'm learning that about you. Where are we meeting?

Gavin: There's a Peruvian restaurant three blocks from your work. How does 1 sound?

Me: It sounds perfect.

Gavin: I'll send you the address.

Gavin: I don't know how you escaped that restaurant without letting me taste you . . .

Me: I don't know why you never let me pay for anything—our last meetup at the coffee shop, the restaurant today. Will you ever let me take you out?

Gavin: No.

Me: I work two jobs to afford these kinds of things, Gavin.

Gavin: Still no.

Me: Lol. Maybe I just need to surprise you then.

Gavin: You do. Every day.

Me: How?

Gavin: The things you say to me, the way you look at me, how you touch me. Not only does it surprise me, but I'm surprised by how it all makes me feel.

Me: ❤

◆ ◆ ◆

Gavin: Are you working tonight?

Me: No.

Gavin: Come over.

Me: Now?

Gavin: Yes.

Me: Isn't Ben there?

Gavin: He just went to bed. I'm about to make dinner, which I would very much like to eat with you or on you.

Me: On me?

Gavin: Fuck yes.

Me: See you in twenty.

◆ ◆ ◆

Me: Holy shit, that was a close call. I don't think I've ever run for an elevator so fast in my life. I thought you said Ben could sleep through anything? We weren't even making much noise, lol.

Gavin: He had a bad dream, that's what woke him.

Gavin: Where are you?

Me: I just got downstairs. I'm about to order an Uber.

Gavin: Don't move. I'm sending Denis. He'll meet you out front of my building.

Me: You're absolutely not doing that. The man is probably home with his family. It's so much easier this way.

Gavin: I'm still sending Denis.

Me: Too late. Uber is here. I'm getting in the backseat noooow.

Gavin: Emily . . .

Me: I heart you for wanting to take care of me.

Gavin: Text me the second you get home.

Me: I will.

◆ ◆ ◆

Me: Home.

Gavin: I'm sorry about tonight. I wish it hadn't gotten so fucked up.

Me: It's not your fault. Ben needed his dad. I love that and I love that you're his comfort. Please don't worry.

Gavin: I'll make it up to you.

Me: No and more no. You're a dad, Gavin, I understand that. I told you I will always respect the way you protect him. It's all good, trust me. Go be with Ben and text me in the morning. ♥

Me: There are no less than five hundred roses at the nurses' station right now. It's like an explosion of long-stem red has completely taken over every inch of desk and counter space, even the floor, they're everywhere. And the way they smell! And how gorg they are, I can't! No one knows who sent them and no one knows who they're for, there's no card or anything. But I have this strange suspicion they came from you.

Gavin: Guilty.

Me: Gavin! I told you, you do not need to make it up to me!

Gavin: The flowers are because I miss you. And if I can't see you, then at least I can make you smile.

Me: I don't even have a sassy reply. Your text just sucked every word out of me and turned me into a pile of mush.

Me: Seriously, no one has ever done anything like this for me before. They're beyond beautiful. Thank you.

Gavin: When can I see you?

Me: I'm off this weekend, but I'm going to the hockey game with Maya and Bettie on Friday. How about Saturday?

Gavin: Saturday, you're mine.

"To many more girls' nights," Maya said as she held her beer in the air, sitting between Bettie and me, directly in front of the ice. "Thank you for everything, Bettie."

"Yes, the biggest thank-you to you," I added.

"My darlings, I hope this is the first of many games we go to together." She clinked her wine against Maya's beer and mine.

"I'll cheers to that." I took a sip and smiled.

While the players were busy warming up, Maya, staring at them, added, "This game is going to be so different than the last one we attended." She knocked me with her elbow several times. "Not that I didn't have a good time last time, it was a blast—but once I saw Jordan on the ice, whoa, things mentally took such a different turn."

"I don't think I'll forget that day for as long as I live," I groaned.

Gavin: I prefer the Tampa T-shirt over the Bears one. Although both look extremely sexy on you.

Me: Why would you say that?

"And look where things stand now." Bettie took a drink, placing her chardonnay in the cupholder.

Maya let out a deep breath. "You're right. I can't imagine my life without him."

Gavin: Because I can see the Bears T-shirt.

Me: What? How?

I tucked my phone under my thigh and looped my hands through Maya's arm. "Bettie, doesn't love look incredible on her?"

Bettie put a hand on Maya's cheek and one on mine. "I'm with the two most beautiful girlies in this arena. Love, friendship, contentment—whatever either of you are feeling, you both look dashing."

"Listen, Ms. Snazzy, you're looking pretty fabulous yourself." I put my hand on top of Bettie's and gave her a stern eye. "And let's talk about how well you're doing. To get to these seats, you had to descend at least twenty steps or more. You tackled them all by yourself—you wouldn't even let us help you."

"I held on to the railing." She batted her lashes.

"So did I," I offered. "That doesn't change my opinion. You're doing so, so great."

She released both of us and waved the air. "I'm getting there." She grinned. "But it sure feels good to get rid of that awful cane. It didn't matter how many scarves I tied to it, it was a wicked eyesore."

"And now it's gone forever." Maya briefly rested her head on Bettie's arm.

"It better be," Bettie said.

Gavin: I'm looking at it right now.

Me: Hold on . . . you're HERE?

Gavin: Turn around. Look up. I'm two boxes to the right.

Me: Why didn't you tell me you were coming?

Gavin: Surprise.

Me: Are you alone?

Gavin: I'm with Jordan. Maya doesn't know. He wants her to have a girls' night, so we're having a guys' night.

Me: And why did you tell me?

"The game is going to start soon." Maya put her beer in the holder between us. "I'm going to run to the ladies' room. Anyone need to join?"

I shook my head. "Unless you want me to go with you?"

"No, stay, I'm fine. How about you, Bettie?"

"I'm good, darling."

"Be right back," Maya announced and headed up the stairs.

Gavin: Because I refuse to leave this arena unless I taste you.

Me: You wild, wild boy. How is that going to happen?

Gavin: Don't you have to go to the restroom?

Me: Now? The game is starting in less than 10 minutes.

Gavin: The game will be over two hours long. I'm sure you can find a window to escape.

I immediately felt Bettie's gaze on me and turned toward her.

"Every time I see you, your smile gets larger." She nodded toward the phone in my lap. "You know, I told you happiness looks beautiful on you. Now I'm starting to think what I see is love."

I let out a loud breath. "Oh, Bettie."

"Am I wrong?"

I slowly raised my shoulders. "No."

She lowered her red glasses to the end of her nose. "He's special, isn't he?"

"He is." I swallowed, my chest pounding. "You know more than Maya."

"I had a feeling. You've been very vocal about her situation. I could only assume she would be the same about yours."

"She will be, when the time is right. It's just . . . not right yet."

I couldn't help but think of Ben's mom and what that must have been like for Gavin. No wonder he didn't date or bring women around Ben. The fear of them leaving—or worse—had to be far greater than the desire to love.

"The beginning is such a special period." She linked her fingers and set them on the armrest. "An important one too. The pieces need time to click. A rhythm needs to be set, communication has to feel its way through the silence. If it were me, I'd keep it quiet too."

"You would?"

"It gives you the freedom to move at your own pace without the questions and pressure and judgment of others. I often hear people say that things should come easy. That the beginning is the least complicated stage. I disagree. Powerful, yes. Unforgettable, yes." Her head bounced, emphasizing each point. "But there's nothing easy about two souls colliding. That's like putting the moon and sun side by side. The energy needs to find a balance, and when it's significant and monumental, that balance takes patience and testing."

My eyes closed, my face scrunching as her words hit. And then they hit again. "Yes." My eyes finally opened. "We're slowly learning that."

"Take your time. No need to rush it."

There was movement from the aisle, and Maya squeezed in between us, taking her seat. "What did I miss?" She lifted her beer and took a sip.

Bettie looked at me as she replied, "Absolutely nothing, my darling."

CHAPTER TWENTY

Gavin

"I shouldn't be surprised you're at this game, considering you own the team . . . but I am." Emily's back was against the wall of the elevator, her hands on my chest, her face pointed up at me. "Maybe I'm more surprised that I agreed to meet you mid-game, knowing I'm going to return to your grandmother looking freshly fucked."

I chuckled. "I can stop the elevator. Take you back upstairs. Return you not freshly fucked." My lips went to her neck despite the offer I'd just made.

I needed a taste, regardless of what she decided.

"And not have you ravage me? Hell no. That's not an option."

"Good choice." I kissed around the curve of her collarbone, the flavor of her skin something I now constantly craved, and pulled away just as the door opened.

"Where are you taking me? And if you say it's a surprise, so help me God—"

"An office. With a door that locks."

I linked our fingers and brought her into the hallway on the ground floor of the arena, a place that was extremely busy, considering it was the middle of a game and we were on the same level as the ice, the locker rooms, the training room, the workout room, and all the other team facilities.

"I'm grateful we're not in the owner's suite." She snorted. It was so fucking cute. "I really thought that's where you were going to ask me to meet you. That you had a fantasy of having me and the game at the same time."

"I thought about it."

She squeezed my hand. "You did?"

I laughed. "And become a meme that will forever live on social media, fuck no." I glanced over my shoulder to look at her. "And let everyone in the arena see your body, also fuck no."

She smiled.

I pulled a set of keys out of my pocket and slowed as we reached the door. This was an office for the executive-level staff of Worthington Enterprises when meetings needed to be conducted here. Since none of those would be happening tonight, we were safe.

"Do you know why I won't let them see your body?" The moment I had her through the door, I flipped on the light, twisted the lock behind us, and pressed her back against it.

"Why?"

"Because it's mine." An admission that shocked me a little as it came out of my mouth—a mouth that went straight to hers to confirm what I'd just said.

I grasped her waist, unhooking the button of her jeans, lowering her zipper, along with her panties, letting it all fall to her ankles. Without my lips ever leaving hers, she slipped off her shoes and stepped out of her pants, and I lifted her into the air, holding her against the door.

It took a little maneuvering, shifting angles and weight, but I was able to unhook my belt, button, and zipper, gaining enough room to slide out my dick.

But my wallet was now around my goddamn ankles, the condom I needed inside.

"Fuck, I have to set you down." I lowered her down the door. "Hang on a second."

"What's wrong?"

"The condom is at my feet."

She pulled herself up to her original position by holding on to my neck. "You don't need one, Gavin. I have an IUD. I'm protected. But if you want to wear one, that's fine."

I went still for a second. "You're sure?"

"That I won't be getting pregnant? Yes. That you don't need to wear one? Also yes."

"You sound like me."

"That was my intention." She tightened her grip, smiling. "I understand if it's your preference. I'm good with whatever you decide—just know that if it was up to me, you wouldn't wear one."

My forehead went against hers.

The idea of feeling her pussy without latex was making me throb even harder. "What are you doing to me?"

"Making things easier." She pulled back to scan my eyes. "Are you inside your head right now?"

The last time I didn't wear a condom, my son was conceived.

But I wasn't going to bring up that situation or speak about another woman in this moment.

So I said, "I . . . don't know."

"It certainly can't be that you don't trust me, considering I ran out of your house and into the elevator with only a bra on so your son wouldn't see me. If that doesn't show you how I feel about your boundaries, I don't know what does."

I exhaled. "Baby, I trust you, it has nothing to do with that. I just need to make sure Ben doesn't get a brother or sister any time soon. In the future, yes, but not now. That's where my head is at—no other place. I want this."

"You have nothing to worry about."

I nodded. "All right."

"You just called me yours." She bit my lower lip. "Take what's yours, Gavin."

My tip was already aligned with her pussy, and I arched my hips forward, breaking through her wetness. "Mine," I moaned.

Her hands moved to my cheeks, fingers spread across my scruff. "Now make me fucking scream."

The hottest words that had ever come out of her mouth.

I held her ass while I propped her shoulders against the door, and I rocked back. Her pussy was pulsing around my tip, and the deeper I got, the more her cunt took hold of me. "Fuck, Emily."

How could she feel better every time I was inside her?

But she did.

And she didn't just take it, she moved with me. She bucked against me. She squeezed my shaft, lifting herself up and lowering to meet me.

It wasn't just the feel of her pussy that was driving me toward an edge.

It was the feel of her body.

The sounds that came from her mouth.

The look in her eyes.

"Faster!" she begged.

I gave her several quick, hard pumps before I pulled her off the door and carried her to the desk in the back of the small office. There were multiple items on its surface—a stapler, paper clips, a cup holding a collection of pens—and I swiped my arm across all of it to clear it away, each item making a noise as it hit the floor.

"You're so wild." She laughed.

I set her on the end of the wood and stood in front of her, keeping her legs spread and around me. Now that she was sitting, I no longer had to hold her weight, which freed up my hands to do anything I wanted with them. They didn't waste any time, immediately going to her neck, tilting her face up toward mine, and I smashed our lips together.

That taste—I still couldn't get enough.

"Ah! More!" she cried.

Her hands were just as frantic, reaching beneath my button-down, running up and down my abs. And the harder I fucked her, the louder she got.

"Gavin! Fuck!"

Her sounds weren't the only sign that told me how close she was getting. I could also feel it by the way her nails were starting to dig into me.

"You're going to make me come!" she yelled.

When her head leaned back, my lips went to her throat. While her pussy was fucking clenching me, I wanted to feel the screams coming from her. I wanted them to vibrate on my lips.

I flicked my thumb across her nipple. It was so hard, it poked through her bra and T-shirt.

But my other hand didn't go to her opposite tit. It lowered between her legs, wetness instantly hitting my skin as I stroked her clit.

"I . . . can't." She drew in air. "Ah!"

"I need to feel you come."

She was narrowing around me, her legs folding across my back. "Gavin!" she shouted again. "Don't stop!"

I had no intention.

Because what she was feeling, I was too.

With my thumb still massaging her, I increased the speed of my thrusts, circling when I was fully plunged inside her, my cock hitting every angle, and as I pulled out, I twisted again. "You feel so fucking good."

She gripped behind my neck. "Yes!"

As the word left her mouth, I felt a change happen. Her pussy was contracting. Her wetness was thickening.

I pushed down on her clit, massaging the bud that was hardening the more I touched it, and I increased the amount of power I used, not just with my hand, but with my dick too.

She felt it.

She reacted.

"Oh! My! God!"

I mashed our lips together, moaning my breath into her mouth while the orgasm took hold of both of us. For me, it was moving through my sac, up my body, and straight out the tip of my cock.

"Emily!" I kept my mouth on hers but unraveled our lips. "Fuck yes!"

Her body stopped moving, allowing me to fully take over, and that was when I knew she was locked up, the tingles exploding inside her, the sensations owning her. What confirmed that was another scream of, "Agh!" against my lips.

She was there.

Peaking.

And so was I.

Emptying myself inside her was a feeling I wasn't prepared for, far different from when I wore a condom. The fucking heat, the intensity, the way she moaned against my mouth and all I could taste was her orgasm—I couldn't get enough.

"Yes," I hissed as the bursts began to slow. "I want more of that." I waited until I knew she was nearing the end before my thumb stilled on her clit. "You liked getting freshly fucked, don't you?"

"No, I love it." She gave me a soft kiss, which turned into a much harder one. "And I'm going to love when you drip out of me."

My chuckle was deep. "You know what I love . . . that fucking mouth."

If my brother was going to take every opportunity he could to burst through my office door without so much as a knock, he could expect the same from me. Payback was a real bitch. So the first thing I did when I arrived at work was walk right into his office without alerting him, earning just the reaction I was seeking.

A pissed-off Jordan.

There were so many things happening at our office—deals in the making, real estate getting purchased—that I needed his full attention. Once we talked things out and I could shift gears to a more personal topic, I hit him with the obvious.

"When are you going to ask her to move in with you?" I crossed my arms over my chest, finally relaxing in the seat across from his desk.

If I aimed the focus on him, I could stop it from shifting to me.

"She's basically already living with me."

"But she's still paying rent at her apartment, yes?" An answer I knew because Emily had told me. "So if a fight happens between you two, she has somewhere to go that isn't, say, your man cave upstairs?"

He nodded.

"You know that's not the same as her moving in." I paused. "Are you afraid of rushing it, or are you afraid she'll say no?"

"Things between us have been in fast-forward since we started hooking up. I want her to live with me. Shit, I want her to marry me. But we're good right now, Gavin. Really fucking good. There's no reason to mess with that."

I was beginning to feel the same about Emily. We were in this untitled phase that came with no pressure. And since I hadn't inserted her into Ben's life, I didn't have to deal with any of his questions or comments about her. That right there would take our relationship to a different level.

"I hear you." I locked my hands behind my head and sank even deeper into the chair. "And Ben's in love with her. So there's that."

"I fucking love seeing them together. She's going to be one hell of a mom."

"She is, for sure." I crossed my legs, foot bouncing in the air, a smile coming over my face as I thought of Emily being a mom. Jesus, she was going to be the best. But this wasn't about Emily and me. This was about Jordan and Maya. "I just want to point out that it's wild seeing you like this after all these years of being single and anti-relationship.

I know you were just waiting for the right woman—and, Jordan, you found her."

He took a deep breath. "I did."

"I'm happy for you, my man."

My phone vibrated from my pocket, and I looked at the screen.

Emily: The roses are still alive and gorgeous. Every time I walk by one of the vases, I think of you.

Me: That's the only time you think of me?

Emily: No.

Me: When are the others?

Jordan brought the conversation back to work, bitching about our most pressing deal and how badly he wanted the transition to be over.

"It's kicking your ass, isn't it?" I asked, regarding how many hours he'd been putting in, but my attention was on the screen of my phone.

As he moaned about the details and decisions that needed to be made, I read Emily's reply.

Emily: Every time I squat to pick up something, I feel you. That sesh last night when Ben was asleep was a wild one. Or should I say, another wild one. The wilds are multiplying.

Emily: And I honestly thought I was going to get banned from late-night sneak-ins after almost getting caught last time. I'm happy that wasn't the case. Lol.

Me: That would mean I wouldn't see you until the weekends and that's a no.

Emily: Are you saying you'd miss me, Gavin?

Me: I miss you right now and I just tasted you last night.

As I watched the bubbles bounce beneath her name, I gave Jordan a random response, not even sure if it made sense. The ringing of his cell was what made me glance up at him.

He shook his head as he swiped the screen. "Hi, Grandma."

"Jordan, my dearest, how are things?"

Jordan smiled at me. "I'm sitting at my desk in the office and Gavin is here with me, so you called at a good time."

"Hi, Grandma." I wasn't going to ask about the hockey game. I didn't want her to think I knew much about it—even though I was positive she knew about us—or that Emily had returned to her seat looking like I'd just devoured every inch of her body, even though I had. So I said, "How's the dancing going?" instead.

"You know I've been giving this new knee a good run for its money. In fact, the other night, I put it to the ultimate test."

"If you're talking about your date with the girls, I heard all about it." Jordan laughed. "Did you have a good time with Maya and Emily?"

Emily: How much do you miss me?

Me: I'm sitting in my brother's office fucking aching for you.

"The best, darling. We had the loveliest dinner, and then I brought those two gals to the game, as you know. A night filled with laughter and wonderful memories. I'm surprised they want to hang out with a weathered bird like me."

Jordan rocked in his seat. "According to Maya, it was one of the best nights she's had in a long time. Her and Emily are already talking about your next outing, which they're planning and insisting on paying for."

Emily had texted me multiple times when she'd gotten home, telling me the same.

My family was already loving her, and they didn't know how much she meant to me.

Emily: I feel the same way—minus the brother's office part. You need to find yourself at the coffee shop across from the rehab center at some point this week.

Me: That was already in the works, baby.

"Who knew I still had that spunk." She giggled. "I heard that you and Gavin were watching the game from the owner's suite."

My jaws ground.

Emily wouldn't have told her.

The only other person who knew was our mother, because she'd been watching Ben.

"We were," Jordan said.

"And you never came down to kiss your grandmother?"

I pointed at Jordan, silently letting him know it was up to him to answer.

"We wanted to give you time with the ladies, Grandma. We didn't want to crash your party. And we didn't want to take any of the attention away from you. It was your evening, not ours."

I pretended to hold a glass and tip it toward my mouth, which made both of us laugh. Once I'd finished tasting Emily, my brother and I proceeded to get wasted in the suite. We'd been in no shape to go see Grandma.

"I understand that, but I want to spend time with my boys too. That means you and Gavin need to make your way over for some milk and cookies. I just made peanut butter kisses. I know how much you love those."

Jordan patted his stomach like fucking Santa. "They're my favorite, Grandma."

"They're not my favorite," I countered.

"Don't you worry, my pumpkin. I'll make you some chocolate chip ones that I know you'll love. They'll be ready tomorrow afternoon at four. I'll see you then."

"I—"

"No excuses," Grandma said, cutting me off. "I'd like you to bring Ben as well, and I'll make my little one some cupcakes. Toodles."

She hung up, and Jordan placed the phone on his desk.

I groaned, "That woman."

"Did you hear how she just sold us? And gave us no choice? What if we had dinner plans? What if we had a business meeting?"

"It doesn't matter what was planned or what wasn't planned—when Grandma calls, we're there. She allows for no exceptions." I rested my arms on my legs.

"We should have used her to negotiate the Clover deal," he said, referring to our most recent acquisition. "She's a million times better than the both of us put together."

I laughed. "You've got that right."

Jordan looked at his phone again, and when he glanced up, I knew the message that had just come across his screen was from Maya.

"Dude, now that's a look of love if I've ever seen one." I created a gun with my fingers and pulled the trigger.

He nodded at me. "When is it your turn?"

There was no way I was going to have this conversation.

I rubbed my hand over the top of my head, ignoring the gel that was in there. "For love? Shit, I don't know." I didn't know why, but I fucking hated saying those words to him. So much so, I stood to leave. "Right now, things need to be all about Ben."

"He's seven."

"And?"

"And Ben wants you happy."

Fuck, not him too.

As I was walking out, I looked at him from over my shoulder. "I am happy."

A statement that couldn't be truer.

"You'd be happier if you had someone like Maya in your life," he told me.

But I did.

And when the time was right, I'd tell him about her.

"Jesus," I moaned, annoyed that he wouldn't drop it. "So you're the master of love now? Throwing it down everyone's throats? After going thirty-three years without it?" I went to the door. "You know one way to get me to stop barging in without knocking? Keep bringing up love, and I'll avoid your office altogether."

I sounded like an angry motherfucker, but that wasn't the feeling inside.

The feeling was the exact opposite.

Jordan smiled, goading me. "You don't think I know that?"

"Asshole."

"See you tomorrow for milk and cookies."

I flipped him off and walked out.

CHAPTER TWENTY-ONE

Emily

Since the restaurant was only half a mile from Gavin's building, I convinced him to send Denis home for the night and for us to walk back to his place. I wanted some air after such a heavy meal. I wanted to feel the coolness of the night and the protection of his hand.

A hand that, no matter where we were, was always on me. This time, his entire arm was draped over my shoulders, his fingers dangling near the top of my breast. I linked my fingers with his and gazed up at him.

There was a warmth inside my chest. A warmth that hadn't come from the bottle of wine we'd just shared or the three courses we'd devoured.

It came from him.

A feeling that had been growing since the very beginning.

One that consumed me whenever I was with him, even when I wasn't.

"What are you thinking about?"

Although I'd been staring, when his eyes locked with mine and the question came out of his mouth, it took me by surprise. "You. This." I took a breath. "Us."

"What about?"

I smiled. "I think I like this little life." A trend I'd seen on social media, something I was sure Gavin hadn't seen, since his accounts were managed by his assistant and the man despised most of the sites. Still, I didn't think that took away from what I'd just admitted.

His lips went to the top of my head, pressing against my hair for several seconds before he kissed me. "Me too."

"I mean, I would like it even more if you'd actually let me pay for something." Teasing him about this topic was becoming one of my favorite things since he was so relentless about it. And knowing how he'd react made me laugh, the movement causing his lips to bump me. "I think we're on our tenth dinner—or something like that, maybe even more—and whenever the bill comes, you get all snappy when I offer my credit card."

He pulled his mouth away. "'Snappy'?"

"You know what I mean."

"Here's more snappiness: I'm never going to let you pay." He kissed me, harder than he'd pecked my head. "Just like I'm never going to let you book a flight—you're going to fly private with me or first class commercially. I'm never going to let you stay in a hotel that isn't a Cole and Spade Hotel." A brand of hotels I'd never booked and couldn't afford, and whenever I flew, my seat was always near the back by the restroom. "I'm never going to let you pay for clothes or makeup or any other shit you put on your body. You're just going to have to take it." He smiled. "Sorry, Emily."

"You spoil me." I soaked in the way he looked at me, the flutters exploding in my stomach. "Why?"

"Because I can." His teeth flicked across his lower lip. "Because I want to."

"I've never experienced anyone like you."

Men had bought me dinner, but this was an entirely different level. Of course, none of them were retired NFL players whose net worth was in the billions.

"This isn't the norm for me either. Remember, I don't do this with anyone." He paused. "I guess I should say I haven't since Ben's mom . . . But Emily, you're different."

I didn't want him to have to talk about her, and I didn't want this moment to grow heavy when everything felt so light and perfect.

I pulled his fingers toward my mouth and kissed the back of his hand. "For the record, if you start buying me tampons, I'm revolting. A line needs to be drawn in the I-buy-Emily-everything-for-her-body sand, and I think that's a good place."

He chuckled. "I can handle that."

We entered through the front of his building and stepped inside his private elevator. As soon as the door started to close, his hands went to my face and he kissed me. My back found the wall, my body arched into his, and I let go.

Because I knew as soon as I gave him my weight, he would take it.

And he did.

He held me like I was nothing more than a handful of pounds, like nothing in this world would ever cause him to release me.

"The hot tub," he said against my lips as he pulled back. "That's where I want you. Naked."

"Now?"

"Now." He rubbed his thumb over my mouth. "And then a shower, where I want you again." He tilted my face up even higher. "And then my bed . . ."

"Where I know you're going to want me again." I licked his fingertip.

"*Mmm.* Yes."

The door opened and he took my hand, bringing me through his foyer and into the living room. I was so focused on him, anticipating when he was going to turn around and strip off my clothes and carry me to the roof, that I almost ran into him when he stopped short.

"Mom," Gavin said in a soft voice, "what's going on?"

Mom?

"Hi, Daddy."

Daddy? Oh shit . . .

Gavin's tall frame and broadness was blocking my whole view, so I moved around him. As my eyes fell over the scene before me, my brain registering exactly what I was looking at—Ben and his grandmother cuddled on the couch under a blanket, staring at me—my heart began to pound.

"Hi, Emily," Ben said since he was just now seeing me. "Are you here to fix my tummy?"

As I looked at Gavin's mom, her expression was filled with shock.

Oh God, this isn't happening . . .

I pulled my fingers away from Gavin's, and as I was about to say something to him, his mom replied, "I called you, Gavin. You didn't answer. I texted you too. I'm sorry . . . I didn't know you wouldn't be alone." The shock continued to grow across her face.

"Gavin, I think I should go," I whispered.

Gavin took out his phone. "Jesus, Mom, I don't know how I missed your call or your text. My phone is on vibrate. I should have felt it." He returned his cell to his pocket. "What's wrong with my boy? Is he sick?"

"My tummy hurts, Daddy," Ben whined. "I feel pukey."

"And somehow, when you packed up his things for the night, you forgot his stuffed hockey stick. You know Ben can't sleep without it."

"Shit," Gavin replied.

As Gavin went to take a step toward Ben, I touched his back to stop him, and he turned and looked at me. "I'm going to go." I pointed toward the elevator.

I didn't know if he'd forgotten that I was here or was too focused on Ben to concentrate on anything else, but his expression didn't register shock.

It showed emotion instead.

"Emily . . ." He shook his head, his throat moving as he swallowed. As the seconds passed, the silence thickened, his eyes became more intense. A type of stare I'd never gotten from him before. And within the quietness that was churning between us, I felt everything. The war. The feelings. The decisions. "I want you to stay."

He . . . *what?*

I wasn't expecting that answer.

Nor was I expecting to enter that stage of our relationship right now.

I was more than ready.

But was he?

"Are you sure?" I kept my voice extremely low.

"Positive." He held out his hand, and I had to force my eyes not to fill with tears as his fingers clasped mine. He brought me to the couch, halting next to the coffee table. "Ben, tell Daddy what's wrong."

The tenderness that came through his tone, the words he chose, even his posture as he looked at his son was making me melt.

"I feel ick."

"Is it something he ate?" Gavin asked his mom.

"We were getting ready for bed"—she rubbed her hand over Ben's hair—"and that's when we realized Uncle J's hockey stick wasn't in the bag. And that's when the tummy and the icks started up with a vengeance."

"Ah. It's all making sense now." Gavin nodded. "I'm sorry I forgot your stuffed hockey stick, buddy. It's my fault, and I should be more careful when I pack your overnight bags. I'm glad Grandma was able to bring you home and make you feel better."

"My tummy." Ben tapped it over the blanket. "Still ick."

I squeezed Gavin's hand. "I'm happy to check him out. But only if you want me to."

"I want you to," he responded.

I released his hand and crouched down in front of Ben and his grandmother. "Hey, buddy." I rubbed his arm to get him used to my touch.

"Hi, Emily." Ben's voice was small. "No button up my nose this time."

"Glad you're giving your little nose a rest." I gently tapped his nose and smiled at him. "Hopefully, I can make you feel better."

As Ben's grandmother was getting up from the couch to give me more room, Gavin said, "Mom, this is Emily." I glanced over my shoulder at him as he added, "She's someone very important in my life." For the second time tonight, I was doing everything I could to hold back tears. "You've probably seen lots of her, since she was Grandma's nurse in the rehab center. Emily, this is my mom, Melinda."

Melinda's expression was so welcoming. "It's lovely to see you here. My mother speaks so highly of you."

"It's nice to officially meet you, Mrs. Worthington."

"Melinda, please." Her grin was even larger. "Ben isn't running a fever. I checked about thirty minutes ago when we got here. That's when I gave him a children's antacid—that's the only medicine I've given him."

"I would have given him the same, that's perfect." As she moved away from the couch, my hand went to Ben's forehead. He still didn't have a fever, and his eyes weren't glossy. "Tell me everything that hurts, kiddo. Are you feeling icky everywhere or just your tummy?"

His lip jutted out. "Just my tum."

"Is it okay if I look at your tum?"

He nodded, hugging the stuffed hockey stick against his neck. "Where's Fenway?"

"Aww, Fenway's at home. If he knew I was seeing you, he'd be wicked jealous. He misses you."

I rubbed his knee before I pulled the blanket back. Ben was in a pair of dinosaur pajamas, and I touched his chest to make sure he wasn't sweating. The fabric was dry, so I gently placed my hand on his lower abdomen and pushed. "Does this hurt?"

"No."

I lifted my palm a little higher. "How about here?"

He shook his head, his dark-brown hair falling into his beautiful eyes.

I shifted my hand toward the right side of his stomach and then the left side. "Any pain in either spot?"

"Nope."

I examined his neck and the glands in his throat, and I helped him sit up a little so I could run my hand down his back. "Are the pains sharp? Do they come and go?"

He nodded. "Ugh."

When I turned toward Gavin, he was whispering to his mom, and she was wearing the biggest smile as he spoke. I was so curious what they were talking about, but when they looked at me, I got the feeling I was the topic of that conversation. And based on her grin, she was beyond pleased with what she was hearing.

I couldn't wait to ask him what their talk was about.

"None of the spots on his stomach seem to be tender," I explained. "Nothing in his neck is enlarged. He doesn't have any pain in his back. My guess is that this could be a case of a missing hockey stick and . . . having to go to the bathroom."

Gavin came over and knelt beside me, his hand holding the back of Ben's head. "Buddy, are you feeling ick because you have to go potty?"

Ben shrugged.

"I'll take him." Melinda returned to the couch, holding out her hand to Ben. Before they walked off, she set her fingers on my shoulder. "Thank you, Emily. I hope to see more of you soon."

"Of course—and same."

I got up from the floor, Gavin did, too, and once Ben and Melinda were out of sight, he immediately pulled me into his arms.

I rested my face on his chest, slowly filling my lungs, the events of tonight finally hitting me. Even though he'd said he wanted me to stay, that didn't mean he wasn't having second thoughts. I was sure his mind was a storm of emotions the same way mine was.

I clenched my eyelids closed and whispered, "I don't know if you were ready for that. I wish it had happened on your terms and not like this—"

"The timing was perfect." He lifted my chin until I looked at him, my eyes opening. "I was going to suggest it anyway. Ben's stomach just beat me to it."

He was?

Oh God.

"Are you sure?" I continued to search his eyes. "The last thing I want is for you to feel rushed and have regret and—"

"Yes, I'm sure." He cupped my face. "I don't feel rushed. I don't have regrets. I want you to be in my son's life, Emily." He grazed my cheeks with his thumbs. "You were incredible with him." As the gravity of that statement hit me, so did his lips, taking mine as though he needed to reinforce what he'd just said. "This feels so right."

CHAPTER TWENTY-TWO

Gavin

As I gently shook Ben awake, his beautiful blue eyes opened—eyes that were the same color as his mother's—and he rubbed them and yawned.

"Hi, Daddy." Once he rolled onto his back, my hand covering most of his stomach, I massaged his tummy as he stretched his arms over his head, his small fists reaching as high as the headboard.

"How's my boy? Did you sleep good?"

"I dreamed of this big dinosaur, and it was flying through the sky, and you know what happened? It landed right by us, and it picked up Fenway and the dinosaur grabbed the poor doggy and flew away with it and Fenway was crying."

I flattened some of his hair. The rest needed water to tame it. "Did you rescue Fenway?"

"I tried to, but it got so high up and I didn't have a dinosaur I could fly on to go get it." His bottom lip jutted out. "Emily was so sad. I didn't like to see her sad."

When Emily had left last night, I couldn't stop thinking about how I was going to talk to Ben about our relationship. I needed his input before I made any decisions. I was pretty positive I knew what my son was going to say. Still, he had a voice and an opinion, and both mattered.

His dream couldn't have been a better introduction.

"I wouldn't like to see Emily sad either." I stroked his cheek with my thumb. "What do you think of her?"

"She's pretty, Dad. And she's so nice. I like that she's like Dr. Kap, but she doesn't stick any needles into me and make me cry."

I chuckled. "She's a little gentler than Dr. Kap, huh?"

He nodded on top of his pillow.

"So you're telling me you like Emily?"

"Lots!"

"What do you think about having her come around more often?" I pulled the blanket down to his knees, preparing him to get up. "Would you like to hang out with her?"

"Yes!"

I tickled his stomach, and once he stopped screaming and laughing, I said, "I thought you would, buddy."

◆ ◆ ◆

Me: Good morning, baby.

Emily: Hi! Morning. 😊

Me: I wish I had woken up to you.

Emily: Me too. But since it was the first time Ben saw us together, especially without my nursing scrubs on, I think it was a good choice to have him wake up to just you. How's he feeling?

Me: He's good.

Me: I've now gotten three texts from my mom about you. Fucking three, Emily.

Emily: I was going to ask you . . . you guys were whispering last night when I was checking out Ben. I get the feeling you were talking about me. True?

Me: We were.

Emily: That's all you're going to say? You need to give me more than that.

Me: I was telling her how I feel about you.

Emily: !!!!!!

Emily: And the texts from Mom, I hope they weren't bad?!?

Me: You've won over Grandma and Mom. They weren't bad at all.

Emily: You know what that means?

Me: Tell me.

Emily: Your mom needs to come to our next girls' night.

Me: I thought you were going to tell me we're meant to be together . . .

Emily: I didn't have to, you just did.

Me: That mouth.

Emily: You love it.

Me: I do.

Me: Do you have to work tomorrow night?

Emily: I have to work for the next three nights.

Me: Sounds like I need to make my way over to the coffee shop.

Emily: I wouldn't hate that. 😊

Me: Your next night off, do you want to come over and hang with Ben?

Emily: I know you said you're sure, but are you really sure? And I know we sorta talked about this last night before I left, but you've now slept on it and had more time to think about it. I just want you to be positive that this is what you want.

Me: Emily, I just invited you to come over to hang with my son. If I wasn't sure, I wouldn't have asked.

Emily: I know. It's just a huge step.

Me: I'm ready for it. I want you to be part of his life.

Emily: I wish I could kiss you right now.

Me: You can.

Emily: How?

Me: Denis and I will be outside the rehab center in ten minutes.

Emily: You make everything happen and you probably don't even realize you're doing it.

Me: See you soon.

◆ ◆ ◆

Emily: Do you have flour at your house?

Me: Yes.

Emily: Sugar? Butter? Oil? Eggs? Vanilla? Baking powder? Milk? Powdered sugar? And heavy whipping cream?

Me: All of it but the heavy whipping cream.

Emily: You don't bake, do you?

Me: My chef does.

Emily: I thought of a fun thing to do with Ben, and I wanted to make sure you have all the ingredients. You probably don't have any piping bags. I'll bring those. Or sprinkles.

Me: I have a seven-year-old with a sweet tooth. I have sprinkles.

Me: Do me a favor, don't forget Fenway.

Emily: He's already packed in my bag. 😊

"I love him so much." Ben hugged Fenway against his chest. My boy had a swipe of flour on his cheek, and I swore the dog had one too. "He's so cute, Daddy. I want a Fenway. A real Fenway. That can bark and do tricks, and we can go to the park and play fetch with him."

I was leaning against the counter in the far side of my kitchen, holding a tumbler of scotch while Emily and Ben were sitting at the island. It had been a full day for the three of us, starting with ice-skating, followed by dinner at home, and now we were on to dessert.

A dessert that Ben and Emily were making together.

I took a sip, trying to process the responsibility of a dog while managing everything else in my life.

"I'll make a deal with you, buddy. When you're old enough to walk the dog on your own, I promise I'll get you one just like Fenway."

"How old is that?" he asked. While Emily checked the temperature of the cupcakes on the cooling rack, Ben set Fenway on the island, running his hand up and down the dog's spine. "'Cause I'm ready to walk."

"Not for several more years." I chuckled.

"Ugh." He pouted. "That's not fair."

Emily's arm went around his shoulders. "Dad just wants to make sure you're going to pick up after the dog. You know, like when it goes potty outside." Emily squeezed him, and he laughed. "You can't leave it out there, you have to put it in a bag."

"I have to pick *it* up?" His eyes went wide as he watched me nod. *"Ewww."*

"Do you still want a dog?" I asked him.

He shrugged. "Maybe a fish."

I laughed even harder. "That, we can do, buddy."

"Ben, I need you to do me a favor." Emily dipped a spoon into the bowl of frosting that they had just finished beating in my mixer. "I want you to taste this and, in your expert frosting opinion, tell me if it needs anything."

He took the spoon and touched the glob at the end with his tongue. *"Mmmm."*

She faced him. "It's good?"

"It's *sooo* good!"

"Does it need anything? Maybe a bit more vanilla?"

He put the whole spoon in his mouth, and with the metal still between his teeth, he replied, "It's extra perfect! I want to eat the whole bowl."

"The whole bowl?" Emily smiled. "Well, we can't have you do that, or you'll get another wicked stomachache. How about we frost these cupcakes and then you can have one?"

Ben's nod was exaggerated. "Yay!"

She scooped some of the frosting into a bag that had a metal tip and handed it to Ben. "You're up, mister. Your job is to frost all three of these." She had placed the cupcake bases on a plate in front of him.

"I'm doing *all* of them? Wow."

"All of them, yes. Let me show you. You're going to aim the tip like this"—she moved his hands toward the bases, placing the tip against the cake—"and squirt. When you're happy with how much frosting it has, you move on to the next one. Sound easy?"

"Yep! Then we get to sprinkle?"

"You sure do." She pointed at the three bowls in the middle of the island. "We have lots of different kinds of sprinkles. Even ones that are shaped like dinosaurs."

"So *coool.*" Ben began to swirl the frosting over a vanilla base, Emily holding the bottom of the cake so it wouldn't move. "This one is for me. I want it to be as tall as the ceiling!"

"How about we stick to triple the frosting, like the ones I sent you?"

"More!"

I took another drink of my scotch, smiling as soon as I pulled the glass away. Emily was a natural. She needed no warming up—she was already so in tune to Ben and what he needed. Ben took to her immediately, holding her hand when we went skating, talking to her while Denis drove us, walking next to her as we entered and left the arena. He wanted Emily to cut his steak at dinner and to squirt the ketchup on his plate. And now, watching them make Ben's favorite dessert, my chest was fucking pounding.

The accidental run-in had worked out just the way it was supposed to.

Emily needed to be in my son's life.

For Ben.

And for me.

"I think the cupcake is on the verge of toppling over," Emily said to him. "Before the frosting makes it too heavy to stand, how about we move on to the next one?"

"I'm gonna eat it all!"

"I have no doubt you will." She laughed. "Now we're on to Dad's cupcake." She glanced at me. "With a strawberry base. His absolute favorite."

"You mean *your* favorite." I winked.

She smirked. "No, I mean, your *new* favorite."

"We'll see about that," I teased.

"Come on, you're going to love it." She held the strawberry base in front of Ben.

"Dad gets *allll* the frosting too!"

"How about you give Dad just a little bit," I requested.

"You're no fun." He stuck his tongue out at me.

Ben quickly finished my cupcake and Emily's, and she placed the bowls in front of him. "I want you to decorate the cupcakes however you want to."

"I get to sprinkle all of them?" His mouth dropped open. "With all this stuff?"

"Of course you do. This is your dessert. You're the chef. We're going to eat whatever you make us, so you can place the sprinkles however you like them."

"I love this so much!"

Emily laughed, and as Ben got to work, she took out her phone. "I'm going to snap some pics of the chef, is that okay?"

"Yep!" Ben, with sprinkles covering his hand, put his fingers on Emily's arm and leaned in to look at her phone. "I know that picture!"

She tilted her phone toward him. "Yes, you do."

"I drew it!"

Emily nodded as she looked at me. "Yes, you did."

He . . . drew it?

"Hold on a second." I took a deep breath as I stared at my girl. "The picture Ben drew you is the wallpaper on your phone?"

She scrunched her face, her expression adorable. "It's hanging on the wall in my bedroom, but since I'm hardly home, I thought making it my wallpaper would mean I'd get to see it more often." She bit her lip. "The only thing missing in the drawing is you." She put her hand on Ben's head, roughing up his dark, overgrown locks. "Ben, you might need to draw me another picture soon, and this time, include your dad."

"Okay! But cupcake first. *Mmm.*"

In that moment I knew, without a doubt in my mind, I fucking loved her.

CHAPTER TWENTY-THREE

Emily

Gavin: Have a good time with Maya tonight.

Me: You're hanging out with Jordan, right?

Gavin: I am.

Me: Why do I get the feeling you guys are going to get into all the trouble.

Gavin: Because that usually happens when we're together. But I'm going to be good . . . I promise.

Me: Ben's with Mom and Dad?

Gavin: He is, which means I'm going to be all alone at my place once I get home from whatever Jordan has planned.

Me: That sounds awful.

Gavin: Doesn't it? Fucking brutal. Don't let it happen, Emily.

Me: You're saying you want me to find my way over to your place once Maya leaves girls' night to go to Jordan's to sleep?

Gavin: That's exactly what I'm saying.

Me: I think I might be able to make that happen.

Gavin: See you later, baby.

As we sat in our living room, the TV silenced, our glasses constantly filled, love was showing across every inch of Maya's face. She couldn't hide it. But loving a man like Jordan Worthington, who was on the road far more than he was home, required some change in Maya's life. That was the main reason I hadn't invited anyone else to our girls' night. I wanted to talk to Maya about Jordan's schedule and convince her to go on the road with him. My girl could be so stubborn at times, fiercely independent and inflexible. Those were things I adored about her. But when it came to her man, if she wanted things to work out between them, she couldn't continue working full-time at the rehab center while Jordan was gone. So I'd come up with a plan for her to switch to per diem. That would give her everything—the ability to travel with him and work while she was home.

Of course, that meant I'd be seeing even less of her, which gutted me, but her happiness was all that mattered to me. My bestie deserved to have everything, especially the vacation Jordan was about to take her on, a nugget she'd just dropped a few minutes ago.

A nugget that I needed to hear all about.

So I sipped my wine and said, "Now, let's talk about that upcoming vacay Jordan is taking you on. Do you have any deets? I'm dying to know everything."

"Um. That makes two of us." She repositioned herself on our couch, sitting on her calves. "He won't tell me anything. The only reason he even told me about the vacation was because I needed to take the time off work."

I wagged my finger at her. "Another reason per diem is perfect for you." Every opportunity I got, like this one, I would continue to drive home this point until she took my advice.

"Anywaaay," she sang, "I know we leave in three days. That's all the information he's given me."

"Oh God, how are you supposed to pack?"

She shrugged. "I don't know."

"Is he going to tell you the night before so you can at least put together your suitcase?"

She put her hand out, palm-side up. "I have no idea."

He would probably have his assistant get everything Maya would need, including clothes, accessories, makeup, and toiletries. But I wasn't going to mention that. I didn't want to come across as knowing Jordan's capabilities, considering I still hadn't told her about Gavin.

A bomb I needed to drop before Bettie or Melinda shared the news for us.

Something was stopping me. There was something so incredibly sexy and scandalous about sneaking around and not telling anyone, only those who had caught us in the act.

But is that normal?

Should I feel this way?

"I can't handle this," I replied, referring to her lack of knowledge about her trip, but maybe I was talking about me too.

"Same! He's leaving tomorrow, and he won't be coming back until our trip—I think. He won't even confirm those details. I just know he needs to travel to New York. Whether he's meeting me here or there—wherever *there* is—I'm clueless."

"That man is killing me."

"You? What about me!"

"The thing is, you know his assistant has planned out every step of this trip, and he's just not telling you because he wants to see or hear your reaction, like when you walked into his condo and it was covered in flowers. He lives for surprises. Meanwhile, we're sharpening our knives over here so we can threaten his life."

She giggled. "But you know what, I love that about him."

"Me too."

She turned quiet, her face becoming serious. "Em . . ."

"Yeah?"

"I'm ready for it to be your turn. For you to find a Jordan."

I found one.

And . . . I loved him.

I rubbed my lips together, filling my lungs, the guilt suddenly coming on thick and strong. So much so, that I downed half my wineglass.

I needed to tell her. I needed to just say the words.

But Gavin hadn't told his brother. In fact, we hadn't discussed telling Jordan or Maya in a while.

Rather than dwell on something I didn't have an answer to, I shook my head, clearing those thoughts away, and whispered, "Girl, you and me both."

◆ ◆ ◆

Gavin was upstairs putting Ben to sleep, something he did whenever I was here during this hour. An undiscussed boundary I'd set so Gavin was the last person Ben saw before he closed his eyes. But what that also meant was, depending on how long it took Ben to fall asleep, I often dozed off while I was waiting for Gavin to come back downstairs. Like tonight, after a full day at the rehab center that had been more taxing than I was prepared for, I woke to the feel of Gavin's soft lips on my forehead.

"You look so fucking gorgeous when you sleep."

I was hugging one of the decorative pillows, tucked into the corner of the couch, a blanket over me. I sat up to hopefully shake the tiredness out. "How many stories did it take?"

"Three. Dinosaurs, dogs, and now he's on an otter kick." He set my legs over his lap and rubbed the outside of my thigh. "I swear, the kid is going to end up being a vet. He can't get enough of animals."

"Except when it comes to taking one outside." I winked.

He laughed. "Jenny told me Ben met a dog in the lobby this morning, I guess one of the residents got a new puppy. Ben didn't want to say goodbye to it. He told me all about it during the dog book we just read."

"Oh yeah, you're going to have a Fenway before you know it."

His hand stilled on my leg. "Hungry?"

I loved that we ate a small snack while Ben devoured his early dinner, and had ours after he went to bed.

"Starving."

"Wine?"

I nodded. "Please."

He got up from the couch, and while he stood at the bar, he poured two glasses of red from an already open bottle and brought them over, taking a seat again. He held my gaze, a unique smile coming across his face. "I want to surprise you, but your situation makes that a little difficult."

"Surprise me?" My head tilted. "And what situation are we talking about?"

He massaged my knee. "How much notice would you have to give work if I wanted to take you away for a long weekend?"

My eyes narrowed as I held the glass near my lips, staring into his eyes. "Where are you taking me?"

He chuckled. "You have to answer my question first."

"Probably about two weeks. That would give me enough time to get my shifts covered for both jobs."

"Now you see why it's difficult to be spontaneous and keep things a surprise."

"Tell me about it, I know." I sighed, my fingers diving into the back of his dark hair. "What do you have up your sleeve?"

"I have some work travel coming up. The first trip is to Nashville. I thought if you could get away, it would be a great vacation. Three or four days, depending on how much time you can get off . . . just the two of us."

My conversation with Maya suddenly entered my head. The guilt I had felt when I told her I was ready to find a Jordan when I had one right here who wanted to take me away.

Nashville was the perfect time to talk to Gavin about it.

"You don't have to convince me," I whispered. "I'm in."

◆ ◆ ◆

Me: I feel like I need to gloat for a second. Who has the best advice in the entire universe? Who deserves a giant 'thank you, Emily, you're absolutely right, going per diem so I can be on the road with Jordan was the best decision I ever made'? That would be me. I deserve that. You're welcome for changing your whole life and making it a million times better. Hehe.

Maya: LOL. Seriously, girl, you were SO right. Thank you, thank you, thank you. Honestly, it was the best decision I've ever made, and I wouldn't have made it or even thought of it if it hadn't been for you.

Maya: And I love you.

Maya: And I think this is the longest we've gone without seeing each other, and I'm not okay. Sob.

Me: I promise you're not missing anything. Well, aside from me. The rehab center and Boston—it's all the same since you left and it will be here when you get back. You made the right choice, babe. You're exactly where you're supposed to be: with your man. ❤

Maya: I can't even put into words how much I'm missing you.

Me: We'll FaceTime soon so you can see my pretty mug.

Maya: Please. I want that.

Me: Love you, babe.

Maya: Love you more.

Maya: I MISS YOU.

Me: Stop. I can't. I feel like half my heart is on the road and it hurts something wicked.

Me: How's my rockstar bestie? How's Jordan? How's all the things?

Maya: The best. All of it. Omg, Em, I didn't think this kind of happiness existed.

Me: I'm crying for you. I'm not even kidding.

Maya: Ohhh, I forgot, I have amazing news!

Me: YOU'RE ENGAGED?!?

Maya: If I was engaged, this isn't how you'd find out. Come on, hello. I'm coming into town and I get to see youuu, that's my amazing news.

Me: HELL YES. When?

I stared at the dates she sent, and my stomach dropped.

Me: You're not going to believe this, but I'll be out of town.

Maya: WHAT?

Me: I know. Waaaah.

Maya: Where are you going?

Me: Nashville.

Maya: Fun! What are you doing there?

Me: Just getting away. A change of scenery kinda thing. 😊

Maya: Ugh! It's not even going to feel like home without you there.

Me: Your next trip back, I'll be here, promise. Or maybe I'll fly out and see you while you're on the road. Ohh, actually I kinda love that idea, I need to make that happen.

Maya: I want that. PLEASE.

CHAPTER TWENTY-FOUR

Gavin

"Jordan," I said as I connected the call, the Bluetooth picking up, so my brother's voice would soon be blasting through the speakers of my SUV. "What's going on, brother?"

"Just checking on things. Seeing how everything is at the office. You must be leaving for the day, no?"

Our corporate headquarters flew by the back seat window as Denis drove toward my place, and I finally reached for the knot at my throat, loosening it, along with unbuttoning the top of my shirt. "All is good."

"That's all you've got for me? That things are good?"

There was a vibration in my hand, and I glanced down at the text on the screen of my phone.

Emily: Blue or red?

Me: What am I picking out?

Emily: A dress I'm buying for Nashville. I can't decide which color will look best on me.

"Since you've been on the road, you're copied on no less than a hundred emails an hour," I said to him. "You get a daily report from our assistant, and you speak to her probably every hour or more. I can't imagine, out of all the things you could ask me, that you're generally curious about the climate at the office."

Me: Red. Always red.

Me: And you're not buying a dress, I'm buying the dress.

He chuckled. "Always such a fucking dick."

Emily: Nice try, but no.

Me: Emily, I'm buying the dress.

Emily: You can fight with me when you see me tonight. And when you fight me, I hope you use teeth because that would be so hot.

"I'm just speaking the truth," I said to my brother. "You must have a reason for calling. Instead of beating around the bush, how about you tell me what it is."

Me: You want me to bite you . . .

Emily: Yesss.

Emily: See you soon.

"All right, then. Here's what's on my mind . . . I'm staring at Maya's engagement ring that I just picked up from the jeweler, and I'm thinking to myself, *When the hell is my brother going to tell me about him and Emily?*"

As Denis's eyes connected with mine in the rearview mirror, my head leaned back, pushing into the top of the seat. "You're proposing. It's about goddamn time."

"Don't avoid the topic. I'll just bring it right back up."

I took off my seat belt and slipped out of my suit jacket. "How do you know about Emily and me?"

"Did you honestly think my security team wasn't going to show me the footage of you and her in my elevator?"

It took me a second to realize what he was talking about.

The night I'd walked into Jordan's place and Emily was on the couch. When I'd offered to drive her home.

When I'd fucking gone down on her in the elevator.

"Jesus Christ," I groaned. "Tell me you deleted the footage?"

"It's gone, don't worry. But I'm going to ask the question again. When were you going to tell me about you and Emily?"

"This has been . . ." Emily exhaled, glancing at the view through the wall of glass from our penthouse suite at the Cole and Spade Hotel in downtown Nashville. "Nothing short of amazing."

As she sat next to me on the couch, wearing the red dress she wouldn't let me buy, my hand slipped behind her neck. While she was focused on the scenery of the city, I looked down her body, my view far more perfect. The dress cupped her tits, tucking most of them in like a pocket, and then showed off the flatness of her stomach and widened just enough for her hips before it ended at the middle of her thighs. It would be a fucking miracle if we made it to the dinner I had planned and I didn't just eat her instead.

"The trip isn't over yet," I told her.

"I don't want it to end." She finally left the windows to look at me. "I've had the best time with you."

My lips went to her hair, and I breathed her in while I kissed her. "You know, it doesn't have to end."

"You mean I can permanently run away from all my responsibilities?" She laughed. "Goodbye, rent. Goodbye, other bills. I won't miss you." She shook her head, and that was when my lips lifted off her. "God, that sounds extremely tempting."

My fingers spread across the back of her neck. "When you move in with us, you won't need two jobs. You won't need any job unless you want to keep them. So yes, Emily, you can run from all of it. And you can run straight to my place."

She searched my eyes. "When I move in with you . . ." Her voice trailed off, silence filling the room for several seconds. "Are you asking me to move in?"

"You're basically living with us now. How often are you at your apartment? A couple of times a week? If that?"

She turned her whole body toward me and took a drink of her wine. "Gavin . . ."

"You could keep your job with Dr. Kaplan if you really want to and pull back from the rehab center." I opened the front flap of my sports coat as I twisted on the couch to face her straight on. "I'm sure Dr. Kaplan would let you work as many times a week as you want. And that way, you'd get to treat kids, just like your plan was all along. But again, only if you want to. You don't have to."

Her chest rose as she took several deep breaths. "You just unloaded a suitcase the size of a dumpster."

I chuckled. "I know . . ."

She searched my eyes. "Do you, though?"

"We need to talk." I let that sink in. "After the conversation I recently had with my brother, it became apparent."

"What conversation?" Her brows rose.

I took a long drink of my scotch. "Jordan asked when I was going to tell him about us. I had no idea how he knew, since I hadn't said anything to him. That's when he proceeded to tell me about the security cameras in his private elevator. Apparently, there's footage of me getting on my knees and licking your pussy." Her eyes began to widen. "Considering that happened a while ago, he's been sitting on this news for quite a bit." I wasn't going to drop the engagement bomb. I didn't think I needed to.

"Gavin, WHAT?" She put her hands over her face. "Your brother saw you? Doing *that* to me? I'm about to die right now."

"He deleted the footage, don't worry."

"But he saw it." Her hands dropped while I nodded, then instantly returned to her face. "Yep. I seriously want to die."

I pulled her fingers away. "Listen to me, I've walked in on my brother during a threesome. I've seen the dude doing plenty of shit over the years. This isn't something you need to worry about."

"I know you think you're helping, but you're not."

"The man is practically married, which means he saw the footage, he immediately deleted it, and he waited for me to tell him about us. I didn't, and that's the fucked-up part about this. I should have told him, Emily."

"Hold on a second." Her hand went to her chest, tapping her heart as though she wanted to slow it down. "Has he told Maya?"

"If he did, I'm sure she would have asked you. Don't you think?"

She slowly nodded. "Yes."

"Baby, why haven't you told her?"

Her cheeks puffed out as she filled them with air, eventually releasing it through her mouth. "This is some of the baggage that's inside the dumpster-sized suitcase." She paused. "During my last girls' night with Maya, she said to me that I need to find myself a Jordan. And instead of saying I already have one, I agreed with her."

"Why?"

She took another drink and set her wine on the coffee table. "I don't know. Part of me thought you didn't want them to know, even though your mom and Bettie know—which, I get, makes no sense. Part of me thought you wanted to keep us a secret. Part of me kinda liked the whole secret thing and found it so hot. Part of me still doesn't believe we're together, and the ridiculously sexy owner of the Bears, who I saw at the game that night with Maya, is really my boyfriend." She rubbed her hands over the bottom of her dress. "And maybe a part of me wanted you to be the one to say it's time to tell Maya and Jordan." She let out another long exhale. "My reasoning is quite possibly a mixture of all that."

I held her chin. "Emily, once I got the approval from my son—yes, I got his approval to have you around more, and I made sure he wanted to hang out with you as much as I do—it didn't matter to me who knew." Her lips pursed the second I mentioned my boy. "The Ben step was the most important. After I got past it, you could have screamed about our relationship from the top of my building." My hand moved to her cheek. "I should have made that clear to you. I should have had this conversation with you, and I'm sorry I didn't. And I feel like shit for not telling Jordan. I should have, I don't know why I didn't. But I can understand how things could have been confusing for you." I gave her a small kiss. "I assure you, I want the whole fucking world to know you're mine."

"Feel this." She put my hand on her heart. "Emotion is literally exploding through me."

"I might as well unload a little more of that suitcase, then." I traced my thumb across her lips, holding her gorgeous bright-blue gaze. "I love you, Emily."

Her eyes closed, and when they opened, they were filled with tears. "You do?"

I wiped the first one before it fell from her eyelid. "I have for a while."

She threw her arms around my neck. "Gavin, I love you too."

I hugged her against me, and when she pulled back, she kissed me. She cupped my face to keep me close until she separated our mouths, then pressed our noses together.

She sighed. "Maya is going to murder me for not telling her."

"Maybe it would be safer to do it over the phone." I chuckled.

"I can't. It feels like something I should do in person. Unless Jordan or your mom or Bettie tells her before I get the chance."

I shook my head. "They won't."

"How do you know?"

"Because of my past. Because of losing Sarah, Ben's mom. They know I don't love easily or at all. And if I ever did, like the way I love you, they would treat the situation as though it were glass." I leaned back to look in her eyes. "I assure you, no one is saying a word about this. In fact, they're tiptoeing, hoping more than anything that you're the one." I slipped my arm around her back, a smile stretching across my lips as I admitted, "And you are."

CHAPTER TWENTY-FIVE

Emily

Every day that passed without my best friend knowing about Gavin and me caused my heart to ache a little more. Maya was missing out on a major part of my life, and I didn't want that for either of us. I got to watch her fall for Jordan and see her love grow deeper. When it came to Gavin and me, I wanted that for our friendship. I wanted to make up for all this missed time.

So I decided I wasn't going to wait until she returned to Boston. I was going to tell her now.

While Gavin was in the shower getting ready for our dinner date, I brought my phone into his bed and tucked myself under the fluffy comforter.

Me: Hiiiii. So I know you're in New York (yes, I'm stalking your location because that's what besties do), but we need to talk . . . I have something to tell you.

"You look guilty."

I glanced up from the screen. Gavin was standing in the doorway of his en suite with a towel wrapped around his waist, drips from the shower clinging to his skin. "I do? How?"

"Are you up to something?"

I laughed. "I just texted Maya, telling her I want to talk. I can't wait another second, Gavin. It's killing me not to tell her, so I'm coming clean, and I'm fully prepared for how she's going to slaughter me."

He walked to the center of his bedroom and stopped, running a hand over his dark, wet hair, his fingers then doing the same to the sides of his beard. "Has she written back?"

The screen showed no reply, and there weren't any bubbles beneath her name, telling me she was typing. "Nope." I didn't want to keep staring at it, so I tossed my phone onto his side of the bed, my gaze focused on his body. How did this man get hotter by the day? How did he get more chiseled? How was it possible that he was mine? And how did the mere sight of him make me wet? "I need you to come here." I sat up and crawled to the end of his bed, flipping around so my legs were hanging toward the floor.

"I'm here." He looked at me through his lashes. "You mean you want me closer?"

With my finger, I waved him over. "Much closer."

He finally positioned himself in front of me, and I pulled at the towel, loosening the way it was wrapped and folded into his waist, and I let it fall to the floor.

He chuckled. "Are you telling me you want to no-show on our reservation that's in twenty minutes? For the record, I have no problem with that."

"I highly doubt it's going to take you twenty minutes." I fisted the bottom of his dick, a hard-on already setting in. "I seem to know what you like, and I'm usually pretty good at it." Aligned right at my mouth due to his height and where I was sitting, I rubbed my lips around his tip. "I give you five minutes. Tops."

"What about what I want to do to you?" He held my jaws, stroking them with his thumbs. "That's going to take far more time . . ."

"You can't have me yet."

"Hold on"—his grip tightened—"you're telling me you're going to give me head, but you're not going to let me taste you?"

"Oh, you can taste me." My tongue circled his mushroom edge and lowered down his pulsing vein. On the way back up, I licked the bead of pre-cum and swallowed it. "But not until after dinner."

"How am I going to wait that long? That's fucking torture."

I smiled. "Sorry."

I kept my eyes on his and surrounded his crown with my lips, tasting the shower on his skin and the spicy ginger-and-cinnamon scent that constantly clung to him. I was only a few inches deep, my hand lifting from the bottom of his dick, which pumped what my mouth couldn't cover, when I heard, "Baby, fuck yes."

He still held the sides of my face, his way of thinking he was controlling my movements even though he wasn't. Because every bit of this was on me—how deep I went and how fast I swirled my tongue and how hard I sucked.

Gavin didn't like the tease. He didn't like the slow, dragged-out bob of my mouth. He wanted my cheeks to cave inward, turning into a suction cup, my tongue spooned on the underside of him and circling the top once I reached it.

So that was what I gave him.

On my way down, the back of my throat anticipated the brief grazing of his girth, and I made sure to calm my gag reflexes while my hand slid over him, the spit that had leaked out making that glide extremely easy. My palm went as far as his sac, squeezing and turning as it reversed back up.

"Ah, *yesss*," he hissed. His abs contracted, his hips arched forward. "God, you know how to suck dick."

I couldn't tell him how much I loved this, my mouth was too full. I could only show him through sounds, making sure they were loud enough that the moans vibrated against him. Each time I released one, his body clenched, he'd attempt to rock forward, and he would let out the sexiest sound of pleasure.

All that did was make me go faster.

Harder.

I timed up my mouth and hand so they were working in tandem. So every part of his shaft was covered at all times, the friction coming from either the inside of my mouth or the skin of my fingers.

The speed was what worked him up—it was what drove him toward the edge. The sucking did, too, when I focused on his tip, adding an extra second or two to that sensitive spot before I dipped again. It was that spot that made him groan, "Emily," the loudest. Because I treated his dick as though his orgasm was goading me, like I would do absolutely anything to draw the cum out of him.

And I would.

Even if that meant spending extra time at the top, using my hand to jerk off the rest, flicking my tongue across the peak.

I wanted his orgasm.

I wanted to watch him unravel.

I wanted to hear his vulnerability.

I wanted it to fill my mouth.

And it took only a few more pulls from my lips before he gave me that.

"Emily! Hell yes!" The signs were all there—the parting of his lips, a feral stare, his head falling back right before he moaned, *"Fuuuck."*

That was when I increased everything I gave him.

The speed, the grip, the power.

What that earned me was a thick, heavy squirt toward the back of my mouth, hitting the roof and falling toward my tongue. His cum was hot, salty, and when he added a second shot and a third, it all began to pool. I quickly swallowed the load, my hand twisting toward the top of him to make sure he was empty, and when a little more leaked out, I swallowed that.

He gave me his eyes, a satiated expression coming over his face. "*Mmm.* That was fucking incredible."

A confirmation that he was done.

I pulled him out of my mouth and wiped the corners of my lips.

As he held out his hands to grab me, I got up and rushed toward the pillows, pointing at him. "Don't even think about it. We're going to dinner. Go get dressed."

"I just want a taste of your pussy." He leaned onto the mattress. "Please. Just a little one."

"You're incapable of only taking a taste. The second your lips touch me, you'll be down there all night." My finger lifted and aimed toward his closet. "Go."

"Fuck, you're mean." He smiled.

I laughed, and as he went to his closet, I found my phone on the bed.

Maya: Omg, I was just going to text you. Want to come to New York this weekend? With Gavin and Ben—assuming they can come—and stay at Jordan's condo and have all the fun with us?

Me: Ah . . .

Maya: Em?

Me: We really need to talk first. Can I call you?

Maya: We're in the bathtub. I'll call you once we get out and you can fill me in on everything.

Me: Put your phone down and go enjoy naked time. Silly girl. XO

Maya: Hi! I'm free, call me.

Me: Ugh, I can't, I'm out for the night. Can I call you in the morning?

Maya: Of course! I'll be up at the ass crack of dawn for a run. Call me whenever you wake up.

The moment my eyes opened the next morning, I quietly got out of bed, doing everything I could to not wake up Gavin, and I closed his bedroom door and went into the living room. Since Ben had spent last night at his grandparents', I could sit on Gavin's couch half naked and not have to worry about covering myself up.

There wasn't any coffee running through my body. I hadn't even brushed my teeth.

I couldn't imagine how terrifying I looked, considering the moment we'd gotten back from dinner, Gavin had eaten me out on this couch, fucked me against the TV wall, and bent me over the dining room table.

It didn't matter.

Maya had seen me at my absolute worst.

And since I couldn't tell her this in person, FaceTime was the next best thing.

I grabbed a blanket from the back of the couch and draped it over my chest and hit the button for the video call, holding my breath as it rang three times.

My best friend's beautiful brown eyes stared back at me, her pouty lips pulling into a smile. "Babe!"

"I'm dating Gavin." The words just fell out of my mouth. "Yes, as in Jordan's brother. We've been dating for a while—I mean, I don't know what is actually considered *a while*, but enough time has passed that I'm sorta living at his place now and Ben is very much a part of my life and Gavin's mom knows and I'm sure that means his dad knows, too, and I think Bettie knows also." My heart was hammering so hard, I put my hand on it. "And I wanted to tell you, Maya. Like so many times. During our last girls' night when you were saying I needed a guy like Jordan, I wanted nothing more than to tell you I was dating his brother. But Gavin and I hadn't talked about airing our relationship and I didn't know if I should say anything and my head was all over the place and I know this is all fucked and you're probably furious with me for not telling you and . . ." I drew in some air, my lungs completely deflated.

Her hand was over her mouth, her eyes wide, almost teary looking.

"You're furious, aren't you? You want to murder me? You can't believe I didn't say anything and you're right, I should have said something. I was so wrong. I wanted nothing more than to share it with you, I swear I did." Had I already said that? Why were the last several seconds a total blur and I couldn't remember a thing I'd said? Was there such a thing as blacking out sober? "Say something, Maya."

Her fingers slowly lowered from her mouth, the emotion still in her eyes, and now I could see it on her lips. "When did this start?"

"That night you and I texted from the Uber, remember when I was called out by Dr. Kaplan's office to do a home visit? And you told me to text you when I got home, and I didn't?" Her eyes widened as I added, "Well, Ben was the patient—oh my God, I'm not even allowed to tell you that, I'm breaking every HIPAA rule. Anyway, my shift ended while I was there, and Gavin asked if I wanted to have a drink and . . . the rest is history." I pulled the blanket up higher, wanting to hide beneath it. "Things between us moved slow. Painfully slow. It took a while before we even had each other's numbers. And then the more time we spent together, the harder and faster we seemed to fall."

She shook her head while she stared at me, staying silent.

"Maya . . . you're still not saying anything."

"I think that's because I'm in shock."

"A good kind of shock? Or an I-will-hate-you-forever kind of shock? I know that with them being brothers, that makes things a bit complicated. Is that even the right word? I don't know." I shrugged. "Weird? I don't know if it's weird. Or if it's extra weird. Or—"

"Em?"

I filled my chest with air, knowing the verdict was about to be given. "Yeah?"

"I have a lot to say about this, but first, I need to get this out . . . We're going to be sisters-in-law." Her head fell back, and when it straightened again, her eyes were filled with tears. "We've always been sisters, but now we're going to officially be sisters."

"I don't know about that. Gavin and I have a long way to go before he puts a ring on my finger—or if that ever even happens at all. But Maya, we're happy." My eyes started to tear. "We're so happy."

She caught the first drip that fell from her eyes. "I'm beside myself right now. I can't even believe it. Never in a million years did I think this was what you were going to tell me." Her mouth dropped open. "Wait a second, you were in Nashville with Gavin, weren't you, you little minx."

I laughed. "I was."

"When I found out you were going, I told Jordan if you went to the game and didn't reach out for tickets, I was going to murder you."

I winced. "Do you still want to murder me? Not just about the game—which I did go to with Gavin, by the way—but about everything?"

I heard the deep breath she exhaled. "Murder, no. But am I hurt, yes. I can't lie to you and say I'm not. We've had so many convos about you finding a man or a man like Jordan—convos that have taken place since you've been with Gavin—and you never said anything to me. Come on, Em, we're stronger than that."

"I've been sick about it. I swear I didn't do it to hurt you. You know I love you more than anything in this world."

"And that's why you should have told me . . . because I am hurt."

I nodded. "I know. You're right. And I'm so sorry."

"If I weren't so far into dreamland right now, I'd probably be a lot snappier and hold a grudge and give you at least a few days of silence to make you really stir." She gave me a stern look. "Ultimately, though, I just love you. I love Gavin and Ben, and what this news means—I love that too. We're going to be a family."

I didn't know why, but hearing her say that—something I'd always considered Maya anyway—made the tears come out even faster. "Babe, we are."

She rubbed her lips together. "And now we're one step closer." She shifted the phone, and suddenly there was a giant diamond on the screen.

Round.

More carats than I'd ever seen.

It sparkled so vibrantly, I could see every color of the rainbow.

I swore my eyes popped out of my head when I yelled, "ARE YOU ENGAGED?"

Her fingers wiggled. "It happened last night." Her face returned to the phone. "I died when he asked me and I died again this morning when I woke up and realized it wasn't a dream—hence my dreamland comment." I could tell she was bouncing. "My best friend is completely in love with the most amazing guy and has the sweetest little boy as a bonus kid. I'm engaged. And now we're going to be one giant family. I swear, life couldn't get any better."

"Maya . . ." I dabbed the corner of each eye. "I can't believe this is all happening. That it's happening for us. That we're getting everything we've ever wanted."

"I can. Because, Em, you deserve it. It's about damn time a man appreciates you and adores you and is obsessed with you."

"How do you know Gavin does any of that?" I grinned.

"They're brothers. I don't care how different they look or how opposite they act, Gavin is a Worthington. And when a Worthington loves, they love hard."

CHAPTER TWENTY-SIX

Gavin

There was a time in my life when it hurt to smile, when the only thing that brought any happiness to my heart was my son. But even when I looked at him, the hurt was still there. Because his eyes, cheeks, the roundness of his beautiful face, and those plump lips reminded me of Sarah.

Even though the resemblance was still there, the hurt was gone.

Seven years had healed it.

And as I glanced across the table, Emily sitting opposite me in this dark, candlelit restaurant, her fingers wrapped around the stem of a wineglass, her lips glossy from whatever she had swiped over them, I couldn't stop smiling.

A smile that wasn't just on my lips—it owned my whole fucking face.

"New York City looks gorgeous on you."

She fanned herself as she laughed. "Yeah? That's what happens when you get me away from being on call and my wardrobe of scrubs. I clean up well." She tucked a blond chunk behind her ear. "Even though I love this"—she glanced down her body at her dress—"if I didn't have a pair of scrubs in my life, I'd miss them."

"You would?"

The candlelight flickered across her skin, and there was plenty of that showing tonight, given that the dresses I'd bought her for this trip were sexier than what she normally wore. This evening's was a deep blue, several shades darker than her eyes, and it showed off the curves of her body that I loved so much.

"I would." She nodded. "I was meant to be a nurse."

"But what if you cut back?"

Her head dropped. "Gavin . . ."

"I mean it. Do you even realize how many hours you're putting in a week?"

She sighed. "I know."

"Juggling your schedule is impossible. Just to come here for Maya and Jordan's engagement party, you had to take on double shifts for next week, which means Ben and I won't see you at all when we get back." I leaned into the chair's cushion, holding my scotch close.

"It's the only way I can have it all—my bills paid, money added to my savings account every month, my—"

"I will give it all to you, Emily." I put the glass down and held on to the edge of the table. "I'll give you everything."

Her mouth opened and her head shook and not a single word came out.

"You know, you still haven't answered me about moving in." I picked my glass back up and took a sip.

She bit her lip. "I wasn't sure if, when you asked me, if you were really asking or if you were just suggesting or . . ."

"It was an ask." I chuckled. "And if you ask me if I'm sure, don't. I'm more than sure. I'm fucking positive." I winked.

She laughed. "I just . . . like to be sure."

I waited until she quieted. "Live with us, Emily. Let me buy you out of your lease. Toss everything you own or put it in a storage unit that I'll pay for, and be with us every night and every morning. I don't want to wake up without you anymore. I don't care if you only spend a few days a week at your apartment—even that's too much."

She took a long drink of her wine, holding it in her mouth even after she set down her glass. "You love me, don't you?"

"I do."

She exhaled. "Because it takes an epic amount of love to want to spend every morning and evening with me. And to make the kind of offers that you have. My lease. My things. Gavin, you do realize how much that is, don't you?"

"Money-wise, it's nothing, I assure you."

She glanced down at her plate, empty since the appetizers hadn't come yet. When she finally looked up at me, I saw the answer in her eyes. "I want nothing more than to live with you. As for the other things, like my bed and bedroom furniture, I'm willing to put them in storage, but I don't know that I'm willing to let you pay for it."

"And your lease?"

Her shoulders slumped. "It would be thousands of dollars, Gavin—"

"Baby, please stop worrying about money when it comes to me. Do you have any idea how much I make at Worthington Enterprises? Or how much money I made in the NFL?" I knew she didn't, so I didn't bother waiting for an answer. "Let me put this in perspective. Paying off your lease wouldn't even dent what I make in a day. I wouldn't even notice the amount missing from my bank account. And what it would cost me, I probably spent that on custom suits last month."

She held her chest. "Jesus Christ."

"Emily, I've got you."

She went silent, staring at me. "I love that you do. No one ever has before. But I've worked so hard, Gavin. Two jobs for so many years to provide the things I want and need—I can't just forget all of that." She went quiet. "I have too much pride."

"What are you saying?"

"I need to contribute. Or I need to at least feel like I'm contributing. Utilities, groceries, the expense of your chef—whatever." She reached across the table, and I lifted my hand from my lap, setting it on the tablecloth, her fingers instantly covering mine. "It's who I am and who I need to be, and I don't want to lose that."

"I hear you. It's not going to be easy for me to let you pay for anything, but I respect that you want to contribute to our home. We'll come up with a plan that works for you." I kissed her hand. "Now that we have that out of the way, are you telling me that you're moving in with Ben and me?"

She was trying to mask her smile. "Yes." And then she gave it to me, full teeth, wide lips. A beauty like no other woman I'd ever seen. "I'll move in with you and Ben."

"Do you know how excited that's going to make him?"

She clenched my fingers before she released them. "I can't wait to see him tomorrow night at the engagement party. It was really nice of your parents to take him with them to New York and let us have a couple of days here by ourselves."

I nodded at her. "What are you going to do about work?" I smiled, letting her know I was bringing the conversation right back to her. "Did you think I forgot that part of the equation?"

She shook her head. "I don't know."

"What do you want, Emily?"

She turned silent. "I have everything I want. That's you and Ben."

I pounded my heart with my fist. "Damn it, that was hot, but I was talking about work."

"It's funny, it was so easy to give Maya advice when it came to her situation with work. I even came up with the per diem idea that solved all her problems." Her head briefly fell back. "But when it comes to me, I can't make a decision to save my life. I know the amount of time I'm putting in is wild. I can't maintain it forever."

"What if I told you I already made an inquiry?"

Her brows rose. "What type of inquiry?"

"I spoke to Dr. Kaplan. He's a family friend, as you know. He made it clear you could work as much or as little as you want. He loves you,

Emily. He called you one of his top nurses. You just have to work with scheduling and communicate what you're looking for, and they'll give you whatever hours you want." I laughed as I took in her expression. "Let me guess . . . you don't know if you just fell harder in love with me or if you want to strangle me. Am I right?"

"You're right."

"I spoke to him because I care. Because Dr. Kaplan and I have that kind of relationship where I can be honest with him. And I thought if I didn't take the initiative to do something about your schedule, I didn't know if you would."

She flattened her hands against the table. "Honestly, I don't know if I would either. I'm so used to going, going, going . . ."

"But you don't have to anymore." I finished the rest of my scotch. "Working with only him, that would give you more time doing pediatrics, which is what you wanted anyway."

She slowly nodded.

"One day, you're going to have to tell me why you gave up labor and delivery at the hospital and went to work at the rehab center."

"Not today." Her voice was a little above a whisper. "Today's too happy for that story." She finished the rest of her wine. "And one day you're going to have to tell me what happened to Ben's mom."

"Today's too happy for *that* story."

"I understand, trust me. I just want you to know I'm never going to try to take the role of being his mother. He had a mother. But Ben will always be extremely important to me, and I'm grateful I get to be in that little boy's life." She wiped the corner of her eye. "And when you're ready to tell me that sad story, I'll share mine, too, and we can have a sob-fest together."

"Deal."

"Tonight's going to end on a positive note." She nodded toward me. "Because of you."

I let out a soft moan of pleasure. "You're saying yes to moving in and you're leaving the rehab center and you're going to work part-time for Dr. Kaplan."

"And because I'm so in love with you."

◆ ◆ ◆

"Look at them together," Grandma said, standing next to me in the private dining room of the restaurant Jordan had reserved for his engagement party. She was referring to Ben and Emily. Emily had just taken Ben to the restroom, and now that they'd reentered the room, Emily was kneeling down, fixing Ben's tie. Ben was laughing at something Emily had said, both of them smiling. "He's dazzled by her."

I murmured, "That makes two of us, Grandma."

"Oh, my darling boy. You have no idea how happy I am to see you in love." She looped her hands through my arm and held on. "I've been waiting for this moment for a long time. I knew it would come. But I'm beyond thrilled that it's with Emily." She gave me a side look and a side smile. "She's quite the gal, Gavin."

"She is."

"You're going to marry her, aren't you?" She released me to adjust the ruffled collar of her dress, clinging right back on once she was done.

"I am, Grandma."

"And you're going to give me more great-grandbabies, aren't you?"

I laughed. "As long as Emily wants that, which I believe she does, then yes." I stared down at her. "You're not demanding or anything . . ."

"I'm eighty-four, my darling. I'm not getting any younger."

"But you're not looking any older either."

She tapped my arm. "There is a reason I love you, and that right there is one of them."

I chuckled as Maya made her way over to us.

My soon-to-be sister-in-law was holding a glass of beer, smiling at Grandma before she focused on me. "Future brother-in-law, I have something extremely important to tell you."

"And that is?" My brows lifted.

"If you hurt my girl, I will hurt you." Even though she was stopping herself from grinning, I knew she was serious.

Maya and Emily had an indestructible friendship. I wasn't at all surprised that Maya was threatening me. I would be disappointed if she didn't.

"You have nothing to worry about," I told her. "That woman is going to be mine forever."

Maya waved her finger at me. "She better be."

"You know," Grandma started, "if he hurts her, I'll also be hurting him."

Maya put her hand on Grandma's shoulder. "I love that you have my back and Emily's."

One of Grandma's arms released me so she could clasp fingers with Maya. "Always, my gal."

"What are you guys talking about?" Emily asked as she and Ben joined us, Jordan not far behind them, my brother putting his arm around his fiancée.

Maya glanced up at Jordan. "I was just threatening to hurt your brother. You know I take my bestie duties quite seriously."

"Maya!" Emily gasped. "You went deep, girl."

"You knew I was going to say something. I mean, let's face it, it was inevitable." Maya laughed at Emily. "He's lucky I only threatened to hurt him. I could have gone even deeper."

"Don't mess with my girl." Jordan pretended to punch Maya's chest. "She might be small, but she's mighty."

"No one is hurting anyone." I raised my glass of scotch. "You've got Dad's back, don't you, Ben?"

Emily kissed the top of Ben's head. "No, Ben's on my side."

"I'm on Fenway's side!" Ben shouted.

Of course, only Emily and I chuckled since no one else knew who Fenway was.

Jordan lifted Ben in his arms. "I wish we could take you to LA with us, little man. It's too bad you have school."

Jordan and I were leaving next week for a three-day trip to the West Coast for a little bit of business, but mostly pleasure. When it had been planned, Emily hadn't agreed yet to move in, so Jenny was staying the two nights at my place.

"I wanna go." Ben pouted.

"At least you have me." Emily put her hand on Ben's back and slowly looked at me and smiled.

"I have an idea." I nodded toward Emily and then at Maya. "That is, if the ladies are up to it."

"I hope you're about to tell us that Emily and I get to have a two-night slumber party with Ben at your house?" Maya announced.

"That's exactly what I was going to suggest," I replied to Maya.

"Yesss." Maya smiled as she looked at Emily. "We're so in, aren't we, babe?"

"That's a hard yes." Emily continued to rub Ben's back while Jordan held him. "Do you want Maya and me to spend the night with you while Dad's gone?"

"YES!" Ben jumped in Jordan's arms.

Emily laughed. "It's settled, then." She looked at Grandma. "How about you and Melinda come over for dinner one of those evenings, and we'll have a girls' night with Ben?"

Grandma lifted her arms in the air and danced, her new knee holding up just fine. "Count us in, darling."

CHAPTER TWENTY-SEVEN

Emily

Gavin: I miss you, baby.

Me: I miss you too. We're having the best time, Gavin. Jenny picked up Ben from school, gave him a bath, got him dressed in his jammies, and stayed here until I got home from work. Maya came over a little before dinner, and now we're eating the cupcakes we baked together. You know, just a little sugar before he goes to bed.

Gavin: It won't keep him awake. Sugar hits him hard in the morning. In the evening, it takes three stories and the kid will be knocked out.

Me: Business stuff all done?

Gavin: We wrapped up the meeting late morning, checked into the Cole and Spade Hotel in Laguna Beach and went surfing. Heading to a cigar bar soon and then dinner at one of Walker's restaurants.

Me: Have the best time with your brother.

Gavin: You do the same with Ben and Maya.

Gavin: Grandma has already texted me twice about your girls' night tomorrow night. Needless to say, she's excited. She's sending over her chef, by the way.

Me: She told me, lol. She doesn't want us to do anything. She really spoils us.

Gavin: You deserve it.

Me: Love you.

Gavin: Love you.

I set my phone on the table and looked at Ben, who was covered in frosting, little bits on his cheeks, a smear on his forehead, some had even trickled down to his pajama top. I grabbed my napkin, laughing as I dabbed the corners of my mouth. "Kiddo, I don't know how you're so good at getting the frosting everywhere, but it's *everywhere*."

He giggled. "Daddy says I have hidden talents—whatever that is—and this is one."

"The four inches of frosting on his cupcake doesn't help." Maya was smiling. "Ben, doesn't it make your teeth hurt?"

"Nope! I love it! I want *mooore*!"

I sliced my strawberry cupcake into quarters and took a bite. "Extra frosting is our thing," I explained to her. "Or should I say, it's his thing. Don't you remember when we went skating at the arena? Well, it's sorta escalated from there."

Ben was licking off clumps of icing that were stuck to his fingers. "I wanna like the strawberry, 'cause Emily makes them so pretty, but I only like the vanilla."

"Maybe one day I can get you to love it." When he shrugged, I laughed again.

Maya took only a bite of hers and pushed it aside, opting for beer instead, pulling her glass in front of her. "Em, this"—she circled the air—"is so wildly perfect. But extra heavy on the wild side."

I knew exactly what she was referring to. "Right? Who would have thought I'd be here? With Gavin. And this amazing little boy." I stared at Ben, popping another bite of the strawberry cake into my mouth. "I'm the luckiest girl alive."

I'd been thinking that a lot lately, and every time I said it out loud to myself or internally or when I voiced it to Maya just now, a wave of emotion came with it.

"You are," Maya whispered.

When her hand moved to mine, I gazed at her. "There are two lucky girls in this room." The overhead light caught the colors in the massive diamond on her finger. "Look at that thing. It deserves its own zip code."

She snorted. "Jordan said he went modest—he knew I wouldn't want anything gaudy. If this is modest, I'd hate to see what gaudy is."

I petted it like it was Fenway. "It's the most stunning ring I've ever seen in my life."

"Yours will be, too, babe."

I waved the air. "We'll celebrate me when the time comes. For now, we're celebrating you, and that ginormous rock, and a wedding I'm dying to help you plan. Can we talk colors and dresses and locations and—"

"I wanna help!" Ben shouted, now with a frosting mustache.

Maya released my hand and raised both of hers in the air. "Ben, I would love nothing more. Will you please be my wedding planner?"

"Yep!" He repositioned himself on the chair, sitting on his bent knees.

Maya's hands flattened on the table. "And you'll help me pick out all the things?"

"Yep!"

"How about colors, Ben. Any ideas for that?" She winked at me.

"Dinosaur colors!"

Maya was taking a drink of her beer and laughed once she swallowed. "So you're saying Emily, as my maid of honor, should wear a dinosaur-themed dress?"

"That'd be so cool." When he nodded, a piece of frosting flung across the table. "You need to have pterodactyls flying around the room and a Tyrannosaurus rex stomping all over the place and, I know, I know"—he jumped in his seat—"little Fenway needs to have fake wings on and pretend to fly, but he really doesn't, he just looks like he's going to fly."

"The stuffed animal Fenway?" Maya asked.

I pointed at the center of the kitchen island. "That one, yes."

"Ben, do you think Uncle J will be able to find us some dinosaurs?" Maya pulled her plate closer to her and pinched some frosting between her fingers and licked it off. "Or can you work your magic and make it happen?"

"Hehe." He lifted the paper wrapper and bit off some of the cake that was stuck to it. "Uncle J can *dooo* it."

"You think so, do you?" Maya pressed.

I took my last bite, the sweetness of the cupcake becoming too much. "I think Maya is going to need your help, Ben. You're the dinosaur expert of the family. You might have to help her hunt for some. Are you down for that task?"

"Yesss." He giggled and patted his belly. "Emily, I'm so full."

"Me, too, kiddo." I checked the time on my phone. "How about you go upstairs and brush your teeth and get ready for bed."

He slumped down in his chair. "I don't wanna go to bed."

I set my plate on top of Maya's. "You don't have to go to bed yet. You just have to get ready for bed. Then we'll snuggle and read lots of books. How does that sound?"

"Okaaay."

"Do you want to go brush your teeth now? I'll be up there in a few minutes to check on you."

As Ben got up from his chair, Maya said, "Good night, buddy. Can I have a hug?" Ben rushed over to Maya and threw his arms around her waist, Maya kissing the top of his head. "Sleep well. Emily and I are going to be in Dad's bed if you need us, okay?"

"Okay!" He took off for the stairs.

I smiled as I watched him disappear. "You know, I've never put Ben to bed before."

"Never?" She crossed her legs, setting her arms back on the table.

"It's always something Gavin does. I've never asked if I can join. I don't know, it seems like a kind of moment that should just be between a parent and their kid."

"But Em, you are going to be his parent." She grabbed my arm and held it. "You basically are now."

Even though she was right and I loved Ben more than anything, the steps before bed felt like a Gavin thing, not a me thing.

I shrugged. "It's funny, I never thought much about it, so I didn't make it a huge deal in my head. Gavin goes upstairs with him, I almost always fall asleep on the couch, and he wakes me when he comes back downstairs after Ben is asleep. But now that I'm really thinking about it, I'm excited for this to be *my* moment." I went silent, my shoulders no longer high but rounding forward. "I know that sounds silly."

"It doesn't. Not at all."

My head dropped, and I looked at her fingers on my arm. "I spend a lot of time with Ben. But something about snuggling with him in his bed and reading him books and hearing his soft, little snores feels so tender and pure."

Her hand went to her heart. "You're going to make me cry."

"Please don't. Because if you cry, I'll cry, and neither of us need to be doing that tonight."

She squeezed me before her fingers pulled away. "Go. I'll clean up. And when you come back downstairs, I promise not to be asleep, and I'll have a glass of wine poured for you."

I blew her a kiss, and as I went upstairs, I could hear Ben singing. I didn't know the song. I could barely make out the words and his voice was pitchy, yet it was the cutest thing ever. I stopped in the doorway of his en suite. He was using his toothbrush as a microphone, staring at himself in the mirror, the dusting of frosting still all over his shirt and face, and now a ring of toothpaste was around his mouth.

He quieted just as I said, "How's it going in here, you little rock star?"

"All done!" He gave me an extra-big grin.

"Your teeth are all brushed?"

He nodded.

"Awesome. Then how about we wash off some of the toothpaste and frosting from your face." I grabbed a washcloth from the cabinet and wet it with warm water, carefully rubbing it across Ben's skin. "What song were you singing?" Once he was clean, I worked on the frosting that was stuck to his shirt.

"It's from the dinosaur show I watch with Dad. I sing it every night before bed."

"Does Dad sing it with you?"

Ben laughed. "No. He won't. No matter how many times I ask him."

When I finally got all the frosting off, I set the washcloth over the side of his sink. "You're all clean."

"Just like my teeth." He smiled. *"Seee?"*

"I *seee.*" I laughed.

"Now, story time." He led me to the bookcase in his room, a built-in display of floor-to-ceiling shelves with a dinosaur mural painted on both sides, and he flopped down in front of it, pulling the first book based on its spine. "I want this one." He handed me a book on dinosaurs. "This one." The second was about birds. "This one *annnd* this one." The next two were about otters.

"Four?"

"Yep! We have a lot of reading to do, Emily."

I laughed as I followed him to bed, carrying the pile of books.

Before he climbed in, he kissed his hand and reached toward something on his nightstand. "Good night, Mom."

As he got under the covers and made room for me, I looked at his nightstand, trying to see what he'd air-kissed. There were several things on there. A dinosaur lamp. A bottle of water. Several books and multiple framed photos.

I placed the books on the side of the bed and sat next to them. "Is one of those pictures of your mom?"

"Yep! That one!" He pointed at the frame in the back. "I say good night to her every night."

There weren't any photos of Sarah downstairs, and although I'd been in Ben's room before, I never noticed his nightstand or the framed pictures on top of it.

"Do you mind if I look at her?"

He repositioned himself next to me, kneeling on the bed. "Nope! I'll help." He almost knocked over the water bottle and he dinged the lamp as he grasped the large, chunky metal frame, lifting it toward the bed and handing it to me.

The frame was cut into two separate sections. The top was a photo of a dark-haired woman, standing by a window. She was looking through it, so only her profile showed, but she appeared to be stunning. She was wearing a long, sheer dressing gown that was open in the center, her hands clasping her beautiful round belly.

But my attention didn't stay on her—it moved to the bottom section of the frame, where an off-white piece of paper was pressed behind the glass with words written in blue ink. As I began to read those words, my heart started to pound.

My mouth went completely dry.

My hands shook so badly, I dropped the frame on the carpet.

No.

It couldn't be.

It was impossible.

There was . . . no fucking way.

"Ben?" There was a churning in my stomach that was getting worse by the second. "What was your mom's last name? It wasn't Worthington . . . right?"

"No, it was Luc—"

"Lucas," I finished for him.

My hand went to my chest, air no longer moving through it.

The room was spinning.

I was dizzy.

A blackness came over my eyes, a heat lifting across my body and coming through the pores of my skin.

When I tried to take a breath, it felt like I was sucking through a clogged straw.

"Ben"—I got up from the bed, leaving the frame right where it fell—"I'll be right back."

I couldn't feel my feet as I flew out of his room. I had no recollection of going down the stairs. I didn't even see Maya until I felt someone grab me. Until her hands were on my arms and her face was directly in front of mine.

"Emily, what happened? What's wrong?"

"Ben . . ." The tears were streaming down my cheeks, and I still had no air in me. "His-s mom. His m-mom is Sa-Sarah."

"Sarah?" She shook her head while she stared at me, and suddenly the realization came across her face and her hand slapped over her mouth. "Oh my God, Emily . . . You mean his mom is Sarah—Sarah. *Your* Sarah?"

CHAPTER TWENTY-EIGHT

Gavin

"Brother, we don't do this enough." Jordan waited until the server poured him a few more fingers' worth, the bottle a single malt Macallan we'd purchased for the night, before he lifted his tumbler and held it close to his mouth. "Every quarter, we should make it mandatory. Two nights, somewhere, anywhere, but together."

"I was just thinking the same thing." Once my glass was refilled, I took a long sip. "Damn, that's good." I set the tumbler down and reached for the handmade ultra-premium cigar, removing it from its package and using the guillotine cutters to chop the end. Just as I was bringing the flame closer to my mouth, there was a vibration in my pocket. I set the flame down and slipped my fingers into the inside of my sports coat, Emily's name showing on the screen of my phone. "It's Emily calling. I just want to make sure there's nothing wrong with Ben."

"Do what you've got to do."

I connected the call, holding the phone to my ear. "Hi, baby—"

"It's Maya."

I put the cigar in the ashtray. "Maya? Is everything okay?"

"Ben is fine. That's not why I'm calling. It's . . . Emily."

"Is something wrong with her?"

"Oh God, Gavin." I didn't like her tone. I didn't like the way she sounded like she couldn't breathe. "I don't even know how to tell you this. I . . . I think Emily should be the one to tell you."

"Tell me what, Maya?"

"She needs you."

"Needs me?"

"Yes. She needs you to come home. Please. As soon as possible."

My fucking heart was suddenly out of control.

I pushed against my chest, remembering a time when I'd felt just like this.

When my entire goddamn world collapsed.

I looked at my brother, pushing my way to the end of my seat. "I'll call our pilot. I'll be there as soon as I can."

CHAPTER TWENTY-NINE

Emily

Seven years ago

There was only thirty minutes left in my twelve-hour shift, and as I sat behind the computer at the nurses' station, inputting the last round of notes, I heard, "Emily, room 612 just got admitted."

I turned around to face the charge nurse. "Is she in labor?"

"She came up from the emergency department. Said she wasn't feeling well, has shortness of breath, and her blood pressure is extremely low." She adjusted the teddy bear that clung to the pocket of her scrubs. "She's thirty-six weeks, so they didn't want to treat her, and sent her up here. I just got off the phone with them."

"Has the ED put her info into the system?"

Her nest of short curls didn't move when she shrugged. "If they haven't, I'm sure they will any minute."

Since I was already at the computer, I attempted to pull up her chart. Within a few clicks, I found her.

Sarah Lucas. Twenty-eight years of age. Her ob-gyn was affiliated with a concierge group in Boston, and aside from the vitals that had been taken in the emergency department, medications she was on, and her medical history, there was no other information listed.

"I'll go check on her right now."

As I was leaving the nurses' station, she said, "You know, you win the award today for the cutest scrubs."

I halted at the end of the high bar top and glanced down at my body. "I found them online. I know it's not Valentine's Day, but the candy hearts put the biggest smile on my face."

"You haven't clocked out yet. Let's not jinx ourselves with all this 'smile' talk. Besides, it's a full moon, and you know what that does to a hospital, even the L&D department."

I sighed and held up my crossed fingers before I made my way down the hall, grabbing a pair of gloves from the box right inside the doorway of room 612. I squirted some antibacterial gel on my hands before I put on the gloves and said, "Hi, Sarah, my name is Emily. I'm going to be your nurse."

She was in drawstring pants, a shirt cut off just under her breasts that showed off her belly, with a zip-up sweatshirt hanging at her sides. Her dark hair was twisted into a messy knot on top of her head, and when she looked at me, while she paced, I couldn't get over the blueness of her eyes or the way her skin glowed or how every mother in this hospital would be jealous at how gorgeous Sarah was this far along into her pregnancy.

But she wouldn't stop moving, going from the window to the bed to the sink by me, back and forth. "Emily, something's wrong."

I'd heard that many times on this floor, almost during every shift, especially if this was the woman's first baby. The third trimester often brought out severe anxiety attacks. Every sensation and symptom either sent them to Google or their doctor's office.

I stepped farther into the room and positioned myself near her bed, using a calming tone when I replied, "How about you take a seat right here." I held my hand toward the mattress. "This way, I can take your vitals and check you out."

She shook her head, her feet still moving. "You're not listening. Something is wrong." She looked at me over her shoulder. "That's why I came to the hospital instead of calling my doctor. Because what's happening . . . isn't right."

"The charge nurse will be reaching out to your ob-gyn if she hasn't already. If he's not able to come to the hospital, we'll send in the attending to treat you should there be anything wrong. Don't worry, Sarah, you're in excellent hands. We have a wonderful labor and delivery department and"—I smiled in the most careful way—"you have me as your nurse." When she continued to move, I joined her at the sink, walking with her toward the windows. "Is this your first baby?"

"Yes."

"I won't leave you until I know what's happening."

It didn't matter that my shift was ending. When I made a promise to a patient, I kept it.

She held her bare stomach. "I know something's wrong." She sucked in a sob. "I just know it." She circled her belly, her touch tender and loving. "I need you to be okay, little guy. Mommy's worried about you."

"The ED took your vitals, and you had low blood pressure. I don't have your medical history beyond the numbers that were taken today. Tell me, do you normally run low?"

"Never."

"So you haven't been running low at all during your pregnancy?"

Her hand slid from her forehead to the top of her bun, and she squeezed the messy knot into her palm. "No. If anything, it's been a little raised."

"How about you let me take it and I'll see if it's gone up?"

She stopped walking and faced me. Now both of her hands were in her hair. "I'm telling you"—she shook her head continuously—"something isn't right."

I rubbed the tops of her shoulders to try to ease her—not as a nurse, but as a woman who could feel her anxiety and just wanted to hug her.

"I hear you. I promise I do. And I promise you're going to be okay and your baby's going to be okay." I paused. "Our job here is to make the feelings you're having go away. Before a doctor comes in, I need to have all the information for them so they can treat you. It's not a lot. Just your temperature and—"

"Ah!" A pool of liquid gushed out, leaving a mark of wetness on the front of her tan pants and on the floor by her feet. "Oh my God!"

"That was your water breaking. You're in labor, that's why you're feeling this way. I promise this is all normal." My hand moved to the top of her back, sliding in small circles. "You're going to have a baby."

"But I'm only thirty-six weeks. I can't have him yet. His dad isn't even here. He's in Maine for the night. This isn't supposed to happen, this is—"

"Don't worry. Lots of babies are born in this hospital at thirty-six weeks. In fact, I helped deliver one yesterday."

She stared at me, her chest heaving. "Emily . . . something isn't right."

"What's making you feel that way?"

"I . . . don't know. It's . . . so hard to breathe."

"Let's get you sitting and connected to some oxygen and out of these wet clothes—all of that will make you feel better." My hand stilled, and I gave her the gentlest push to help lead her toward the bed. "Once I have you settled, I'm going to go check on the status of your doctor." When she didn't move, I whispered, "Sarah, everything is going to be all right. Remember, I'm not leaving you."

We locked eyes for several seconds. It was as if she was weighing my words, and eventually she allowed me to bring her to the bed, propping herself on the edge. I left her there for just a moment while I fetched a gown from the closet. But as I was approaching to help her undress, she began to rock.

"No. *Nooo.* This isn't right. I'm so cold. I'm covered in chills. I shouldn't have the chills. I shouldn't feel like I can't breathe." She cupped her stomach.

I reached for the oxygen tube and nasal cannula that were housed behind the bed, flipped the switch to turn it on, and fitted it inside her nose. "This is going to make you feel better. Take several deep breaths for me." I bent down to the floor, taking the slides off her feet. "Remember, deep breaths. In and out. Just focus on your breathing."

She held her chest as I tried to help her out of the zip-up, her arms not moving to let me take it off. "There's heaviness."

"Do you mean a heaviness that feels like anxiety?"

"I'm not an anxious person. I've never felt anything like this before." Her head dropped, and she tapped the same spot on her chest. "Like a pile of lead is sitting right here, and it keeps getting heavier."

I left her sweatshirt alone and went and put her shoes in the closet. "You've never had a baby before. With that comes loads and loads of anxiety. Your body is experiencing something completely new and unknown." I stood in front of her, and as I went to reach for her sweatshirt again, she grabbed my hand.

"Emily, I need you to listen to me."

I nodded. "Okay."

She shook my hand, like she was trying to get my attention, even though she was all I was focused on. "I need you to get a piece of paper and a pen. Don't think I'm crazy. I need this. I need you to do this."

With my other hand, I pulled out a pad and a pen from my pocket. "I keep these in here at all times."

"I need you to write something down for me." Her hand moved from her chest to the oxygen in her nose, pushing the tubes higher up.

I wiggled my fingers out of her grip and held the pen to the pad. "Tell me what you want me to write."

"I love you. I will always love you. You're the greatest thing that's ever happened to your dad and me. I'll never be far, I'll be watching. I'll . . ."

As her voice drifted off, I glanced up from the blue ink, and Sarah's eyes were closed. Her skin was turning pale. Her lips were moving, but nothing was coming out of them.

"Sarah?" I slid the pad and pen into my pocket and put my hands on her shoulders, and when that got no reaction, nor did shaking her, I went to check her pulse. "Sarah?" The tips of my fingers had barely landed on her neck when she fell back against the bed.

"Fuck! *Nooo!*" I sprinted to the doorway of the room, looking out onto the hallway as I screamed, "Code blue!" I ran back to her side, lifting her feet from the floor and turning her legs so I could lay her on the bed.

I was still in the process of getting her fully on the mattress when the emergency response team came in. The code I had screamed, which had also sounded an alarm across the unit, told the medical staff my patient was in cardiac arrest. While the doctor and other nurses surrounded her, what they needed to hear was everything I knew about Sarah Lucas.

"Twenty-eight years old, thirty-six weeks pregnant. Water broke about four to five minutes ago," I told them, my heart beating so fast, I was sure I sounded breathless. "Patient was complaining of shortness of breath, so I hooked her up to oxygen. She also said there was a heaviness in her chest. BP was borderline high during her whole pregnancy and was taken in the ED and registered low, so they sent her up here."

Sarah's skin was turning even whiter, her lips now blue.

Arms were moving faster than I could see, and directions were being ordered. I stayed still until I heard, "Emily, start chest compressions while we take her to the OR."

My schooling taught me what was happening inside Sarah's body, but in my two years of nursing, I'd never witnessed it before.

If I were to guess, many of the nurses in this unit hadn't ever seen an amniotic fluid embolism either, a rare and extremely dangerous occurrence when either amniotic fluid, cells, or something else entered the mother's bloodstream.

It would be a miracle if we could save her.

And the only way to get the baby out was an emergency C-section.

I got on the bed and straddled her body.

Come on, Sarah. Come on, Sarah.

One of the nurses handed me a bag-valve mask, and after I pulled the oxygen from Sarah's nose, my shaking hands hooked the mask to Sarah's mouth. Once the seal was tight, I followed the count of chest compressions, followed by two breaths.

Come on, Sarah. Come on, Sarah.

Your little boy is going to be born soon, you cannot leave him.

I checked for a pulse. "I'm losing her!"

"Get the crash cart," I heard.

I lifted her half shirt, and when I was handed the paddles of the defibrillator, I set them on her chest. "Clear!" The shock entered her body, and I could feel it under my knees as I knelt on the bed.

Everyone watched the heart rate monitor. When there was no change, the doctor yelled, "Again!"

"Clear!" I shouted.

Sarah, come back to me.

Sarah, please.

Saaarah!

"We need to take her to the OR now!" the doctor announced. "Emily, restart chest compressions!"

The nurses, along with the doctor, were pushing the bed out of the room. I felt the movement, but the only thing I was looking at was Sarah's face, the color of her skin, waiting for a sign that she was coming back to life.

Sarah, you can do this.

Sarah, you've got to fight.

Sarah, you cannot leave . . .

At the door that led to the hallway of the OR, another team was waiting, each of them dressed in surgical scrubs. As they took over, the emergency response team backed away, one helping me off the bed, while someone else took over the compressions and air flow.

I stood at the entrance of the hall as they wheeled Sarah through, watching them run her to the OR until the door fully closed, cutting off my view.

Vanessa, another RN in my unit, put her arm around my shoulders. "The first AFE I've ever seen. Thank God. I hope I never see one again."

Heaviness.

That was what I felt.

In my chest, neck, behind my eyes.

The heaviness Sarah had described and it was now mine.

My toes were cramping, my knees wanting to buckle.

"She's not going to make it, is she?" I held my chest as I spoke.

Vanessa shook her head. "I don't think so, no."

I knew that . . . I just needed . . .

I didn't know what I needed.

Every second of the last several minutes was replaying in my head.

Her pacing.

Her shortness of breath.

Her anxiety.

Her chills.

Her impending doom.

She knew.

But I didn't.

She knew . . . and I didn't.

And I'd promised her she was going to be okay.

I'd fucking promised her.

"I didn't know." I couldn't breathe. "I had no idea this was an AFE." I swallowed something—it wasn't spit, it was heavier, thicker, it burned as it went down. "I thought she was having anxiety and then her water broke . . ."

"Of course you wouldn't have known, honey. No one would have. AFE comes on too fast. It presents symptoms similar to labor. There's nothing that could have been done to stop this or prevent it." Her hand went to my cheek. "This is one of those situations where even the best medical professionals are helpless."

The door next to us swung open, and one of the surgical nurses exited, pulling off her hair covering and removing her mask. "The C-section will be starting at any second."

"You're not doing it?" Vanessa asked her.

"Another emergency came in. I have to scrub in for that surgery."

"How's the mother? Sarah Lucas?" I asked.

The nurse began to walk away, stopping just long enough to say, "We couldn't resuscitate her on the table." She shook her head. "She's gone."

No.

Nooo.

Fuck no.

I reached inside my pocket, realizing I still had gloves on, and I didn't bother to take them off as I removed the notepad, handing Vanessa the sheet of paper I'd written on. "Sarah knew something was wrong," I forced out, not letting myself cry. "She knew she wasn't going to make it."

"She probably just didn't feel well and, like all first-time mothers, feared the worst." She glanced down at the paper in her hand.

"She had me write that for her."

She slowly looked up at me. "It's for the baby . . ."

A baby who will never know his mother.

"I can't give it to the father when he arrives." The heaviness was doubling. Tripling. "I . . . have to get out of here, Vanessa."

"I'll give it to him."

She went to give me a hug, and I wiggled away, the thought of arms wrapping around me too much, and I raced for the stairs. I didn't want to wait for the elevator. I didn't want to be boxed in. When I got outside, I expected the air to pull me into its warm arms. For a wave of relief to wash over me.

But it didn't come.

It made my stomach churn.

It made my heart rate climb.

I rushed over to the dumpster in the back of the hospital, my hand flattening against the cold metal side, my stomach emptying. And when I couldn't retch anymore, I began to walk.

I didn't know I had reached home until the walls of my bedroom showed me I was standing inside of it.

My nursing scrubs fell to the carpet.

My elastic was pulled out, my hair falling to my shoulders.

Sarah, I'm so sorry.

I'm so fucking sorry.

When I got into the shower, I made the decision.

I couldn't ever go back to that unit again.

CHAPTER THIRTY

Gavin

"Emily . . ." I reached for her hands the moment she turned silent, a couch cushion separating us, a distance she insisted on after Jordan and Maya carried Ben out of my condo and took him to theirs. That was the first word I'd spoken since she told me her backstory with Sarah. A story that began when Sarah was admitted to Emily's wing and ended when Emily no longer had the heart to return to the hospital. A story that caused her to break down and cry multiple times. "I need a second . . . this is a lot."

"This is more than a lot. There isn't a word to even describe what this is."

My mind was bouncing all over the place, absorbing the details she'd just given me, filling in the small holes I'd been carrying for the last seven years with her firsthand account.

When my breath finally returned, when I could somewhat put my thoughts together, I said softly, "I can't believe you were her nurse. That it was you who wrote that note. That . . . you were even there."

Her knees were bent, and she held them to her chest. "Does that change everything?"

Every tear she'd shed tonight wrecked me a little more.

I couldn't just see her pain—I could feel it.

"Change what, baby?" She looked as small as the pillow beside me. "Us? No. What happened at that hospital does not affect us."

"But how can you say that? Sarah was under my care. She came in presenting symptoms. She . . ."

While she recounted the past, her tone, her emotion, her choice of words all told me she was blaming herself, her last statement no exception.

"Symptoms a first-time mother would have when she was going into labor. Emily"—it was my turn to be vulnerable, so I twisted my body toward her and rested my bent leg on the couch—"I arrived at that hospital after getting the worst call of my entire life, and once I held my son, I broke the fuck down. I wept like no man should ever have to weep. But once those tears dried, I sought out answers. I needed to know why this happened to Sarah. I needed to know exactly what happened to her. I spoke to the charge nurse who had been working that shift, the OB who performed the surgery, I even spoke with the head of the goddamn hospital." I stretched my arm over the back of the couch, my fingers close to her shoulder. "Everyone who had a role in treating Sarah did what they were supposed to. I don't blame anyone, I especially don't blame you."

"I promised her, Gavin." Her voice quivered. "I told her she was going to be okay and that her baby was going to be okay." She held her forehead. "Do you know how much it hurts . . . that I didn't keep that promise?"

"It was a promise you couldn't make. No one, including me, faults you for not being able to uphold it."

Her fingers clenched into a fist. "But I gave her my word."

"Stop blaming yourself, Emily—"

"That's all I did. Blame myself. Hate myself." She pulled at her T-shirt, yanking the collar down. "I couldn't even stand the feel of myself." She rested her forehead against her knees, and when she finally pulled her face out, she added, "I used up all my vacation time that I'd accumulated at the hospital—three or four weeks' worth, something in that range. And soon after that ran out, Maya wouldn't let me stay in bed anymore. She basically had an intervention. She said I needed to get out of my head and forgive myself. That's when she got me the job at the rehab center."

"Why would you treat yourself that way when you knew there was nothing you could have done?"

Her knees lowered, and she crossed her legs in front of her. "Maybe. Just maybe if I had . . ."

"No." I moved closer, sitting on the cushion that was between us, and I put my hands on her thighs. "There is no *maybe.* I know more about amniotic fluid embolisms than anyone should. I know the survival rate is beyond slim. I know what happens inside a woman's body for one to occur, and I know what happened inside Sarah's. By the time she came up to the labor and delivery floor, she was already too far advanced. There wasn't a medication or surgery that would have worked, neither would more chest compressions or defibrillation." I shook her knees. "There is absolutely no reason for you to ever blame yourself."

She went silent, but I knew what was happening in her brain was far from quiet.

"Is it weird if I say a part of me wants you to yell at me for this? Scream at me. Tell me I fucked everything up and I'm the reason Ben doesn't have a mother. I don't know . . ."

"Would it make you feel better?"

"No."

"Here's what I'll tell you instead." I held her cheek. "I'm relieved you were the one scheduled to work that day. I'm relieved your face was the last one Sarah saw. And I'm relieved that you were her nurse, because I know how she was treated and looked after, and I can't say I would know that if any other nurse had been with her." My thumb brushed her skin. "I've seen the way you care, Emily. How you work on patients. The love and attention you give them." My throat was getting tight. "In Sarah's last moments, she was lucky to have you."

My thumb caught the new set of tears that were falling from her eyes. "When I saw the note in Ben's room, I lost it, Gavin. I left Ben up there and ran downstairs. It wasn't pretty." She leaned into my hand, her voice cracking, her chin tremoring. "Maya had to put Ben to bed. I couldn't handle it. I couldn't handle anything. My brain was spiraling, questioning if you would think I knew Sarah was your girlfriend or that I had purposely put myself in your life to somehow heal. I promise, neither of those are true. I didn't know until I saw the note."

"I believe you—and I never thought either of those things." I pulled her legs onto my lap, moving in as close as I could get to her. "Emily, we're two people who have experienced a debilitating tragedy. We were just on opposite sides of it." I hugged her legs against me. "In some strange way, we're connected because of it."

"That's a positive way to look at it."

"That's the *only* way to look at it."

She slowly nodded and found my fingers and squeezed them. "Can I ask you something about that day?"

"Of course."

"Why were you in Massachusetts? Didn't you live in Florida and play for Tampa at that time? And why were you in Maine?"

I huffed out a mouthful of air. Out of all the questions, she'd picked the easiest ones. "Sarah was hot. I mean, she was literally sweating all the time during her pregnancy, and Florida's weather was making her miserable. It was an abnormally warm spring on the Gulf Coast. Sarah was from Alabama. We met in college, and since their summers were as intolerable as Florida, Boston made the most sense, even more so since I owned a home here—a different one, not this one. I didn't have to report to training camp until late July, so our plan was to spend my entire offseason here. We transferred doctors, switched up her birth plan, and we made this our home." I looked away from her, toward the windows that showed a view of every angle of Boston. "At thirty-six weeks, we thought there was plenty of time. Maine was a last-minute trip with a few friends from high school to do some fishing off the coast of Bar Harbor. Only a four-hour drive, a distance that seemed like nothing at the time. But"—my head dropped—"I couldn't take that long to get back and had my jet come get me, and that forty-or-so-minute flight to the city was the worst forty or so minutes of my whole fucking life."

"I can't even imagine." Her voice was so soft, I barely heard her. "I can't . . ."

"She was already gone when I got the call. The OB was performing the emergency C-section. I didn't even know at that time if Ben would make it. When I arrived at the hospital, he was in the NICU. Even though he was born late preterm and weighed six pounds, they kept him in there for a week as a precaution." I paused, releasing a loud exhale. "I would have taken him home immediately, but honestly, I was in no shape to take him anywhere. My mom stepped in during those first couple of months while I got my shit together."

"Never in a million years did you think you'd be doing it all alone." Her hand slid through my hair. "That you'd have a newborn and be mourning the woman you loved and the mother of your child. I can't wrap my head around what those months looked like and the grief that consumed you."

"It wasn't easy."

"It had to be impossible." Her fingers tightened in my hair.

"I just focused on Ben. He's all that mattered to me, along with football. My mom came to Florida, helped us get adjusted, and I hired Jenny, who deserves the world and then some." I rested my elbow on the back of the couch, setting my chin on my palm. "Ben and football—that's what my life looked like for a long time. I had no interest in love. Even the thought of it was too much. And then you came into my life and changed everything." I smiled. "You made me want more. You made me want to let love back in. And you made me feel love." I leaned forward to kiss her. "And I'm so incredibly in love with you, Emily."

Her eyes gradually opened after my lips left her again. "I love you more."

I brought her hand up to my mouth, holding her knuckles close to my lips. "I want you to remember that we survived what happened, we came out the other side, and that's something that will always hold us together."

She bent her knees, leaning them onto my chest. "I hope so."

"One day, when Ben's old enough to understand, we're going to tell him how you tried to save his mother and you were the one who wrote that note." I kissed the back of her hand. "He's going to look at you like a hero, the same way I'm looking at you right now."

"I'm no hero."

"You are to me."

She pulled back, half smiling, half shaking her head in disbelief. "No—"

"You want me to stop? Because I can keep going. I have lots more to say about you."

She put her hands on her face and stared into my eyes, "No, don't ever stop."

CHAPTER THIRTY-ONE

Emily

Flowers were everywhere, just like the last time Gavin had them delivered to my wing at the rehab center. But this time they came with a card, and every nurse and patient knew they were for me. And this time, there were even more of them. There were so many, I put a vase in every patient's room, on each table in the cafeteria, and I sent bunches home with the staff.

Gavin was trying to make my last day here as memorable as possible, and he certainly did. The only downside was that I wouldn't be here tomorrow to enjoy the roses, but it made me smile to think my colleagues, some who I'd spent the last seven years with, would get to enjoy them.

"I'm going to miss you," my charge nurse said as she pulled me into her arms once I'd collected my things from the nurses' station, the rope that kept her glasses on scratching against the side of my face.

"No crying." I leaned back to look at her. "You promised."

"I can't help it. We've been through a lot together, girlfriend. A marriage, divorce, two kids, a new relationship for you. Shit, that's a whole lifetime."

"This isn't goodbye." I held her hands. "This is *I'll be back in a couple of weeks to bring you all lunch.* Besides, I'm not going anywhere. I'll still be in Boston. You can text me for all the reasons and haul my ass out for drinks."

"Don't think I'm not going to."

"You better." I winked.

I gave her another hug and I made my way around the unit, saying goodbye to the people who I'd shared so many shifts with, even some who had been working my first day here when I was still a mess over Sarah.

And when I got outside, Gavin's SUV was parked directly by the door.

Denis smiled at me through the window, getting out to open the back seat. "Good afternoon, Emily. How was your last day?"

"Sad. Emotional." My shoulders lifted. "But perfect."

"I'm sure they're going to miss you." He patted my arm.

I peeked into the back, Gavin's handsome face smiling at me from the farthest seat. "What are you doing here?" I couldn't hide my grin. "I thought I was meeting you at home?"

"Surprise."

My hand gripped the doorway. "Don't you have meetings all afternoon?"

"I canceled them. The office can survive without me."

I laughed as I slid in, Denis closing the door behind me. "Can they, though? With Jordan on the road so much, they need you there to hold things down."

He pulled his phone out of his suit pocket. "That's what this is for." He wrapped an arm around the back of me and hauled me toward him. "If I want to pick up my girlfriend from her last day of work, nothing is going to stop me. Not employees, meetings, or any of my brother's unhandled bullshit."

I moaned a little while he kissed me. "I know I already thanked you for the flowers, but thank you again. I can't even express how gorgeous they are. You're the most popular person at the rehab center right now. Don't be shocked if you get fan mail."

He chuckled. "You're welcome." He held the back of my neck. "You're doing okay?"

Something he'd asked me at least every day since my connection to Sarah had been discovered. He just wanted to make sure my mind wasn't going back there, drowning myself in a blame game that occasionally still returned.

I couldn't say those thoughts were fully gone. They never would be. But hearing Gavin's side of the story absolutely made me feel better.

I nodded. "It's been an emotional day. I didn't cry, so that's a bonus, but it was hard to say goodbye to everyone. That place has been like a second home to me." I ran my hand over the buttons of his shirt, feeling his muscles beneath. "Maya popped in and brought lunch. She's in town for a day, I guess, before she meets your brother somewhere. It was awesome to have her there."

"Did she say where she was meeting him?"

I shook my head. "No. Why?"

"Just curious."

He was up to something.

My brow furrowed, and I shifted my focus to the windshield. "Denis, why aren't you going in the direction of home?"

"You know he's not going to answer you," Gavin said.

I sighed. "Denis, at some point, you've got to give in a little and lean toward Team Emily."

Denis laughed. "I am Team Emily. I have been since the very first time I took you home. But I'm loyal to the man who signs my paychecks."

I turned toward Gavin. "I have an idea. Maybe my monthly contributions should help pay Denis's salary. That way, this SUV is equal territory."

"Denis's salary is two hundred and fifty thousand. Are you going to give me a hundred and twenty-five to cover your share?" He smirked.

"Damn! That's what you make, Denis? I'm in the wrong field."

Both men laughed.

"I expect a lot out of my team, and they're compensated for it," Gavin admitted.

"He's the best, I get it, and he's worth every penny." I smiled at Denis through the rearview mirror. "But seriously, you two, why does it feel like we're going to the airport?"

Gavin's hand lifted to my cheek. "Because we are."

"Is Ben meeting us there or something?"

"Ben's not coming on this trip." His fingers lowered to my chin. "It's just going to be us."

I stared into his eyes, looking for answers. Not that it ever helped. The man was like a lockbox—the only way to get information was for it to come out of his mouth. "How long are we going to be gone? I'm going to miss little man."

He shook his head. "You're not getting that info out of me."

I looked over the seats—there were two suitcases in the back. "One of those is for me?" I glanced down the front of me. "Since the only thing I have is the scrubs on my body and some lip gloss in my purse."

"You know I'd never take you anywhere and not bring what you need."

I played with the back of his dark hair. "You take such good care of me." I loved that about him. The constant thoughtfulness whenever we did something or went somewhere. "So why did you choose today to run away?"

He ran his hand over my thigh. "We have something to celebrate. Yesterday you weren't able to fly away with me. Today you can. Tomorrow you can, too, and every day going forward. Of course, we wouldn't leave Ben that much, but now we have the flexibility to go wherever, whenever."

"Hold on a second, mister." I tapped his chest. "I'm going to be working for Dr. Kaplan, let's not forget that. I'm not going to be totally unemployed."

"Ah, but Dr. Kaplan is different. That's a work-as-you-want kind of gig."

"And I plan to work. Lots." I gave him an evil smile.

He held my neck, tilting my face back, biting his lip before he replied, "That's up for negotiation."

There was a black American Express card in my wallet that Gavin had given to me with the instructions to buy whatever I wanted, to never ask, and to use it for everything. I had no intention of using it for everything or anything. But the man endlessly made me feel spoiled, and he made it clear that he really wanted to take care of me.

"Kiss me," I ordered.

As he did, I felt the SUV slow, and when our lips separated, I saw Denis pulling into the airport, going through the locked, armed gate of the private wing where Gavin's jet was stored.

And that jet was quite a sight—all black, incredibly sexy, and waiting on the runway. Denis parked beside it and opened the door to the back seat.

I climbed out first, just as he was saying, "Have a wonderful trip. I'll see you both when you get back."

I thanked Denis, Gavin did, too, and we ascended the steps of the jet.

Gavin led me toward the back and lifted some folded clothes off one of the seats. "An outfit for you to change into."

I took the pile of soft cotton, giggling at him. "Do you ever forget anything?"

"Not when it comes to you."

I gave him a kiss and brought the clothes to the back of the plane in the bedroom, shutting the door before I quickly removed my scrubs and put on the leggings and oversize off-the-shoulder top. When I returned, the flight attendant was placing drinks on a table in front of the couch Gavin was sitting on.

"I've prepared a glass of wine for you, Ms. Wren," his flight attendant said as I joined him. "I'll be serving some light snacks per Mr. Worthington's instructions once we're in the air. Is there anything aside from water that I can grab you in the meantime?"

"No, this is perfect. Thank you, Gretta." I picked up the wine, Gavin holding his scotch. "Cheers to a surprise vacation that I know is going to be amazing."

Would I ever get used to this life? This way of travel? I doubted it.

Once he clinked my glass, I added, "I'm guessing Maya and Jordan are meeting us, since they're not on the plane?"

"In a few days, yes. We're going to Jordan's home in Windermere Island in the Bahamas—I'm sure Maya has told you about the place."

"She has." I folded my legs in front of me. "She said it's extra dreamy."

"Dreamy, huh?" He smiled. "We're going to have a few days to ourselves before we fly there to meet them."

"And where are we spending those few days?"

His brows rose. "Do you want me to tell you?"

"Hmm." I took a drink of my wine. "How about I take a guess."

He loosened his tie and removed his jacket, Gretta delivering two bottles of water before she disappeared again.

"Go for it," he offered.

"There's a part of your life you haven't shown me yet. A place you spent a good amount of time in. A place I want to see and a place I think you want me to see." I set the glass down. "I think we're going to Tampa."

"That's your final guess?"

I nodded. "Yep."

He held my face. "In a little over three hours, you'll find out if you're right."

CHAPTER THIRTY-TWO

Gavin

"I love it." Emily stood on the patio of my house in Tampa, turning around in a circle to get the view from every angle. This was the last of the tour now that I'd shown her the twelve thousand square feet inside. The patio overlooked Tampa Bay. "What's not to love, really. This house is so you—masculine, but light and cozy, with hints of you and Ben in every room."

I pulled her close, my hands immediately going to her ass. "I want it to have hints of you too."

She smiled. "I'm sure I can make that happen."

"Would you want to spend time here? School vacations? Summers?"

"Yes, yes, and yes." She held up a finger, which she pressed against my chest. "But doesn't it get extra steamy here in the summer? Like the kind of humidity where you can't even breathe?"

I laughed. "You're saying you wouldn't like that?"

"I'm saying I enjoy when every part of my body *isn't* dripping with sweat." She smiled.

I tightened my grip on her, squeezing those fucking cheeks. "Our stadium was outdoor. I used to play in that heat almost the entire season. You get used to it."

"You didn't die—I mean, obviously, you're standing here, so no, you didn't die—but how did you tolerate that kind of heat while playing at that level? It sounds like Jordan had a much better gig, being indoors, standing on a block of ice, not baking under the sun like you."

"We played less than twenty games a season. Jordan played over eighty. I'll take the heat over the beating his body took."

Her eyes widened. "Damn. I don't blame you. But I don't envy you either." She laughed.

"That's what air-conditioning is for, and swimming pools." I nodded toward the dock that framed the side of the house, the lot on the corner of a canal, and the bay where my fifty-four-foot yacht was parked. "And that."

"That's your boat?" She stayed in my arms but turned around to face it. "Wait, don't answer that, of course it's your boat. I don't know why I would be so silly and ask."

"I like toys, Emily. The bigger, the faster, the better—and she's all those things."

She reached up and wrapped her arms around my neck. "I have no experience with boats aside from the touristy ones that go out of Boston Harbor."

"Those are nothing like that beast right there."

"Probably a dumb question, but aside from how pretty it is, what makes it so special?"

"Why tell you when I can show you." I took her hand and led her off the patio to the dock and helped her get on board. "First off, you can't see the engines—they're underneath where we're standing—but the horsepower on this vessel is cranked up and double than most yachts."

"Which means?"

I laughed, holding her chin so she looked up at me. "It goes hella fast."

"Tell me more."

I opened the sliding glass door to the galley and brought her inside, where there was a full kitchen, living room, dining area, and captain's seat.

"I don't even feel like I'm standing inside a boat. I feel like I'm in an apartment. You could live on this thing, it has everything."

"It has more than you even realize." I pointed out the dishwasher, the separate freezer, the wine fridge—things I'd had added while the boat was being built—along with the two hidden TVs across from the couch, the extendable table, the electronic window coverings, and mood lighting. "We're going to take this on trips. The Keys, the Bahamas—that'll be part of our summer adventures with Ben."

"I cannot wait." She kissed me. "I'm assuming the sleeping quarters are downstairs?" She was now looking at the staircase.

"I wouldn't call them *quarters*. The rooms are fairly large for a boat."

"Rooms? As in . . . plural?"

"There are three bedrooms, three bathrooms, and a laundry area."

"Jesus," she groaned. "I want to see your bedroom."

I took her down the steps, my stateroom located at the bottom of the staircase. I slid open the door, bringing her inside the large space that held a king-size bed, a couch, a small desk, two nightstands, a tiny walk-in closet, and a full en suite.

"This is bigger than my bedroom at my old apartment."

"So you're saying you'd be comfortable traveling in this to the islands and spending a week or two on it at a time?"

She snorted. "You're kidding, right?" She moved closer after peeking at the en suite, her arms locking behind my neck. "I could permanently live on this and wouldn't be mad at that at all."

"After all the kids are out of the house, I can make that happen."

"Kids." She released a breath that was full of pleasure. "I love the sound of that."

My hands went to her face. "Kiss me."

I fucking loved that she did.

And the more her mouth stayed on mine, the more I realized there was no way I could leave this cabin without tasting her.

My hands dropped to her ass again, and I lifted her into the air and set her on the end of the bed. Before my body went on top of hers, I worked on getting her naked, removing her oversize shirt, unclasping her bra, tearing the leggings down to her ankles, slipping those off along with her nursing shoes.

As soon as there wasn't a single piece of clothing covering her, she started undressing me. Since I was still in my suit, I gave her some help, loosening the tie enough that I could slip it off my neck, unbuttoning my shirt while she focused on my belt and pants. When everything dropped to the floor, I removed my socks and shoes, and I grabbed her waist and moved her higher on the bed. That new position put my face right in front of her pussy.

"Gavin," she moaned, her hands sliding into my hair as my mouth landed on her clit. "Oh my God."

I didn't waste time teasing her, giving her tiny flicks and brushes from my nose, winding her up until she was begging, even though I knew she loved that.

What I gave her instead was the fast friction of my tongue, along with two fingers inside her pussy, eating her like I wanted her to come.

Because I fucking did.

But goddamn it, she tasted so good, I didn't want this to end.

"Don't stop!" she screamed.

I wouldn't.

I knew what my mouth did to her, I knew how hard she came whenever I put my lips there. I wouldn't ease up until she was shuddering.

Except it didn't take long for that to happen.

Within a few more licks and finger-fucks, her stomach was trembling and she was shouting, "Gavin!"

Just the sound and view I was after.

Fuck yes.

"Ah!" she shouted. *"Ahhh!"*

God, she was beautiful when she came. Full of soft curves and silky skin, wild locks of blond and the most stunning blue gaze.

I didn't let up until she was past her orgasm, when her body went completely still, and I kissed her clit before I lifted her off the bed and positioned her in front of the couch. I didn't have her sit. I kept her standing, facing the cushions, my fingers crawling up her back and pushing just enough at the top to bend her over.

"Baby, hold on tight." With her ass high, I could aim my tip at her cunt and thrust in. *"Fuuuck."*

I knew she was extra wet because of my mouth, but what I was never prepared for was her tightness, the way her heat took hold of me and didn't want to let go.

"*Mmm*, more," she sang.

"That's what you want?"

"Yes!"

I gripped her hips, using them to drive in and pull out, going in a little deeper each time, and when she finally had all of me, I twisted my hips, arching upward, adding pressure to every angle and friction to her G-spot. "You feel so fucking good."

"So do you." She looked at me over her shoulder, and while she stared, her eyes feral, she demanded, "Harder."

Her wish was my fucking command.

My fingers bore down, squeezing her waist the same way her pussy was clenching my cock, and I rocked into her, stroking her with double the power and speed I'd used before, slamming her pussy like I wanted her to come again.

And she did.

"Oh fuck!" Her arms were extended out in front of her, her legs spread, and she was moving with me, meeting me in the center. "Agh!"

The shudders weren't just in her stomach—I could see them in her spine, her entire body shaking.

"That's it, baby."

Her wetness thickened, her pussy narrowed, and when I could tell she was well past the peak, I pulled out, and I made my way around her to take a seat on the couch. Once I did, I pumped my dick a few times and held out my hand for her to take. "Climb on. I want you to ride the cum out of me."

The sexiest smile came across her face as she took my fingers and straddled me, her knees pressing into the couch cushion below, her hands clasping my shoulders.

I gripped the base of my cock, aiming it toward her pussy, her body high and ready for my tip. She rotated in a circle, grinding over my crown, and as I broke through, her pussy fucking hugging me, I moaned so goddamn loud. "Emily . . ."

"I know." Her head fell back. "I feel the same way."

My hands flattened against her back, my mouth on her nipple as she began to buck against me. The harder she pounded me, the more I sucked, taking that firm bud into my mouth and gnawing the end with my teeth. I moved to the other side, making sure both tits got equal attention, and when her nails pierced my skin, I knew she was close again.

So was I.

I reached down, thumbing her clit, and she yelled, "*Ooo*, yeah!"

As she swayed her body forward and back, I folded my arms around her, and I arched my hips upward. "Goddamn," I groaned. "Keep fucking me."

As soon as those words left my mouth, her speed increased. "Gavin! I'm going to come!"

"Let me hear it. Let me fucking feel it."

Each of her moans drew my orgasm that much closer, and when I felt her pussy contracting, I could no longer hold it off. *"Ughhh,"* I hissed before I meshed our lips together. "Ah, yes!" The surge was moving through me, drawing the cum to my tip, and every time her cunt pumped me, I filled her with another shot. "Fuck, Emily . . ." Stream after stream came out of me until there was nothing left.

She was spent, too, her breath releasing in pants, her eyes and lips looking so satiated, her movements slowing until she was frozen on top of me. "Wow."

"That was"—I shook my head—"I don't even know how to describe it besides calling it incredible."

"Agreed." Her nails pulled back, and she wrapped her arms around my shoulders. "Boat sex. I can now add that to my list of things I never thought I'd do. It fits perfectly under elevator foreplay." She smiled and laughed.

"What about supply-closet sex? Shouldn't that make your list?"

"And office sex at the Bears arena." She nodded.

I laughed. "Oh yes, that was a good one."

"Aw, my Gavin." She put her lips on mine. "I'm starting to believe you have something against having sex in a bed."

EPILOGUE

Gavin

A year and a half later

At the beginning, the months following Sarah's death, I heard her voice. I'd hear it in my dreams, bolting me awake. And in the dark, when I was drinking to forget. But after a few months, when I finally put the bottle down and I returned to the land of the living, I stopped hearing her. I also stopped feeling like she was watching over me.

But I never stopped believing she was watching over our son.

From somewhere far above, she was extremely proud of everything she saw. Of his accomplishments. His athleticism. The way he was maturing. His kindness, tenderness, and the way he loved.

Ben wasn't just a good boy. He was an honest boy. Genuine. Sweet and caring.

Like his mother.

Although I'd never married Sarah, I'd never proposed—things that would have happened in the future had life worked out differently—I made her a promise the moment we found out she was pregnant. I promised I would take care of them both.

I never told Emily we had that promise in common, that she wasn't the only one who felt like she'd let Sarah down.

I did too.

I couldn't protect her. I couldn't prevent what had happened inside her body.

But from the moment our son was born, I did everything in my power to keep him safe. To keep him healthy. To keep him surrounded by people who loved him fiercely.

Six months ago, as Emily stood across from me at the altar in Punta Cana with Maya at her side, Jordan and Ben at mine, surrounded by an audience of our family and friends, she recited vows. Ones that not only included her promise to me but also to Ben.

In Emily's mind, she wasn't going to let Sarah down again.

And she didn't.

Every day that passed, she proved to be the most incredible mother, and I was the luckiest guy in this world.

Every time my eyes landed on her, I was reminded of that.

Like now, as she walked out of the sliding glass door to join Ben, our golden retriever, Fenway, and me on the patio of our home in Tampa. She was wearing a long dress, her blond hair wild from the humidity, and she had very little to no makeup on.

She couldn't possibly look more gorgeous.

I pressed my lips to the top of Ben's head, keeping them there as Emily walked over, stopping in front of the table that separated her from the couch we were sitting on.

I roughed up Ben's hair and pointed at the two boxes in Emily's hands. "What's that?"

"Some gifts I got you guys. Fenway has one, too, but I don't think I'll be able to get him out of the pool to open it." She laughed as Fenway's tail acted like a propeller, waving back and forth in the water as he went from one end of the pool to the other.

I took the box she handed to me, so did Ben.

"It's not my birthday, Mom."

Sometimes he called her Mom. Sometimes, Mom-E. Both had been Ben's idea, and I swore Emily melted every time he said one or the other.

"Aren't I allowed to give you a present when it's not your birthday?" She smiled, her hands going to her hips. "Well, open them, you guys."

My box was smaller than Ben's. Long and narrow, like one built for a necklace. Ben's was thicker, and square. Each one was wrapped, so they required a little maneuvering, and I tore off the paper and lifted the lid.

What I saw inside made me speechless.

It made my fucking heart explode.

It made me appreciate my wife more than I already did—something I never thought was possible.

I slowly looked at her, my eyes closing, my pulse hammering so hard, I could feel it in my throat. "Emily . . ." I whispered.

When I opened my eyes, her lips were sucked inward, an attempt to stop herself from smiling.

Ben took a few more seconds to get inside his box, and he removed a T-shirt, letting the bottom unfold, reading the words that were printed on the front.

"I'm going to be a big brother!" He dropped the shirt on his lap so he could look at Emily. "Is that true?"

She nodded. "It's true." She pointed her gaze at me. "Dad has the proof in his box."

She'd had her IUD taken out two months ago. We didn't think she would get pregnant this fast.

But in that belly, covered by her loose dress, was the blessing we'd both been wishing for.

I pulled out the pregnancy test, showing it to Ben, wrapping my fingers around the hard plastic as I got up from the couch and surrounded her in my arms. "We're having a baby." I squeezed her, holding my lips to the top of her head. "You just made me the happiest man alive."

"You know, I feel the same way." She smiled even harder. "I'm also kinda hoping it's a girl. I'm surrounded by three males. I need some pink in my life."

We both laughed, and I cupped her face and kissed her.

But the kiss didn't last because Ben threw his arms around us and shouted, "I'm going to be a brother!"

We opened our stance to position Ben between us, and I looked into the eyes of my son, wondering if the baby in Emily's belly was going to have her eyes the same way Ben had Sarah's.

"You're going to be the best big brother," I told him. "But you know, with that role comes a lot of responsibility. Do you think you can handle it?"

Emily laughed as Fenway jumped out of the pool, jealous he wasn't getting attention, and he put his wet paws on our arms.

"I would say these two guys"—she kissed Ben's cheek and got a huge wet lick from Fenway—"are up to the task."

Acknowledgments

Nina Grinstead, Maria Gomez, Sasha Knight, Ratula Roy, Kim Cermak, Sarah Norris, Brittney Sahin, Nikki Terrill, Kimmi Street, Christine Miller, Valentine Grinstead, Mom, Dad, and my Brian: I love y'all so much for reasons that go far beyond words—even my words. Every single one of you had a massive part in this, whether it's this book or my life or holding me together so I can write. I hope you know how much I appreciate every one of you.

My Midnighters, you are such a supportive, loving, motivating group. Thanks for being such an inspiration, for holding my hand when I need it, and for always begging for more books. I love you all.

To all the influencers who read, review, share, post: Thank you, thank you, thank you will never be enough. You do so much for our writing community, and we're so grateful.

To my readers: I cherish each and every one of you. I'm so thankful for all the love you show my books, for taking the time to reach out to me, and for your passion and enthusiasm when it comes to my stories. I love, love, love you.

About the Author

Photo © 2021 Moments by Jade Photography

Marni Mann is the *USA Today* bestselling author of more than forty novels, including the Billionaires of Boston duology, the Hooked series, the Dalton Family series, the Weston Group series, and the stand-alone novels *Even If It Hurts*, *Before You*, *The Better Version of Me*, and *Lover*. Marni knew she was going to be a writer since middle school. While other girls were daydreaming about teenage pop stars, Marni fantasized about penning her first novel. She crafts unique stories that weave together her love of darkness, mystery, passion, and human emotions. A New Englander at heart, she now lives with her husband in Sarasota, Florida. When she's not nose deep in her laptop and working on her next novel, she's sipping wine, traveling, boating along the Gulf, or devouring fabulous books—and chocolate. For more information visit www.marnismann.com.

About the Author